Praise for Whiskey & Ribbons

"While the primary refrain of Cross-Smith's fugue is one of grief, this is a hopeful book, a lovely break from the clatter of bad stereotyping."
—LOS ANGELES TIMES

"A vital addition to the canon of New Southern literature."
—CHICAGO REVIEW OF BOOKS

"Her prose goes down fast and packs a punch."
—CHARLESTON POST & COURIER

"Cross-Smith so strongly conveys what's inside [her characters]. With *Whiskey & Ribbons* she's created a glow, bright and throbbing."
—ATLANTA JOURNAL-CONSTITUTION

"*Whiskey & Ribbons* lingers in the mind like a sad, sweet song."
—SHELF AWARENESS

"An authentic portrayal of relationships—romantic and familial; in joy and in sorrow."
—BOOKLIST

"An absorbing delight."
—FOREWORD REVIEWS

Whiskey & Ribbons

Leesa Cross-Smith

Whiskey & Ribbons

A NOVEL

HUB CITY PRESS
SPARTANBURG, SC

First printing, March 2018.

Cover design: Meg Reid
Interior design: Kate McMullen
Proofreader: Kalee Lineberger, Jaque Lancaster
Cover photo: © Susana Blanco / Arcangel
Printed in Saline, MI by McNaughton & Gunn

Latria Graham's interview with Leesa Cross-Smith appeared originally in Electric Literature.

First hardback printing: March 2017
First paperback printing: August 2019

Library of Congress
Cataloging-in-Publication Data

Cross-Smith, Leesa, 1978—
Whiskey & Ribbons / Leesa Cross-Smith.
Other titles: Whiskey and ribbons
Description: Spartanburg, SC : Hub City Press, [2018]
Identifiers: LCCN 2017032053
 ISBN 978193823542 (Paperback)
 ISBN 9781938235382 (hardcover)
 ISBN 9781938235399 (Ebook)
Subjects: LCSH: Brothers and sisters—Fiction.
Loss (Psychology)—Fiction. | Widows—Fiction.
Domestic fiction.
Classification: LCC PS3603.R67945 W48 2018
DDC 813/.6–dc23
LC record available at https://lccn.loc.gov/2017032053

This project is supported in part by an award from the National Endowment for the Arts.

HUB CITY PRESS

186 W. Main Street
Spartanburg, SC 29306
864.327-8515
www.hubcity.org

For you and you and you.

Fugue Late 16th century: from French, or from Italian *fuga*, from Latin *fuga* 'flight,' related to *fugere* 'flee' and *fugare* 'to chase.'

Fugue [music] a contrapuntal composition in which a short melody or phrase (the subject) is introduced by one part and successively taken up by others and developed by interweaving the parts.

Fugue [psychiatry] a state or period of loss of awareness of one's identity.

Requiem for

EAMON MICHAEL ROYCE

End of Watch

July 11

Finale

Da capo

NOAH MICHAEL ROYCE

Born

July 27

I.

Evangeline Royce

MY HUSBAND EAMON WAS SHOT AND KILLED IN THE LINE of duty while I was sleeping. I was nine months pregnant with our son Noah. Me, a full-bellied cashew in our windows-open bedroom, our summer bed. Eamon heard the call over the police radio—domestic dispute. He was on his way home to me, but decided to swing by the disturbance since he was close. I think of him making the drive, the gentle peachy July morning light illuminating his last moments, his last heartbeat, his last breath. The God glow and invisible shadow of death, haloing him. The kid who shot him was only sixteen. He'd gotten in a fight with his stepdad. The kid jumped from his bedroom window and shot Eamon. Eamon's cop buddy Brian had just parked his patrol car in the grass. He put the kid down.

Brian and another cop came to the house, woke me up. I don't remember walking to the kitchen where Dalton found me, shaking, peeing across the floor like an animal. He came as soon as I called. I don't remember calling but he told me I did. Dalton had been long-adopted by Eamon's parents—they were brothers. Brian and the cop left. Dalton wouldn't leave me.

We cut our hair together the Sunday after the funeral.

Finale.

Da capo. From the beginning.

That was six months ago. Noah is six months old; he is a living, ticking timer for how long Eamon has been gone.

Where did you come from? I ask Noah sometimes. *Where is your daddy?*

But last night.

Da capo.

Dalton and I kissed.

I kissed him.

I kissed Dalton.

He was playing piano and I sat on his lap, facing him. Wine as dark as a dragon's heart was involved, gold-bright whiskey too. We were nearing drunk. We were waiting at the right stop and the drunk train was five minutes away.

Dalton is an exquisite pianist. His mom was a concert pianist, a piano teacher. He can play anything. He played through several songs before deciding on the jangly part of "Piano Man" with hilarious gusto because he knows I like it and Dalton is a natural entertainer. He plays piano as if he's busking for tips and not in our living room, the two of us, alone. I say *our* living room because he lives here now with Noah and me.

Last night it was snowing and snowing and snowing and snowing but before that, it iced. I'd dropped Noah off at my parents' as a twofer. They'd get to spend sweet time with their only grandbaby and I'd get to have some time off from being Mama. On the way home, I got a flat. Luckily, Dalton was driving past and saw me, changed the tire. But before he changed the tire, I rode with him to drop off a girl named Cassidy who comes into B's, the bike shop he owns.

Dalton changed the tire and we came home and made hot chocolate. My mom called, told me the storm was getting worse and I should stay home because it would be safer for Noah to spend the night with them. Deal.

I properly grilled Dalton about Cassidy and whether or not he was into her. He said no. I asked him questions the way only a girl best friend and sister-in-law can and I listened well, even when I was convinced he was lying to me. He said no, but maybe he meant yes.

Grief radiates. Since Eamon was killed, my bones ache with sadness. There is a gritty black tea stain on my heart, every organ.

But sometimes.

Sometimes when I'm with Dalton, sometimes when Noah gives me his biggest smile—*Eamon's smile*—sometimes the tea stain pales. Even when it's quick, even when it comes back darker. I still ache for the lifting. How can I not ache for the lifting?

Cassidy or any other woman could potentially throw a wrench in that lifting. If Dalton leaves us, if Dalton loves her. If Dalton ever loves her more than me, more than us. So yes, I grilled him. And later, I kissed him. It was a kiss of ownership. It was a hot, dripping wax seal. The kiss was a lock and a key. The kiss was a creaky gate in the wind.

At first Dalton wouldn't kiss me back. He stopped playing and looked at me.

"Evangeline," he said.

Sometimes I was Evangeline. Evi. Sometimes, Leeny or Evangeleeny. I was never only E. Eamon was E.

Dalton said my name. I said nothing.

I kissed him again.

3

He was a sublime kisser once he kissed me back. His kiss was a song. The piano started playing itself with the small of my back, the apple curve of my ass as Dalton repositioned us. *Adagio, discordant.* I was well-trained in classical ballet, taught it to tiny girls and boys who smelled like baby powder and oatmeal, but no—there was no grace here.

I was kissing Dalton Berkeley-Royce in the house I used to live in with my husband Eamon. I was kissing Dalton, my brother-in-law, my friend. *Only.* I'd known him as long as I'd known Eamon because Dalton and Eamon were a package deal and everyone knew it. Dalton's mom died when he was in middle school. After that, he was raised by the Royces, with Eamon. I knew their history as if it were my own. Eamon was mine, Dalton was his. Dalton and I were always close. He was my brother from the moment I married Eamon and now Eamon was gone. Disappeared. Dead. I was a widow—a word so ghostly and hollow, a word that *should've* been a palindrome but wasn't, those w's with their arms stretched wide, begging for mercy.

I wanted to grow wings and fly into Dalton's mouth, scratch and claw both of us, bleed inside him. Teardrop-spill all over him like honey. The snow was still falling. Falling still. The house, quiescent. Lilac mint whiskey kisses. Heartbeat-breaths. Thrumming piano strings, slowing. Slower. *Nocturne.*

Dalton pulled away. I didn't. He put his hands on my shoulders, hot-pink heat flashed my cheeks. The fireplace clicked.

"Let's talk about this first," he said.

I shook my head no and kissed him again, saw the glitter sizzle and spark when I closed my eyes.

Caesura.

The phone rang.

My mom. Making sure we weren't out driving in the snowstorm, making sure I was safe at home like I said I was. I was paranoid I'd mention something about the kissing. Accidentally say the word *mouth* out of place or mention Dalton's tongue. Dalton's lips. They weren't Eamon's. Eamon's mouth was fuller. He had

4

a bottom lip I could've chewed on for a week. I could still feel it between my teeth. Eamon was gone forever, but he was every-where. How did that happen? I even heard his sea-god timbres in the blue of Noah's cry.

I had my mom put Noah's ear to the phone so I could tell him goodnight. When the call was over, I covered my face and cried.

"Heyheyheyhey," Dalton said quietly, like he always did. As if he could stop me, catch me before the tears took off, pause it all before I rained.

But it didn't work.

I rained and rained and rained because it's what I do. I've gotten good at it. Rain Queen.

I tried to catch my breath, but couldn't. Dalton went into the kitchen to get me a glass of water and I slid down the living room wall and rained more.

Dalton crouched to be closer to me, his long legs, his knees spread wide.

"Evi, drink this. Glass of water. I put lemon in it. Drink a little for me, please?" he said calmly. Also something else he always did. Especially when I wandered during the space between.

The space between: there were sixteen days between Eamon's death and Noah's birth, as if their spirits had spent those sixteen days together in the sky, an airy boys' club somewhere I couldn't reach. They rested for sixteen bars—sixteen bars of music transposed into sixteen thick, dark days that felt like sixteen *hundred* endless nights—*au repos*.

Backyard-wandering, full-moon pregnant in my turquoise maternity dress and tobacco-colored cowboy boots, I'd lose my way. Dalton would find me. He was always finding me. He'd try to lure me inside with lemon water, with sticky, stinky cheeses or a small green bowl of almonds, the darkest chocolate chips. He would shake the bowl, like I was a kitten waiting to hear the rattle of food. Once inside, I'd get in bed and sleep for hours, usually waking up to Dalton making food or cleaning or working on a bike in the garage. Sometimes he'd put down towels and work on a bike in the living room, the TV or music turned down low so he wouldn't wake me. He became my protector, *our* protector, Noah still womb-safe and warm.

The wandering didn't happen so much after Noah was born. Noah grounded me. Kept me still. A welcomed weight.

"Drink a little more for me, please," Dalton said again. He was sitting next to me on the floor with his back against the wall.

I shook my head no.

"Leeny. For me, *please*," he said.

So I did.

"It's supposed to keep snowing," I said, my cry-throat thick.

"Okay," he said, rubbing my back as I leaned forward.

"I miss him so fucking much," I said, pushing my fists into my temples.

"Me too," he said.

He cried too. It's what we did together. So if someone were to ask me if I'd been *intimate* with Dalton, I'd say yes. Sobbing together was its own unique form of intimacy—a thread wrapped around us so tight it was cutting off our circulation from the rest of the world.

Dalton stood up, held his hand out for me. We went into the kitchen. He bent over and drank water straight from the faucet. I got a satsuma from the counter, felt its cool weight in my hand, peeled it, and turned on Otis Redding on my phone. Playing Otis Redding or Sade or Phil Collins or Journey made me feel like Eamon was still here. Those were his favorites. Not guilty pleasures. *Pleasures*. Now they were mine.

Before Dalton and I had made our way to the piano, we'd slow danced in the kitchen to "Chained and Bound." I turned it back on and ate my satsuma. Dalton was leaning against the counter, watching me.

6

"I'm tired and I know I'll be tired for the rest of my life," I admitted. "I don't want you to feel like you're trapped here with me, with Noah," I said.

"You don't get it," Dalton said.

I shrugged.

Dalton pushed himself off and sugar-kissed my candied mouth. These were different from the piano kisses. These kisses were hungry. Dalton was eating. We were breathing like we were fighting. The Otis Redding ended and "One More Night" by Phil Collins came on.

Dalton stopped, pulled away. "Fuck," he said turning from me, "I don't know what to do." He laced his fingers on top of his head.

I went into the freezer for the whiskey.

When Noah fusses in the middle of the night and I don't hear him, Dalton stands in the refrigerator light and gets out a bottle of my breast milk. Many times, I've gotten up to pee and found Dalton in Noah's room, both of them sleeping, their heads lolling to the side, the empty bottle on the floor at Dalton's feet. I feel guilty when my bladder wakes me up, but my baby doesn't. I feel guilty for being grateful Dalton lives with us now so I don't have to do it all alone.

Dalton loves Noah so much and has a thousand nicknames for him. *Noah-bear, No-no, Noahlicious.* Sometimes he'll put Noah in his sling and take him out to the garage so they can do dude stuff together while I nap. Sometimes Dalton takes Noah over to Eamon's parents' to visit on the days when I can't leave the house. The days I can't leave the bed.

Eamon never got to hold his baby and it feels like a thick, itchy eyelash stuck in my eye. Forever.

The prelude from Bach's "Cello Suite no. 1" was playing in the kitchen while I drank, checked the weather. We had five inches of snow and they were expecting ten more overnight. Dalton made his way to the piano, asked if I had any requests. While I was thinking, he started playing a Rachmaninoff piece I recognized. It was soft. It sounded like the snow.

"You always want—" he said before launching into the opening piano of "Hold Me" by Fleetwood Mac.

"I do always want Fleetwood Mac, yes," I nodded and sat next to him on the bench.

He started playing "Gypsy," my favorite.

But I put my hand on his to get him to stop. Eamon hated Fleetwood Mac until he married me. He had no choice. He knew I'd never marry a man who didn't love Fleetwood Mac as much as I did. Hearing "Gypsy" was too much. Dalton stopped playing and put his hands in his lap.

When Dalton's mom Penelope died, Eamon's mom Loretta made sure Dalton continued with his piano lessons. Penelope and Loretta met after both of their little inner city churches merged—one black, one white—in a town where black and white people didn't worship together often. Louisville was an extremely segregated city, and for a black church and a white church to decide they wanted to do something completely different was a bold statement. Penelope and Loretta loved the early-eighties-rebel-hippie-radicalness of it all and fell in love with one another quickly in Sunday school class a year before they both got pregnant. Penelope used to teach Eamon piano lessons too, although they didn't stick. Loretta told Dalton it was important for him to keep playing piano, even though his mom was gone—piano could be a way for him to connect to her, always.

I worried about Dalton's hands. Like what if he got them caught or cut on a tool or they got stuck in the spokes when he was fixing something? How could he play piano? He didn't play professionally but he could've. He could play the classics, he could play jazz, he could teach if he wanted. Once I saw an ad for a pianist to play Christmas songs at the mall and I showed it to him and he gave me a look. He'd done it before in college, and in the past he'd played in the lobbies of fancy hotels on weekends.

"Okay, this," he said. He played the outro of "Epic" by Faith No More.

"I like that," I said.

He finished the song.

"Hey. I'm sorry I kissed you again," he said.

"Don't be. I started it," I said.

"Yeah, but I meant in the kitchen," he said.

"Are you? Sorry?"

"Do you want me to be?"

He took the glass of whiskey from my hands, downed the rest.

"I have to accept the fact that the rest of my life won't make sense," I said.

I wasn't waiting for him to say anything. I was drunk, I was sleepy, I kept thinking I heard Noah crying but remembered he wasn't with us. He was safe and warm at my parents' twenty minutes away.

Dalton started playing "Moondance."

"You play by ear. How do you have all of these memorized? How do you play when you're drunk?" I asked. Sometimes he used sheet music, but most of the time he played without it.

"I've seen the sheet music for most of these at one point or another. I've practiced all of them. I hear the music and it makes sense to my fingers. It's just what I choose to do with my brain. I got a lot of room up here," he said, tapping the side of his head.

I listened, he played. I put my head on his shoulder.

"By the way, our life makes sense to me," Dalton said.

I closed my eyes so I could keep it in. Dalton's words accompanied by the piano. A new song.

He played some Oscar Peterson. At one point I stood up and started swaying. Dalton stood up with me and we danced together again, to nothing. The last thing Dalton played was "Desperado." Yes, it was depressing. That's how we'd been operating since the summer. My life is depressing now. Before? Eamon was alive and Dalton and I goofed off whenever we were together. He was always over at our place or we were over at his. Dalton was easy to be around and everything about him was familiar and comfortable to me. He was the only person I could stand to be with those tender days the week after Eamon's funeral when I would sleep and sleep and sleep and sleep and sleep and cry and cry and cry and cry and cry. He cooked for me and made me tea. African Honeybush in the morning, rooibos in the afternoon, and when the sun went down, vespertine chamomile with lavender. We sat together in silence and watched PBS. I especially liked the mind-numbing shows about woodworking, gardening. I liked listening to them list the names of things. At two o'clock it was American holly. African blackwood. Ash. Lacewood. Redheart. Bolivian rosewood. Burmese rosewood. East Indian rosewood. Honduras rosewood. At three o'clock it was Acantholobivia euanthema. Dhalia hybrida. Monsonia crassicaule. Zygocactus bridgesii, also known as false Christmas cactus.

Back when I was knitting Noah's baby blanket. *Knit one, purl one, knit one, purl one. Dear God, You promised to never leave me and I feel left. Knit one, purl one, knit one, purl one, knit one, purl one, knit one, purl one. Purl one, knit one, purl one, knit one, purl one, knit one, purl one, knit one. Dear God, I cannot do this. I don't want to. Fuck it.*

Back when ballet and teaching were the furthest things from my mind but the French terms I'd heard and known for most of my life still pirouetted across my brain—the sound of flowers, blooming. The sound of petals, falling. *Arabesque. Développé. Échappé sur les pointes. Fouetté. Glissade. Grande jeté. Pas de chat. Port de bras. Relevé. Rond de jambe. Temps lié sur les pointes.*

Back when I couldn't have a single thought without hearing *Sergeant Royce had been on the force for ten years. He is survived by Evangeline and their unborn child.* The words, rearranging themselves in my head—an ammonia migraine of syllables. *Royce, unborn. He survived. Eamon Evangeline, ten. Their. He is Eamangelon. Evameline. And their child, force.*

⚓

Still, snow. Dalton played "Desperado" slowly and whenever he got deep into playing something he bit his bottom lip and closed his eyes. I watched him do it. Thinking of the kissing. Thinking of the fact that tonight was an accident. Thinking of the fact that there were no such things as accidents.

I didn't know if it was the snow or the kissing or the feeling like we were a fresh broken egg shattered on a cold concrete floor. Dalton played the piano every day—but it was like he couldn't stop. Like if he stopped playing, we'd fade away. So, he played.

Caesura.

Thundersnow.

We both turned to the window at the same time. The lights flickered.

I don't believe in ghosts but in that moment I *felt* Eamon near although I couldn't read it properly—like I'd been asked to touch something but couldn't *feel* it because I had on thick gloves. Eamon could feel a million different ways about me kissing Dalton or he could only feel one. Could he feel? Nothing made sense and I couldn't make it, no matter how hard I tried. It was exhausting, infuriating, pointless. It made me feel impossibly small. The only thing anchoring me was Noah. And Dalton, but I knew he didn't belong to me like Noah did.

Later when we were sleepy enough to go to bed I told Dalton he could sleep in my bed if he promised no funny business. Right after Eamon was killed and before he moved in, Dalton would sometimes sleep on the floor in front of my bedroom door. Now, Dalton slept in the blue bedroom down the hall. When I came home and he wasn't expecting me and he had his shirt off, he'd put it back on. He was a gentleman, deliberately.

"No funny business," he said, shaking his head.

"Are you still drunk?" I asked.

We'd stopped drinking an hour or so before, sat in front of the fire playing cards. I won both hands of Go Fish. Dalton annihilated me at War. He tried to remember the complicated rules to Asshole but we weren't sure we had enough people so we gave up. We played one round of Two-Handed Rook. We also shared two cigarettes sitting on the kitchen floor with the back door propped open. We never smoked together before and now we did. We were a new beast. One thing when Noah was with us and a whole new thing when it was just the two of us. Sometimes I couldn't help myself from wondering what my parents thought about us, what Eamon's thought about us. Maybe everyone assumed Dalton and I had gone crazy together. But in truth, what other people thought about us wasn't important. Eamon was dead so my list of important things had been considerably shortened.

"I'm *kind of* drunk," Dalton said, leaning against the frame of my bedroom door.

"No funny business," I said again and Dalton nodded, slowly.

I got into bed and after a minute, Dalton slid in behind me. He was in his T-shirt, his pajama pants, same as me. He wrapped his arms around me. Eamon was the only man I'd ever been with. Dalton and I had never been in the same bed together, never joked about it. There we were, spooning. Not forking. The bedroom, softly ticking. The snow, whispering down from the February sky, glowing ballet slipper-pink.

Eamon Royce

WHEN I MET EVANGELINE I WORKED SECURITY AT THE megachurch, and yes, it was as glamorous as it sounded. The coffee was free and I had a cush spot by the exit door. I stood there, watched things. Nothing ever happened, not even close, but that was what I got paid to do—stand there in my uniform and keep an eye on things, make people feel safe while they worshipped. The first time I saw her, my mind was somewhere else. My phone had been blowing up. Lisabeth.

You always do this.

Fuck you Eamon!!!!

Never speak to me again.

Why aren't you texting me back???

Where are you?!?!?

Have you seen my orange yoga pants?

I hate you so much right now.

Call me later.

Whatever.

Whatever Eamon.

I was putting my phone into my pocket when Evangeline walked over to me, but I didn't know she was Evangeline yet. I knew she was ridiculously beautiful, in purple—the same color of this grape jam my grandma used to make. Once I realized I was comparing the color of her dress to my grandma's jam, I realized I was paying too much attention to her already. I had half a girl-friend but Evangeline was a *goose*.

Dalton and I had code words for girls. We came up with them in middle school and still used the words when we were alone. We'd trained ourselves to think that way forever ago and I found myself thinking about it when I saw a beautiful woman. We made sure the words were inconspicuous. We didn't want the girls or my mom to be able to decode them. *Kitten* would be a dead giveaway so we never used it. A *goose* was the highest level. It meant the girl was both pretty *and* hot, which could also mean *cute* and hot, but that was debatable. We'd decided on *goose* because it was a silly word that would never cause suspicion. A *squirrel* was a girl who was hot but maybe not so pretty. A *duck* was a girl who was pretty but maybe not so hot. A *caterpillar* was a girl who wasn't particu-larly pretty or hot but we weren't ready to count her out yet. Like maybe we could give her a couple years. A *ferret* was a girl who had no hope, so move on.

Evangeline was a *goose* all the way. Lisabeth was a *goose* too. An angry *goose*. My phone vibrated in my pocket again. I turned it off without looking at it. Gave my full attention to the *goose* in front of me.

"Hi. The little ones will be performing this morning so we're going to bring them up through here and over this way," she said, showing me with her arms. No wedding ring. The *goose* was unmar-ried. "So if you could make sure no one sits in these two rows that would be awesome," she finished, dropping her arms to her sides.

"Okay," I said, nodding.

"What happened to Russ? He's our usual security guy," she said, tilting her head at me.

"Oh, he moved to Florida. So now, it's me," I said. The sanctuary was filling up quickly. The worship band tuned. I turned to look over at them. To at least give a semblance of doing my job. I didn't want to do my job though. I wanted to talk to Evangeline. Leeny *Goosey.*

"Aw, we'll miss him. He was sweet," she said.

Two of the little ones she'd referred to came up to her, started playing peekaboo on either side of her legs.

"Hey, you two, where's Miss Donna? Go find Miss Donna since it's almost time to start," she said to them in a calm, measured voice. They ran off as suddenly as they'd appeared. She smoothed down her dress in the back.

"I'm Eamon. Royce," I said, pointing to my last name on my uniform. "And I'm not sweet at all so you will never confuse me with Russ."

I didn't smile.

But she did. It was glorious.

"Oh I'm sure you're sweet enough. We'll see. I'm Evangeline," she said, waving.

A couple people stepped to the rows Evangeline had asked me to protect and I kindly told them they were reserved for her Sunday school class of little ones. The lights dimmed, the worship band started playing.

"Nice to meet you, Evangeline," I said.

"You too," she whispered, turning from me.

I didn't turn my phone back on. I hadn't thought about Lisabeth in two whole minutes. I stood with my back against the wall, deliberately not looking for Evangeline, but it didn't matter because she was already everywhere.

When I got home, Lisabeth was still on fire.

"It's the middle of the day," I said, closing the door behind me. "How can you be so angry in full sun? This is like, nighttime anger."

We didn't live together but she had a key. She was in the kitchen wearing one of my old T-shirts over nothing else but a pair of panties. My body reacted. Her legs—gamine—her wild hair tucked behind her ears. This fight could end in fucking. I'd be fine with it. I'd always be fine with it. Or not. Maybe it was time for me not to be fine with it.

"Eamon. Eamon! You are an asshole," she said, pointing at me.

"Okay," I said, shrugging.

"That's it? Okay?"

"What do you want me to say, Lisabeth? Tell me what you want me to say and I'll say it and we can get it over with," I said. I began walking to my bedroom, taking off my uniform.

"I don't want to have to tell you what to say!" she said, following me.

"Honestly? I don't even remember what this is about. I've been racking my brain all morning and I swear to you I have no clue," I admitted. I put my gun in the top drawer like always. I took off my duty belt, started unbuttoning my uniform shirt. I wasn't looking at her.

"You said you'd come to dinner at my parents' tomorrow night and then you said you had to work. I asked if you could switch with someone. You said no. You don't remember this?" she asked so calmly it almost scared me. How did she turn off the crazy so fast?

"Ah," I said, remembering. I didn't want to go to dinner at her parents' because going to dinner at her parents' would be a lie. This relationship was ending. Both of us knew it. The shot clock was running out. Any second now we'd hear the final buzz.

"So you can't switch with someone?" she asked.

I took my shirt off, my undershirt too. I took my pants off, my socks. I stood there in my boxers, scratching my head.

"No, Lisabeth. I can't. And it's not a big deal," I said.

"It *is* a big deal to me! You refuse to hear it."

"I'm tired," I said.

"I'm leaving," she said.

I let her go.

Later I met Dalton out for beers and wings.

"U of L has no three-point shooting. That's the problem," I was saying as we watched the basketball game flash on the flat screens surrounding us.

"That's the problem," Dalton echoed, reaching for a fry.

Dalton and I knew each other well enough to not have to talk all the time. We both had our quiet moments and could spend extremely long periods of time together in silence. We'd always been that way. But also, when we needed to talk, we'd talk. And I kind of needed to talk.

"Hey. I've ended it with Lisabeth, I just haven't told her yet," I said.

"Wow," Dalton said, but his tone was *duh*.

"I'm trying to avoid a long drawn-out conversation," I said, watching the door. It was a habit I had and not one I was likely to change. I was a cop. I was aware of these things even when I wasn't wearing my uniform or driving my patrol car. I couldn't turn it off and didn't want to. It was how my brain operated. A group of young boys came in, scrambling through their wallets, flicking through their glowing phones.

"She's crazy," Dalton said. He leaned back in his chair, threw his arm around the empty one next to him.

"I know. That's what I used to like about her," I laughed.

"Now you got to pay the price. Hook up with another crazy girl and that may make the transition easier," Dalton said.

"Frances got a friend?" I asked, referring to Dalton's sometimes-girlfriend.

"I know exactly how to piss Frances off and I can't help myself," he said.

"Mom thinks you're being lazy in your relationship. You know how she feels about Frances," I said. My mom had tried to make it work with Frances, invited her over, reached out to her, but no matter what she did, those two couldn't get along. It wasn't happening.

"Mom's right," Dalton said, in easy agreement.

"I saw a *goose* at church. That's what I want. A new *goose*," I said, watching the guy from our team ferociously dunk on the flat screen. I made a celebratory fist before finishing my beer.

"Who's this?"

"Evangeline," I said, giving her name a bit of flair.

Dalton raised an eyebrow. "Fix your Lisabeth problem first, yeah?"

"Yes, sir. Fix your Frances problem first, yeah?" I said back to him.

"Fixing this beer problem right quick," Dalton said, getting up and heading to the counter for round two.

For the next couple weeks I stayed busy with work. Louisville's crime rate in general was super-high compared to other cities in America. Louisville was the biggest city in Kentucky. A city of over a million people where the odds of being a victim of a crime was one in twenty. Our police department never got a real break. I tried my best to leave work stuff at work, came home in my uniform most days, showered the stench of my shift off me—the sadness and grime of the streets, the at-times blessed tedium of routine traffic stops. Lisabeth had this sharp minty body wash in the shower and I specifically used it when my shifts were over because it made me feel extra-clean. Like I could wash off the blood and evil of the world. Start new. But on Sunday mornings I saw Evangeline at the church. I started volunteering for Sunday nights too, hoping she'd be there. She was. Our relationship had progressed from police officer and Sunday school teacher to Eamon and Evangeline, but I'd never seen her outside of church. She always made a point of coming up to me, saying hello, thanking me for my service. Sometimes she'd remind me where the coffee was. I'd act like I didn't know, because I liked listening to her explain things. She pointed a lot and I thought it was maybe because she was used to working with such small children, guiding them this way and that. She told me she taught ballet. I resisted the urge to tell her she looked like it, but she did. She had a ballerina body and walked with her feet turned out a bit. Evangeline was a light beauty. At times I'd be overwhelmed with wanting to pick her up, carry her out of the sanctuary, carry her to my patrol car, take her anywhere she wanted to go, just me and her. I found myself thinking about her a lot more than I should've.

The first time I saw Evangeline outside of church was at the theatre. I'd promised Lisabeth I'd go with her to see *Les Misérables*. I'd fallen asleep right before the end of Act I and made no real apology about it, seeing as how I'd been working a lot of nights and Lisabeth knew that and still wanted me to take her. She'd tried explaining the musical to me on the way to the theatre but none of it stuck. My feelings about Lisabeth hadn't changed, but I hadn't broken up with her either. She still came to my place, I still went to her place, we still had sex, I still thought she was sexy in the morning wearing my shirt. I knew we wouldn't be together forever, but she didn't. I felt guilty about how I looked forward to my conversations with Evangeline so much, how my palms would start to sweat when I saw the top of her head at church. She had this long, curly hair that looked like fluffy, twisted feathers.

"This guy Javert, he's a cop—so you have something in common," Lisabeth had said to me as I was parking my truck in the garage next to the theatre.

"Hold up. I thought he was the bad guy," I said.

"He is."

"So how do we have something in common? You think I'm the bad guy? No, honestly—be honest with me," I said, almost too serious. I didn't know if she would be able to let it go or not. I didn't know if I wanted her to.

"He's a cop, but he's constantly chasing after our hero, Jean

Valjean. What do you mean I think you're the bad guy? Why are you trying to start a fight? What is this about?" she asked.

I turned the engine off, we got out. I instinctively took her hand as we crossed the street. I was still doing things like grabbing her hand, walking on the outside nearest the traffic when we were together. The thought of anything awful happening to her made me want to weep and I saw awful things happen on a regular basis. The day before the theatre I'd been called to a fatal car accident, directed traffic as the coroner zipped the body into a bag. I didn't want to hurt Lisabeth. I didn't know what I wanted. Maybe I didn't want anything. My crush on Evangeline was just that. A crush. I was too old for a crush. I felt foolish and guilty.

"This isn't about anything. I'm sorry. I was being silly," I said, covering her hand with both of mine and kissing her knuckles. She smiled at me and we went inside, took our seats.

At intermission I went to the bathroom and to get two drinks. A bourbon for me, vodka cranberry for Lisabeth. I was walking back with them and saw Evangeline. She made wide eyes at me and spread her arms out like an airplane swooping in.

"Eamon! Hi!" She hugged me. We'd never hugged before. I was careful not to spill the drinks on her dress. It was short, tiger-orange. Her legs were amazing. Little ballerina legs. *Little Evangeline.*

"Hey! So you follow me around now?" I said. "I'll allow it."

She pulled away and we stepped aside. I leaned against the wall. She put her hands on her hips.

"I figured you for a secret musical theatre fan," she said, winking.

"I'm that easy to spot? Damn. I gotta up my game," I said.

"You're not here alone," she said, pointing to both drinks.

"Oh, you don't double-fist at the theatre? It's the only way to do it. You haven't lived until you've double-fisted it through *Les Misérables.* Actually, nope. I fell asleep right before intermission. My, um, girlfriend wasn't too happy," I said, immediately regretting it. I shouldn't have made it seem as if Lisabeth were a burden. Not kind of me. Not a good look.

"The line is so long," Evangeline looked over at the bar.

"You can have my bourbon. Here," I said, holding it out for her.

"No. No. It's fine. I'll see if I can get one before the lights blink," she said.

I made a face at her.

"They'll blink the lights when it's time to get back to our seats," she said.

"A-ha. You know things I don't know," I said. I took a small sip of my bourbon, wishing she'd taken a drink. An accidental intimacy. "Who are you here with?"

"My best girlfriend and her niece. This is like the seventh time I've seen *Les Mis*. I'd live at the theatre if I could," she said.

"You grew up doing this stuff? Obviously dancing..." I said. The line was moving. The lights hadn't blinked yet. I didn't want them to. I wanted blinding beacons swallowing us for the rest of our lives.

"Pretty much. I started dancing when I was three—grew up a theatre kid, a dance kid. It's an entirely different world," she said.

"My brother—he's a pianist. His mom was a concert pianist. He's amazing. He could play for stuff like this," I said, motioning to the auditorium, the ceiling and walls.

"He's your half-brother?" she asked. I'd mentioned Dalton's mom, not mine. She caught the confusion.

"He's my adopted brother. My parents adopted him when we were in middle school, after his mom died," I said, probably saying too much, although I saved the word *suicide* for people I knew well. I wasn't going to pour *suicide* all over Evangeline, have it bleach her nice theatre dress.

When it was her turn to order, she got a glass of white wine.

"It's on me," I said, setting down one of my cups, taking out my wallet.

"No way," she said.

"Yes way," I said, handing the bartender a twenty dollar bill, telling him to keep the change.

"Well, thank you. You are a gentleman and a scholar, Eamon Royce," she said.

"You're welcome. My pleasure."

The lights flickered, turning the hallway into a submarine.

"There they are," she said, pointing up.

"I guess I'll see you Sunday?" I said.

"Yes! So good to see you, like, out in the world."

"Absolutely."

I went back to my seat, gave Lisabeth her drink. I finished mine. The lights went down, the curtain went up. I thought about Evi. How she smelled like clean, clear, life-giving water.

I worked. Wrote tickets. Arrested some dudes in a bar fight, had to go to court and testify for a couple cases. On Saturday, Mom made roasted chicken and potatoes, invited Dalton and me over to eat with her and Dad, asked us if we wanted to bring our girlfriends and we both said no. She got a kick out of that. Mom liked having her boys to herself.

"I worry about you," Mom said as soon as I got to my parents'. It was how she started most of our conversations. Especially if she'd recently heard anything about a cop anywhere in the world getting hurt or caught a glimpse of a dramatic police procedural on TV. She put her hand on my cheek, gently slapped it. Dalton and I had ridden over together, he was behind me. After Mom hugged me, she threw her arms around his waist.

"I want you to quit. Work in a cubicle somewhere. Your daddy and I can help you out if you need money. I worry about my baby out there in the streets," she said.

She was especially worried about me working downtown and the West and South Ends, where crime was the worst. She'd call to check up on me whenever she heard about shootings in the projects or whenever meth houses exploded out on the edge of the county. I worked some of those, spent significant amounts of time in the worst, most crime-ridden areas in the city before I returned to my nice, safe neighborhood and almost felt guilty for being so isolated from the crime when I wasn't on duty. I could be at my parents' place, their backyard sprawling out into the golf course behind it and forget for a quick second that at that very moment, two guys were probably beating one another to a pulp in a back alley somewhere downtown over a dice game or two dollars.

"I'm not in the streets, Mom. I'm right here. I'm in your kitchen," I said, lifting a piece of chicken off the plate and putting it in my mouth. She slapped my hand like I knew she would. Like she always did.

"Don't touch. It's resting," she said.

"It's delicious," I said back to her.

"Dalton, tell him just because he looks handsome in a uniform, it doesn't mean he has to put himself in danger every day," she said.

"Someone has to do it though, right?" I said to both of them. "I mean, if something was going down right now, you'd call the cops, right? That's me. I'm that person. Someone has to be that person, right?" I looked back and forth between their faces as my dad stepped into the kitchen.

"Leave the boy alone," my dad said. It was his go-to response.

"As long as you're my baby, I'll worry. People are crazy, Eamon Michael," my mom said.

Dad and Dalton hugged, sat down at the table, started talking. I remained at the stove with my mom. She bent over to get the potatoes out of the oven. I took the mitts from her hands, got the dish out myself, put it on the counter. She went to the cabinet, got down four plates.

"Who's drinking what?" she said, holding up two bottles of wine. A Shiraz, a Chardonnay.

"Beers," Dad said. I didn't think my dad had ever had a sip of wine in his life. He was strictly a beer dude and not a big drinker anyway. But Mom? Mom loved her wine.

"Dalton, you'll have wine with me won't you?" she said sweetly.

"Absolutely. I got it," he said, hopping up and going in the drawer for the wine key. He opened the red for both of them, poured it into two glasses. My dad offered me a brown bottle of beer and I took it, set it at my place at the table. I made a plate. I was reaching for a biscuit when Dalton got next to me, grabbed his plate.

"I do agree with her though. I'd be lying if I said I don't worry about you too," he said.

I looked at it this way: I'd turn in my badge when I felt like it was time to turn in my badge and not one moment sooner.

"What if I wanted you to close the bike shop?" I asked him.

"Why are you closing the bike shop?" Mom asked. She had the ears of a wolf when she wanted to.

"I'm not. Ma, I'm not," Dalton said. "We were just talking."

"I love the bike shop. You should go work at the bike shop," she said, pointing at me. She sat down. Dad was across from her, already eating.

"The boy doesn't want to work at the bike shop, Loretta," he said. Dad pointed at me with his fork. My dad had retired from the force some years before. None of this was new to my mom, none of this was new to any of us.

"It wasn't my intent to fall in love with a police officer. I used to worry myself to death at night. I couldn't sleep! The moment your daddy retired, you jumped right in. I didn't get to take a breath," she said.

"Mom, Ma. Mom, stop," Dalton said. He put his plate on the table and put his arms around her. "Eamon's fine. He's right here, he's fine. Everyone's fine."

"Mom. I hear you. I hear you. I love you," I said, going to her.

My dad let his chin rest in his hand. "Loretta. Let's eat. I'm sorry if I upset you," he said.

"No. I'm sorry. I'm sorry," she said, using her napkin to dab at the corners of her eyes. It felt like a scene from a movie. I didn't feel like being in a movie. We sat, we ate, we talked. The timer went off and the peach pie was done. I got it out of the oven.

We ate more. We didn't talk about my job anymore. Mom asked Dalton lots of questions about Frances. She didn't ask too many about Lisabeth and I was relieved. I felt bad for Dalton because he didn't have much to say about Frances, but Mom kept pressing him.

"I'm probably not marrying her," Dalton finally said after Mom asked if they were going to ever get engaged.

"I've never told you this before but the things I *do* like about Frances—those things remind me of your mother," Mom said.

"Really?" Dalton said.

"I miss her," Mom said. Was it a full moon? Mom was usually emotional but tonight it was off the hook.

Dad and I went into the living room to watch the end of the basketball game. Mom spilling out sometimes made Dad uncomfortable. When he couldn't stop it, he did what a lot of men did. He left the room. Dalton didn't. He always stayed behind, talked to her. Listened. The game was almost over by the time they joined us on the couch.

"And Lisabeth? That's still going on?" she asked me.

I gave Dalton a look, wondered if he sold me out. He looked innocent enough.

"Nothing is happening," I said. I let my mind wander to seeing Evi Sunday morning. The first time since bumping into her at the theatre. Maybe something would feel different. Maybe we unlocked a new level to whatever it was we had. I hoped.

Sunday morning, no Evangeline. I did my job and even listened to the sermon this time. "Seeds of Grace" was what he called it. When I got home, Lisabeth was there. She'd just gotten out of the bath. She was on my couch with a towel on her head. She was watching a tiny-home renovation show on HGTV. I asked if she had time to talk.

"About what?" she asked, using the remote to click the sound down.

I sat in the recliner. We were catawampous in more ways than one.

"I think you know about what," I said, not intending to sound like such an asshole, but...

"Why are you like this? What did I do?"

She cried. I knew she would cry. I hated seeing her cry. I was wholly unoriginal. A dick. A man. Made her cry, then hated having to deal with it.

It started raining hard against the windows. Seemed overly dramatic.

"Lissa, you didn't do anything. We tried. I'm not shitting you, I think it's important we tried." I meant it.

"There's someone else," she said.

I held my hand up at her. Instant reaction. It was the same thing I did whenever I told a perp to be quiet and he started talking anyway. It was the same thing I did whenever I'd already asked a neighbor twice to calm down and hold on while I talked to another one. I didn't want to treat Lisabeth like a criminal. She wasn't. I put my hand down. Told her there was no one else.

"You know me. Look at me. This isn't about anyone else. This is about us," I said.

"Eamon. There's someone else for me. For *me*. This isn't about you."

I was confused. She turned the TV off, headed upstairs to my bedroom. I followed her.

"What?"

"I met someone else. Not you. I mean, I don't know if you met someone or not but I did. *Me*. You probably never considered that," she said. She went in my top drawer. I hated when she went in my top drawer. It's where I usually kept my duty belt, my wallet, my badge, my gun. Everything. But I was still in uniform, my gun was on my hip. Everything about the moment was ridiculous. I wanted it over. I wanted her out. I wanted to sit down in my own damn house and turn on ESPN, have a glass of whiskey, neat. I'd call Dalton. Or maybe my buddy Brian. I didn't know if Sunday was a good day for a break-up, but it seemed as good a day as any.

The first day of the week, a new week, a new break, a new life.

Lisabeth and I had been dating for a year. Now we could both start new. Happy fucking new year. She had another man. She had another man? I wasn't pissed before, but now I was.

She closed the top drawer, went into the second. She started gathering her underwear, lacy thongs and a couple pairs of superhero ones I'd bought her as a kitschy joke.

"So who's this dude?" I asked. I leaned against the doorframe, feigning calm.

"You don't know him," she said, not looking at me.

"So tell me who he is, so I can know him." Shrugged.

"Oh, you're standing there with a gun and you're this big bad cop and you're questioning me? I'm supposed to tell you everything? I'm not scared of you."

"You shouldn't be scared of me. Why the hell would you say something like that?" I stepped closer to her, closer to the dresser. I took my gun from its holster, opened the top drawer. Lisabeth had to step aside. I put my gun in the drawer, my wallet, my duty belt. I started unbuttoning my uniform shirt.

"Don't try to use an authority thing here because it won't work."

"What are you even saying?" I said, taking my shirt all the way off.

"I'm saying okay, Eamon. I've moved on, we've both moved on. We should've done this a long time ago," she said. The tears stopped and came back again, stopped again. She looked good standing there in her underwear, going in the bottom drawer for her yoga pants, her knee socks. She reached into the closet behind her for one of her old tote bags, started filling it up.

"Hey. Hey, come here," I said, reaching for her.

She dropped her stuff, melted into my arms. I smelled her head—flowers and something bubblegummy. She looked up at me and I kissed her. Slowly at first, then softer. I was okay with doing this one last time. I knew it was for one last time.

"Who is he?" I asked, touching her.

"You don't know him," she said, touching me.

"That guy Mark from work?" I asked, unhooking her bra. One-handed. Swag.

She shook her head no.

"Luke from work?" I asked.

"You think I'm a work whore. I'll have sex with any dude if he works with me?"

"No!" I said.

"It's Nadia's boyfriend's friend," she said.

My brain tried to make sense of it. *Her sister's boyfriend's friend.* I think I met that dude once over at her parents' house? I remembered someone tall, in flannel, maybe his car was green.

"Oh," was all I said.

"I haven't had sex with him."

"Okay."

She gave herself to me and I took her. Afterwards, I let her leave.

I poured my whiskey, texted Dalton, texted Brian. They both showed up. We watched basketball and didn't talk about anything important at all, which is exactly what I wanted. When they left it was late. I slept good. Hard. A little drunk too.

I worked. Fought the bad guys. I arrested arsonists and a rapist, a middle school teacher caught with kiddie porn on his work computer, a couple dads woefully behind on their child support, some drunk-driving college kids, abusive husbands, gas station thieves. I came home to an empty house and it was okay. I saw Evangeline the next Sunday and the next Sunday and the next Sunday. We talked more. I felt more comfortable with it now that I was single. I went over to my parents' with Dalton for another Saturday dinner. I told Mom I broke up with Lisabeth.

The next Sunday, there was a late member meeting after the night service. I liked how the church Sundays added structure to my week. I worked a forty-hour week like most people—eight-hour shifts, weekends, holidays—none of it bothered me. I had Mondays and Tuesdays off. It was fine. But it was nice to add those Sundays to my schedule. I didn't even mind working overtime on Sunday nights whenever there was an event at the church. I liked how the sanctuary smelled like communion wafers and baptism water. I grew up going to church most Sundays anyway, had slacked off when I was in college, but I felt comfortable there, could feel the Spirit of the Lord hovering above and around us.

I was standing by the exit doors as everyone made their way out after the meeting. It was raining and Evangeline was walking towards the building, holding her phone to her ear.

"I locked my keys in my car," she said into the phone.

We made eye contact. She held her hand up at me, mouthed *sorry* for no real reason.

"I'm at Oak Grove Baptist. The giant church off the highway?" she said as if she weren't sure. It made me smile.

"I got this. I can help," I said to her, pointing at myself.

"Are you sure?"

"I got this. Which car is it?" I asked, looking through the rain.

More members made their way out, thanked me, walked into the dripping night.

Evangeline told the person on the phone thank you, slipped it into her purse.

"Thank you for this, Eamon. Um, it's the black four-door in the third row, right there," she said, pointing.

I went to my car first, then hers. In a minute, I had her door open. I reached inside, got her keys out of the ignition. I went back to her underneath the awning.

"How did you do that?" she asked as I handed her the keys.

"Police magic."

"Police magic," she repeated.

I showed her the wire coat hanger I had hidden behind my back.

"Dry cleaning police magic," I said, ditching the hanger in the garbage can next to us.

"Thank you, hero. Kentucky's finest," she said, winking.

I wanted to ask her out to dinner but I was in uniform. I prayed that if she was at church the following Sunday for God to give me a sign, let it be sunny and I'd ask her. It was supposed to rain and snow all week.

The following Sunday was the sunniest day of my life. I switched a shift with my buddy. He worked security for me. I showed up at the church in Sunday street clothes—a white Oxford, grey pants, brown boots. Evangeline saw me, called me a hero again. She said I looked sharp.

"Thank you. So do you," I said.

"What's the special occasion? Where's your uniform?"

"Actually, can I talk to you for a second?" I asked. Adrenaline flash.

"Sure. What's up?"

We stepped aside, the same way we did at the theatre. Did she know what I was about to ask? Could she sense it? Women's intuition?

"Um—I was...wondering if you'd let me take you out to dinner or for a coffee if dinner is too much? If you don't like coffee...tea or a Coke...a milkshake with two straws?" I said. I turned the charm up to eleven.

"I'd like that," she said, nodding.

"Isn't that what women always say in romantic comedies? I'd like that?"

"Do you watch a lot of romantic comedies, Eamon?"

"I would if you wanted me to," I said, turning the charm up to one hundred.

"I'd like that. Yes. Yes to dinner and maybe coffee after? Or a milkshake with two straws?" she said. The lights dimmed. Dimming, flickering lights—they seemed to follow us.

"Put your number in my phone, please. Is tomorrow too soon? I'm off Mondays and Tuesdays. I work weekends. I don't know your schedule. Are you free tomorrow?" I was talking too much. I handed her my phone.

"I'm free tomorrow," she said, taking it, beeping in her number.
I took my phone back, called her so she'd have my number too.
"Tomorrow. I'll call you," I said.

"You don't have a girlfriend anymore?"

"I don't."

"Would you like to sit with me this morning?"

"That's okay?"

"Come on," she said.

I followed her.

From the beginning of our relationship I knew wherever she'd go, I'd go.

Dalton Berkeley-Royce

FRANCES WAS FUCKING HER HEART OUT ON TOP OF ME. Cursing, wild-eyed. This was the picture I had in mind whenever anyone would ask me why we were still together. *This is why we're still together.*

We came at the same time. It was kind of our thing.

"I thought maybe I was pregnant last month," she said, slapping her back against the cool sheets of my bed.

I sat up against the headboard, scratched through my hair. It was long. It was down, hanging past my shoulders. If I wanted, I could preciously put it up in what Frances and Evangeline called a man-bun.

"What the hell?" I said. Suspicious. Jocular. Suspiciously jocular.

"I'm not. I'm not!" she said. She reached over to get her cigarettes from her purse. I didn't mind when she smoked one in my room, but only after sex. I loved Frances. I'd kid around with Eamon about her being crazy because that's what men did. We kid around about women being crazy or maybe sometimes we were serious but deep down we all knew the truth. Women weren't the crazy ones. We were. I loved Frances. I hadn't decided how much I loved her yet but I knew I loved her at least a little.

She was funny and beautiful and smart and mean when she needed to be. It was hot when she was mean. Maybe that meant I needed therapy, maybe that meant she needed therapy. Loretta had mentioned more than once that Frances reminded her of my mother. My mother, Penelope. Penelope was my mother, Loretta was my mom.

In my bike shop, I restored and repaired classic and vintage bikes. Bianchi, Peugeot, Trek, Specialized, Surly, Ibis, BMX, etc. Some for customers, some to sell. Taking things apart and putting them back together again was a comfort for me and had been my whole life. Penelope was depressed a lot when I was a kid. She'd go for days and days without getting out of bed for anything other than the bathroom or the occasional cup of soup or cigarette. Instead of TV, Penelope would keep me busy with either piano lessons or bikes. Any old bike she found in the trash or at Goodwill, she'd throw it in the back of her station wagon, bring it home for me.

"Fix it," she'd say, sweetly smiling at me. Even when she was fighting the thick black fog of suicidal thoughts, the lead-heavy boots of wanting to give up.

And I would fix it. I could fix the bikes. From the beginning of my life I've always tried to make broken things better. I'd take them apart. Penelope never minded the mess because she took her sleeping pills, disappeared to the bedroom for hours at a time.

I would take the bikes apart in the kitchen, sometimes in my bedroom, sometimes in the living room, sometimes on the front porch, the deck, the garage. It wasn't long before the neighbors caught on, began dropping off bikes for me. Either to repair or to use the parts for scraps.

I called my bike shop B's. B for bikes. B for Penelope and Dalton Berkeley. B for my heart.

"You're absolutely not pregnant, but you thought you were?" I needed clarification. Frances lit the cigarette, took a drag, offered it to me. I accepted it, smoked and handed it back. Smoking was stupid, but let the record show I was a sucker for a good ritual.

"I thought I was. Maybe. I'm not. I mean, would it be the *worst* thing?" she said. I could see the feist sparking behind her eyes— gold flecks against black velvet.

"Not the *worst* thing, but not the *best* thing either, right? I mean we agree on that?" I said.

She sat cross-legged next to me, using her empty can of Diet Coke as an ashtray. It was spring, the air was rich, pulsing with fecundity. We had the windows open, the curtains she'd picked out for me were trembling in the wind like delicate butterfly wings. Watching them made me want to play piano. They looked like a song. *Pianissimo.*

Penelope and I would play a game when I was a kid and make up piano songs according to our moods or a song about how my hamster would sound running on his wheel at night or a song about the little bright blue and yellow birds nesting in the tree out-side my bedroom window. Penelope would play Vivaldi's "Spring" Allegro for me, tell me all about how it sounded like the things outside our windows—the birds, the storms, the wind, the rain, the leaves, the sun returning. I could hear them. I could hear all of them. She taught me to play them too. I could play them poorly by the time I was six. I could play them well by the time I was ten. I could play them perfectly by the time I was twelve. A man at church used the word *prodigy* once. Penelope made a *zip the lips* motion. Later she told me if I heard words like *prodigy* or *genius* too often I would think I didn't have to practice, didn't have to work hard. Penelope taught piano at the university and they put on a concert in her honor the month after her memorial service, asked me to play. I played Rachmaninoff's "Piano Concerto No. 2" and there was a full orchestra behind me. Loretta had bought me my first tuxedo. I wore it with my black high-top sneakers. Eamon had given me his lucky baseball card to keep in my pocket—a signed 1995 Marty Cordova.

Sometimes Penelope would turn on the string Vivaldi recording. We would lie on our backs on the floor with the windows open and listen. Just, listen. Penelope died and the key of my life changed. The notes went both sharp and flat. Slowed. *Adagio. Grave.* I felt a blue ache on that bed next to Frances, thinking about Penelope. It'd been fifteen years since she'd taken enough pills to stop her heart. I watched the curtains, heard Vivaldi in my head. My fingers played the air. I thought about the baby Frances and I weren't having. I didn't want to have a baby with Frances. Yet? I didn't want to have a baby with anyone. Yet? When the time was right, wouldn't I feel it? She wasn't pregnant. It wasn't happening. There I was, grateful I didn't have to think about it. There I was, thinking about it.

Frances snapped her finger in front of my face.

"Where'd you go?" she asked. She asked it often when I stared off. Not so much because she wanted to know, but she liked me knowing she was aware of my non-presence. I'd been a bad boy. I'd drifted.

"Sorry. I'm sorry," I said, readjusting myself. I reached over, grabbed my underwear, slipped them up my legs.

"You'd hate it so much if I got pregnant? If we had a kid, got married, did all those normal things people do?" she asked, smoking.

"I didn't say I'd hate it. I want to be prepared for it. That's all. I'm not big on surprises," I said. The music was gone. I wanted it back. My fingers were itchy. I pulled my jeans up, put my T-shirt back on.

"Well good thing I'm not, right?" she said.

"Frances," I said. It was all I said. If I loved her I'd want those things too, right? Surprise or no, I'd want them. I couldn't process it properly so I stopped trying.

When she was gone I played piano with the windows open. I played piano, I took a shower. I went outside and my neighbor Miss Margaret told me she loved listening to me play.

"So remember to keep the windows open, okay?" she said, smiling her flirtiest eighty-year-old smile.

"I sure will," I said and I thanked her.

I went down to the bike shop to get some work done.

Eamon stopped by. He stopped by a lot, happily played the role of leaning cop, drinking coffee.

"You're such a cliché," I said to him.

"Body of a god and a ten-inch cock or cop drinking coffee? Both? Let's go with both," he said.

"If you've got ten inches I've got fourteen," I said, closing the register. We were only talking like this because the shop was empty. A customer had just picked up his bike and left. My only other employee, my buddy, Detroit had the day off.

"D! D-Money. Come on, bruh. Come on." Eamon laughed at me, shook his head. He stood there, using my Chemex, drinking my Ethiopian Yirgacheffe. I felt a rush of love for him—I had felt skinless about family since I was thinking about Penelope so much earlier in the day.

"I could be wrong. It's been a while since we measured," I said. We literally measured them when we were freshmen. Eamon had me beat by half an inch. He was also six days older than me. There is a picture of Penelope and Loretta, both in overalls, both nine months pregnant with us. They are holding hands. Loretta had it hung next to the staircase at home.

"If Evangeline will have me, I'm going to marry her. Watch," he said.

"She'll have you," I said.

I told him Frances thought she was pregnant last month.

"Well, listen. You'd be an awesome dad. The kid would be lucky to have you be his dad," Eamon said, pointing at me.

I felt my eyes get hot. Sure, we'd seen each other cry plenty of times. I wasn't even sure I felt like crying. I couldn't properly express how I felt in that moment but I knew Eamon telling me I'd be an awesome dad was some love right there. Brotherhood. Goodness. I'd never known my biological father. He ran off on me, on Penelope. Penelope's parents had died before I was born. She was an only child and so were they. I would've been a walking Charles Dickens novel if not for the Royces. Theirs was a gigantic, loving family—the kind of family you see in the movies.

"Don't cry, because I'll cry," Eamon said.

"Fuck you."

"You know I'm right."

I was practically an orphan, biologically. Never had a blood family outside of Penelope but always had the Royces. The thought of having an actual family of my own was overwhelming. Good and bad. I didn't want to think about it all the way yet. That's why I drifted to the music in my head when Frances brought it up earlier. Here it was again right in front of me.

"Ask. Ask Evi to marry you. She'll say yes," I said, shifting. I didn't want to cry.

"I'm doing this tonight," Eamon said. He nodded and was staring off into the middle distance before meeting my eyes again. He clapped his hands together and smiled at me.

Eamon and Evi had been dating for almost seven months and if it were any other woman, I would've been surprised Eamon was taking the leap so quickly. But this wasn't any other woman. This was Evangeline.

"All right, there's a ring I've been thinking about. That's where I'm going right now," Eamon said, slapping the counter. "Dig. Bring Franny if you want. Let's go out to dinner. I've got to work like—" he looked at his watch. The static of his police radio clicked, the robotic voices repeating letters, numbers, secret codes. "—two more hours. You and Franny meet us at West's at eight." He took a sip of his coffee, headed towards the door. "Mighty fine cup of coffee," he said, smiling. He never called Frances *Franny* but Eamon always got cheekier when he was excited.

"You ready for this?" I asked him.

"I'm ready for this."

"You already told Mom?"

"Reading my mind."

"See you at eight."

"All right, brother," he said, leaving.

I did inventory, worked on a couple bikes, thought about how Evangeline was going to be my sister-in-law and how much fun it would be to dance with Frances at the reception. Frances was a blast at weddings.

West's was a mid-level classic American bistro on the hip side of town. Frances and I stood out front, waiting for Eamon and Evangeline to arrive. I hadn't told Frances about Eamon's engagement plans. I didn't want her to get jealous. Eamon and Evangeline hadn't been together for as long as Frances and I had. Most times Frances said she didn't care about getting married and maybe that was true but I didn't want to have the conversation on the way to the restaurant. I didn't want to have the conversation at all. But I loved her, right? I loved her. I loved how she looked. Some kind of amazing black dress with a slit up the side—a slick knife sheathed in onyx. This is another scene I would show someone when they asked why we were still together. *She wears black dresses with slits up the sides and black heels like it's her job. She's New York City sexy and here we are in Kentucky. She's a goose, trust me on this.*

Her lips were reddest-red. I put my hands in my pockets and looked away, saw Eamon and Evangeline holding hands, walking towards us. The city lights and car headlights zipped up and down next to us, the streetlamps flickered, the neon restaurant sign buzzed overhead.

We were electric, all of us.

"Hi!" Evangeline said first. She and Frances hugged. Evangeline hugged me. I was stoked for Eamon and Evangeline. They looked great, they smelled great. Eamon was taking himself off the market and he was taking Evangeline with him. One day I'd like to have what they had. They *belonged* to one another. They *belonged* together. I let those sentences rattle around in my head as Frances and I walked in behind them. Eamon gave the hostess his name. We were seated.

Eamon and I were equally matched. We'd play Twenty-One in our driveway and I'd win one game, he'd win another. I was better at piano but he was faster than me. I was better at football, he was better at baseball. We both lost our virginity to our high school senior girlfriends on prom night. He liked to call me a handsome motherfucker and it was easy for him because he was a handsome motherfucker too.

Eamon and I were not jealous of one another. Neither one of us were the kind of guy to be okay with being jealous, with wanting what another guy had. Too lazy for us. Eamon got his degree in criminal justice, I got mine in English. Eamon joined the police force and I bartended and played piano gigs sometimes, taught a couple lessons here and there but mostly lived off the money Penelope had hoarded away and saved for me until I opened the bike shop with it.

Eamon and Evangeline getting engaged, married, making all of this legal—it got me thinking. I wanted that too. I wanted to feel a way about Frances that I didn't feel. Yet. I kept waiting for it and the sexiness and the smoking and the dinners and the dresses and the lips and the eyelashes and the perfume and dangly earrings and sleeping in the same bed clouded all of it sometimes.

I was thinking about this as Eamon winked at me and pulled the ring box from his pocket after dinner. He opened it. Evangeline gasped, put her hand to her heart.

"Evi. Evangeline. Will you do me the honor of being my girl

forever? My wife. My bride," he said, calmly. My heart was racing. Frances covered her mouth with her hand. I watched her, I watched them. The people at the table next to us started clapping.

"Yes, Eamon. Yes," Evi said, slapping his shoulder. Frances clapped so I clapped too.

"You know he knew about this," Eamon said, motioning to me. Evi smiled as he slipped the ring on. Frances glared at me. *Uh oh.* I knew her pissed look and I knew me keeping this surprise a secret meant for an uncomfortable ride home. *Worth it.* I smiled at Frances before giving my attention back to the happy couple. Our waitress brought out a small round chocolate cake dripping with shiny, slick icing. It was getting late, there was a piano player in the corner who had taken his seat on the bench. I made a guess of whether he'd play jazz or classical. He busted out "Satin Doll." Duke Ellington. Jazz Piano 101. He was good. I liked hearing the music twinkle-lift through the air. The night felt charmed already, the music made it even better. I was so happy for Eamon and Evangeline I didn't care that I could feel Frances's eyes burning a hole in my shirt. Like I could feel the grey of it turn soot-black, ringed with hissing orange fire. She'd be mean, she'd get over it. This wasn't about her.

Later after we'd finished the cake, Evi focused her attention on me. I looked at the starry diamond on her left finger. Eamon put up the paper all right. It was huge. I could almost smell how expensive it was from across the table—a whiff of something clean and clear-blue.

"Have you ever played piano in a restaurant like this, Dalton? I can't believe I don't know this," Evi said, shaking her head and widening her eyes.

"In college I did." I finished my beer. Frances was looking at her phone. "I made sweet tips playing in places like this and like, stores during Christmastime. And sometimes I'd play in the pit during a show at the arts center."

"It's crazy I've never seen you there before. I'm in *Romeo and Juliet* there next month."

Eamon had told me this, but I'd forgotten. I wanted to start remembering things like that since Evi was going to be my sister-in-law. It was important for me to know these things. I felt like we knew one another well anyway, but I wanted to crank it all up a notch more. My family was expanding. Whenever Evi and Eamon had their kids, I'd happily be an uncle to them.

"The ballet? You're Juliet?" Frances asked, putting away her phone.

"I am." Evi blushed.

"Fucking A," Frances said. *That's my girl.*

"It *is* fucking A," Eamon chimed in. He leaned back, let his arm rest on the back of Evi's chair.

"We'll come see it," Frances said.

"Absolutely we will," I said.

Eamon invited us all back to his place. Frances got into my truck.

"Um, fuck you for not telling me this was like an *engagement* dinner," she said, making a disgusted face. She kicked her heels off, rolled down the window.

"It was a secret," I said, shaking my head. I laughed at her and she punched my arm. Hard. My Frances.

"Dalton, I'm serious. We're stalled out, you and me. You don't tell me things," she said.

Eamon and Evangeline were one car ahead of us. I waited to see if he would turn at the light. We'd debated before whether it was faster to turn at the light to get to his place or go up three streets, then turn. Eamon went straight. I turned at the light. We'd see which one of us got to his place first. I could drive to his place with my eyes closed.

I closed my eyes, held them closed as long as I could, until the adrenaline kicked in. I opened them and the traffic thinned out in front of me.

"I tell you things," I said. Yes, she was right. We were stalled out, but it didn't bother me. Did it?

"It's not fair *Evangeline* has everything," Frances said. She said Evangeline in a sing-song whiny way I'd become accustomed to. In her defense, when Frances wasn't around, Evangeline had on occasion called her *Francey, Princess, Princesa, Francey-Pants.* They knew how to behave civilly but theirs was an accidental friendship. An accidental frenemyship.

"You want Eamon, is that it? You're jealous?" I teased.

"Oh please. You know he's not my type," she said. I looked at her. She rolled her eyes. I pressed down harder on the gas. I wanted to beat Eamon home and prove to him I was right about the shortcut. The engine gunned.

"Don't be jealous of her. Don't be jealous of anyone," I said.

"Should we get married?" she asked. She used her serious voice. This wasn't Mad Frances or Jealous Frances or Funny Frances. This was Serious Frances.

Two more minutes and I'd be at Eamon's. I ran a yellow. I loved that Frances didn't say one word about my crazy-ass driving. A plus for her in the *Sure We Should Get Married* column.

"Do you *want* to get married?" I asked her. Not a question a man should ask a woman. A man should know the answer to that question without asking. A man should be able to look into the eyes of his lover and see what he was searching for. I saw a lot of things when I looked into Frances's eyes. I saw sex and fighting and trust and knowing she'd answer when I called, knowing she'd text me back. Knowing I could call her an hour beforehand and she'd be ready, come out to dinner with me. I saw love and frustration in her eyes. We'd been together like this since the moment we met at the restaurant where I'd bartended back in the day. The first night, my first shift, she came right up to me and started bossing me around. *Garbage goes here, glasses dry here, don't leave wet towels over there and clean up your shit.* That same night, we closed the restaurant together and afterwards, stood by my truck, talking. We got into my truck, talking. She kissed me. She said *fuck it* before putting her hands on my face. Maybe those should be our wedding vows. Quick, to the point. *Fuck it.*

We had cooling periods, weeks at a time when we wouldn't

talk at all besides the occasional *have you seen anything good on Netflix?* text from her or *I do miss you but this break is good for both of us text* from me. I never really dated anyone in between. I was reluctant to call Frances my girlfriend, even when we were decidedly *together.* We needed an airier word. *Girlfriend* was too rigid. *Lover* made more sense. Roomier. *Girl* seemed too possessive, more possessive than I intended. *Frances* fit perfectly. Frances was my Frances.

I looked over at her, wanting to see if I could decipher something new in her eyes. The neon-colored chunks of city lights flashed against the windshield glass of my truck as I power-rattled us down the road.

"Neither one of us wants to get married," she said, turning from me and looking out her window.

We were quiet. I got to Eamon's house just as he was pulling in his driveway. *Dammit.* I pulled behind him.

"The so-called shortcut is *not* faster. How many times do I have to tell you before you listen to me, son?" Eamon said as soon as he got out of his truck. His keys jingled as he shoved them in his pocket.

Eamon's house was hardwood and slate-grey walls downstairs. Upstairs, everything was white. The house was swank, the neighborhood was swank. He'd worked hard, earned it. He'd recently had the kitchen redone. Evi would be moving in soon. Right now she lived halfway across town in an apartment but spent a lot of nights at Eamon's. The house I rented wasn't far from Eamon's but Eamon owned his. Eamon owned a home, was engaged now.

Frances turned on Eamon's stereo, put on Björk. She made herself at home, no matter where we were. She acted like she owned every place we walked in. It was like she wasn't born with any inhibitions at all and she didn't care if people thought she was rude. Why would she? The thought had never occurred to her.

The music was down low. Trip hop, Frances's favorite. She was a Portishead song in a black dress, deep bass in black heels. Her sexiness was calculated. Undeniable. Made me sweat. I scratched at my beard. She and Evi were on the couch. Frances bent her elbow, leaned her head on her hand and looked like an Egon Schiele sketch, all long limbs and angles. She had her long, thick hair twisted up behind her, like an unbloomed black orchid. I watched her release it, let it fall before I turned back to Eamon. He was in his liquor cabinet, pulling out fat wide-bottomed glass bottles of brown liquid, two clears.

"I admire you for getting all this done. This house looks awesome," I said.

"Well the feeling is mutual, man. I admire the hell out of you. Look at what you've done with B's," he said as he pulled the last bottle out. He looked at me.

"Now you'll be a married man," I said, wishing I already had a drink to toast with. The conversation *felt* like a toast.

Eamon swiveled and clawed the glass tumblers out of the cabinet. He began pouring whiskey into all four of them. The ice-clear gin and vodka were after-options. First shots were always whiskey at Eamon's.

"Beautiful ladies, dearest ribbons, please do join us in the kitchen for a quick toast," Eamon said. He was a natural leader. People did what he said. Evi walked in. Frances sauntered—a cat, vaguely interested.

"Hey you," I said to her, close to her ear. She smacked my ass softly before reaching for her glass.

"Women, you are sleek and gorgeous. You hold us together, you're the ribbons. We're men. Dangerous only if you take us too seriously. We're the whiskey. To whiskey and ribbons," Eamon said, lifting his glass.

"To whiskey and ribbons," Evi and I repeated.

"Whiskey and ribbons. Sláinte," Frances said, staying true to her Irish father's roots.

We did our shots, we did another. The girls were getting drunk already. Together they were the ones who suggested we play strip poker. It wasn't us. Promise.

"I'm terrible at poker. I don't even know why I'm doing this. I don't know how to play! Maybe because we're engaged? Oh no, I didn't call my mom! I'm a horrible daughter!" Evangeline said, covering her mouth with her hand. She sat cross-legged in the kitchen chair, tucked her feet underneath her while Frances dealt our hands. Frances was one of those women who knew how to do everything. Poker, sous-vide steak, getting red wine stains out of white fabric using nothing but a spoon and a sugar packet.

"Your mom is fine. You'll tell her tomorrow," Frances said, annoyed.

"I'm with Frances. You're not a horrible daughter," Eamon said, nodding his head towards Frances as he took another sip of his whiskey.

"She'll forgive you," I said to Evi.

"Okay. Lowest hand has to take off a piece of clothing. Simple," Frances said.

I had to strip first. I took off a sock—a navy blue and light blue polka-dotted number Frances had given me for my birthday.

"Wait. Evangeline, are you still a virgin?" Frances asked, shuffling the cards again. I watched her hands. Her fingernails were long-ish, a deep raisin color. She got them done every Wednesday evening. Her toes too. Whiskey always clicked a small key in Frances's heart and unleashed the prowling tigers of curiosity, cruelty, honesty. Any of us were fair game, but I was protective of Evangeline. Eamon and I could take it. Evi was tenderhearted, kind.

"Babe. Don't," I said. I was working on a glass of whiskey and ice, maintaining a pleasant buzz. Eamon had brought out his cigar box. I nodded, dug into it. Eamon did the same. I watched him smirk at Frances.

"I am!" Evangeline said, holding her mouth open, making her eyes wide.

"She is," Eamon said.

"Bullshit. How do you stay here all the time and you guys haven't had sex? Eamon's hot, you're hot. You're engaged," she said, loudly.

We played. Frances pointed at him when she said, "Eamon, you lose. Strip."

"All right," he said, the unlit cigar between his teeth. He bent down and took his sock off.

"It'll take forever to get you boys naked." Frances rolled her eyes.

Evi downed the rest of her drink, hopped up from her chair. I heard her rattling through a kitchen drawer, heard the refrigerator door hum open and kiss closed again. She came back to the table with a plate of cheeses, some thinly-sliced meats, green olives. A fresh bottle of cold white wine, opened, the color of pear flesh.

"Technically I *am* a virgin and will remain so until our wedding night. But it's not like we don't do—stuff," she said, picking the conversation back up after sitting at the table again.

Evi lost the next round and Frances informed her to strip. Evi was only wearing a dress, so she stood up, lifted it over her head and let it drop to the floor. I looked away. "It's not fair since y'all are wearing more clothes than me. Both of you take off your pants. Or your shirts. The whole one sock thing isn't going to fly," Evi said, popping an olive into her mouth. I didn't make eye contact, out of respect for her, out of respect for Eamon. From the corner of my eye I could see her hot-pink bra strap, neon against her brown skin. I stood and did as I was instructed. Took off my pants. Eamon unbuttoned his shirt, took it off. Took his white undershirt off too. I was wearing a pair of plain white boxer shorts, another *here let me dress you* gift from Frances.

"So *that's* why Eamon asked you to marry him," Frances said, winking at Evangeline. I was glad she did it. She'd softened herself, wasn't being entirely awful. Simply nosy.

Eamon shook his head, laughed. He wasn't an easy person to get riled up. Frances made attempts to push his buttons but it rarely worked.

"I'll eff his brains out on our wedding night," Evangeline said, raising her eyebrow.

Frances grabbed all the cards from the table, finished her drink and poured herself more wine. She was fully dressed, had won every hand so far. She began dealing to all of us again. Eamon propped open the back door and we lit our cigars.

I lost my shirt, everything but my boxers. Eamon stood next to the table, cupping his dick in his hands. Evi was in her underwear, Frances still in her black dress.

"Is the game over now?" Eamon asked.

"Sure," Frances said.

"Dalton, play piano. Poker's done. Piano time!" Evi demanded and clapped.

I half-jogged over to the piano, sat on the bench. Played the first thing that came to mind. "Moon River."

Evi gasped.

"Did Eamon tell you to play this?" she asked.

I shook my head no, kept playing.

"Aw, it's like my *favorite*," she said, putting her hand to her heart. "You're my Huckleberry Friend, Dalton. I love you."

"I love you too, Huckleberry Friend," I said, winking. "He told me you like this one."

I started playing "Hold Me" by Fleetwood Mac. It was pretty, easy, and almost everyone loved it. Everyone but Eamon, who had this weird unnatural hate for Fleetwood Mac. The stereo was still on. Frances went over to it, turned it off.

Somewhere between the kitchen and the piano, Eamon had managed to get his underwear back on.

"Eamon hates Fleetwood Mac," Evi said, pouting.

Eamon shrugged.

I started playing a piano version of "Niggas in Paris" instead.

"That's what I'm talking about," Eamon said, laughing into his fist. "That's my brother right there," he said, pointing down at me on the bench. I could tell he was properly buzzed, nearing drunk, but not there yet. Eamon wasn't an easy drunk. He was balanced, always in control, but I recognized when he was loosened up.

"You're a half-white boy raised by a black family so of course you know hip hop piano covers. It's like, your *brand*," Frances said, rolling her eyes. She leaned against the doorframe.

Eamon kept laughing.

"Do you *like* Dalton, like at all? Because sometimes I'm not so sure," Evi said, sitting on the couch. She wrapped herself up in the fuzzy black blanket next to her. She yawned. I felt like I could look at her again now that she was covered back up, so I did. She was the perfect woman for Eamon. Everylittlething about her. If I could've bargained with God to handcraft Eamon's dream girl, dream wife, she would look and act exactly like Evangeline Cooper.

"Do I *like* Dalton? Do I *like* Dalton Berkeley-Royce?" Frances pointed to herself, then to me.

Eamon plopped on the couch next to Evi, they kissed. They kept kissing.

"No. Wait. Before you two go to bed to *not* have sex, I want to answer your question properly," Frances said. She stepped to the middle of the room. I started playing more quietly. *Pianissimo.* If Penelope and I were playing our *Sounds Like* game I would've said the piano sounded like the end of a summer storm, the raindrops slowing. Frances held her hands up, the stem of her wine glass slipped between her knuckles. She could drop it, she could shatter it against the hardwood floor, the piano, the wall, the windows. She could pour the pear-gold all over herself, all over me, throw it all over Evi because she was jealous of her. She walked over to the piano while I played, set the glass on top of it.

"I more than *like* Dalton. I *love* Dalton. We'll figure it out. We'll figure it out," she said. So sweet. She nudged me and I scooted over. She began tinkling out "Heart and Soul" and I played my part.

"I'm going to bed, y'all," Evi said after a while, wrapped in her blanket.

We stopped playing.

"Y'all stay. Sleep down the hall. I'll make breakfast in the morn-ing," Evi said, standing. She yawned again.

"Can I borrow your eye makeup remover?" Frances asked.

"Yeah. Come on," Evi said. Frances followed her and they dis-appeared upstairs.

"Hey. I want to talk to you about something real quick," Eamon said after he was sure they couldn't hear. He motioned for me to come over to the couch so I did. He was smiling wide. Wildly.

"What's up?" I said, smiling back. I was super-buzzed but not drunk. Close. Maybe too close. The coffee table seemed to ship-wobble in front of me. I steadied myself against the armrest.

"Promise me something," he said.

"Okay."

"If something happens to me—if something happens to me, you'll take care of Evi. Swear to me. Like even if I'm dead and gone and she marries someone else and moves a thousand miles away, you'll check in on her. Make sure she's okay?" he said, earnestly. The smile was gone.

"Absolutely. Of course, man. Of course," I said.

"Promise?" he asked.

"I promise," I said.

"All right," he said, holding out his hand for me.

I knew exactly what to do. Same thing we always did.

We bumped fists, shook, hooked pinkies, bit our thumbs. The secret handshake we'd made up in his treehouse when we were seven years old. We'd been friends and brothers since we were in the womb, like Jesus and John the Baptist. We were David and Jonathan. No discussion needed. Of course I'd take care of Evi.

"Nothing's going to happen to you, though," I said.

I could hear Evi and Frances in the bathroom above us, dissolving into a fit of bright bubbly wine giggles.

I nodded again.

I'll take care of your girl.

II.

Evangeline

ICE STORM. BLIZZARD. SNOWED IN. WE DON'T HAVE TO think about doing anything. The pantry is stocked. We don't have to go anywhere. I pump and put my milk in the freezer. Dalton's phone buzzes on the table and I think about not looking at it, but I do. It's Cassidy. I decide to answer it. I know Dalton won't care.

"Hi Cassidy, this is Evi, Dalton's sister-in-law. We met yesterday. Dalton's sleeping," I say quietly.

"Oh hi, Evi. I wanted to leave D a message," she says.

D? I roll my eyes and tell Cassidy I'll take it for her.

"Okay. Please ask him if he wants me to go open up the shop today or if we're staying closed because the roads are so bad. It's supposed to snow more, I think. I don't care either way," she says.

I don't know what she's talking about.

"Oh. Do you work at the bike shop now?" I ask.

"Well, yes and no. I haven't worked a full shift yet," Cassidy laughs.

I fake laugh.

"I remember. You're the new bike mechanic," I say.

"I am. And the only chick, but Dalton's great," Cassidy says. I can practically hear her taking off her panties over the phone.

"He is. He *is* great," I say. I hear Dalton coming down the stairs and I turn to see him, sleepy-eyed and scratching at his head. "Oh you know what, Cassidy, he's up now. Here he is."

I smile, hand Dalton the phone and start making coffee. Dalton leans against the counter, talking into his phone while he's rubbing his eye. He lifts his shirt up to scratch his stomach. I see the trail of hair from his belly button to the elastic of his pants. I force myself to look away and turn back to the coffee pot.

"Nah. Let's sit tight. No one will be out today anyway. I'll call you tomorrow and let you know about Monday," he says. I hold up an empty mug as a question. He nods his answer.

I want to hear what else he says to her but I don't want to be so obvious about my eavesdropping so I open the utensil drawer to pretend like I'm looking for something. I hear him talk about some place and I assume it's a new restaurant. I guess Cassidy is telling him where she wants to go when they go out to dinner. Is he still doing that after the kissing last night? Even though I invited him into my bed for the first time? Nothing happened. But still.

I slip a pair of chopsticks out of their paper pocket envelope and put them back in and turn around as Dalton finishes his conversation.

"Good morning," he says as he reaches out for my arm, pulls me to him.

"Hey. Good morning," I say. He wraps his arms around me and squeezes me until I make a noise of mercy and he lets go. I grab Eamon's grey sweater off the kitchen chair and as I slip it over my head, Dalton tickles my armpit. Tells me how much he loves my armpit hair. I fold at the waist and wiggle away from him, tell him

I know. He tells me that a lot. Pets me when I let him. He calls them my little puffs. *Let's see the little puffs* he's been saying this winter. I stopped shaving months ago.

"I'm stoked about this snow day," he says. He pours his coffee and stands in front of me blowing across the top of the mug.

"Are you stoked about your new bike mechanic too? The same bike mechanic who just so happens to be the same girl who you've kissed and who also calls asking you out to dinner?" I ask, turning my back to him, cuffing the long scritchy wool sweater sleeves to my wrists. I add some all-natural no-calorie sweetener and a pour of almond milk to my coffee. I turn around to look at him as I take a victory sip. Dalton tilts his head and doesn't say anything.

Until he does. "Is this really what you're doing? What *we're* doing?"

"What?"

"Come on," he says.

"Come on, what?" I say, staring into my coffee.

"If it's a problem—" he starts.

"It's not a problem. Do what you want, Dalton. You do what you want. I do what I want."

"When do I *not* do what I want?"

"I guess never." I shrug.

"I want to be here. With you. With Noah. Like this," he says. "Last night was different."

I shrug again. I don't know what to say. I'm scared to care. There's the truth. I said it to myself. But I'm not saying it aloud to him this morning. Once I start talking about it, I know I won't be able to stop. I can't put it all back once I let it out—a cup, spilled.

"You do agree with me that last night wasn't a normal night for us, right?" Dalton bends down to look right into my eyes. It's a tiny act of aggression I don't hate, the woosh-like striking of a match. I look at him and nod.

"Of course. Cut it out," I say.

"*You* cut it out. Don't start shit about Cassidy. I told you it's not like that anymore."

"It's too early for fighting," I say.

"I miss Noah-bear this morning," Dalton says, switching gears. God bless him. Noah Michael is both the unluckiest and luckiest little boy in the world. To lose his daddy before he ever got to meet him, to have so many different people who love him this much already.

Dalton sits down at the piano. He's changed shirts. From blue-grey to one the deep green-green of the trees in Vietnam War movies.

"We should drink all day and sleep and watch crap and eat junk," he says, turning to look at me. I'm thinking of walking over to him and throwing my arms around him and kissing him again. But I won't. I go behind the bathroom mirror and get two orange ibuprofens because I have a morning-after-crying-and-whiskey-and-wine headache. I throw my head back, swallow the pills. He keeps playing.

When I get back to the living room, Dalton starts playing ballet warm-ups. The same way he did when he came and played for my Littlest Sprouts three-year-olds class, back when I was teaching. Back before I got too pregnant. A class full of tiny girls in pink. They loved Mr. Dalton playing the piano for them. It felt fancy. Usually I hooked my phone up to the speakers and played our warm-ups.

I stand in first position, holding my coffee. Once upon a time, I was three too, I was a Littlest Sprout too and my dance teacher would play our warm-up music on a record player. I used to think my dance teacher and I were psychically connected when we'd move at the same time. I stopped teaching once I got too pregnant. I lost dance and Eamon at the same time and it felt like losing everything.

I do a proper *demi-plié* as Dalton plays, keeping my heels on the floor. I've been doing them for twenty-seven of my thirty years. I stay turned out, do another plié before taking a sip of my coffee. I am trying not to cry and Dalton knows.

I go and sit down next to him and put my fingers on the keys. He automatically puts his hand on top of mine and pushes my fingers down for me. His finger covers my wedding ring I wear on my right hand now. I wear it on my right hand because I didn't want to wear it on my left anymore because Eamon is dead so we can't be married. But I couldn't bear the thought of not wearing it and I didn't want to wear it around my neck because I was scared I would lose it, so I moved it to my other hand. Dalton presses my fingers up and down and I think about Eamon touching this cool wide white key like this and reaching his finger up to tap the skinny black one next to it like I am now. Now.

"Call your mom, check on Noah—then Irish coffee. Irish coffee and pancakes," Dalton says after we stop playing piano.

I nod and he puts his hand on my leg.

The night after he moved in, we sat down next to each other on the couch. We were being quiet and the TV was on but neither one of us was watching it. It was a PBS period piece. *Sense & Sensibility, Jane Eyre, Pride and Prejudice, Belle, North & South, Persuasion, Emma, Poldark.* I watched them as if they were somehow keeping my heart beating, keeping me alive. I'd seen them all too many times to count, could mouth the words without looking at the screen.

Nothing specific happened to bring it on, but Dalton hung his head and cried. I put my hand on his back and cried too. Dalton put his hand on my leg and looked at me. He said he was sorry. He started using his T-shirt to wipe his eyes. I asked him what he was sorry for and he said for crying. I liked his hand on my leg because I guess it could be a small, seemingly meaningless thing but it made me feel less alone.

I'd felt alone before but this was a new kind of alone. This widow-who-just-had-her-baby alone was deeper than anything I'd felt before besides the grief. As if the superheroes of darkness, loneliness and grief had teamed up to take me on. All of them, capes billowing high in a gust of evil wind, holding hands and partnering up to devour and torture me, but never let me die.

"I got snowed in at Eamon's on our first date. You know that, right?" I say to Dalton. We're on our second Irish coffees. Called Mom first and had her hold up the phone to Noah so I could do Mom-things like tell him I love him and wait for him to make any sound resembling a *hi* or *Mama.* I told her we'd check the roads in the morning and I'd call.

"I know the story, but tell me again. I know E's version," Dalton says, smiling at me.

"What's that supposed to mean?" I smile and swat at him, careful not to spill my drink.

"It means E told me y'all got snowed in. What's up with you always assuming the worst?" he says, still smiling.

"Do I?"

Dalton shrugs.

"No, seriously. Do I?"

"Quit it. Tell the story. Tell me the first date story," Dalton says, leaning his head back on the couch and closing his eyes. I look at his watch. It's only nine-thirty in the morning. I'm so glad.

On our first date, Eamon and I went out for pizza. He claimed the best spot was over the bridge in Indiana and he wanted to take me there. It'd snowed the night before so I wore my L.L. Bean Boots and when he showed up at my place, he was wearing the same boots.

"I guess I should've called first. This is so embarrassing, right? Don't girls fight over stuff like this?" he joked and winked at me.

"Absolutely. Everything you've heard about girls is true. Whenever boys aren't around, we have pillow fights in our underwear and kiss in a flurry of feathers," I said as he opened the truck door for me.

"I knew it. I'm always right," he said.

"Not the best way to start off the first date, in case you were wondering."

"What's not?" he said after he'd put his seatbelt on.

"Claiming you're always right," I said, making my eyes little slits and smashing my mouth into a straight line. It was my meanest face. I was trying not to laugh while I did it.

"What? A man can't do stuff to make a pretty woman laugh anymore?"

"I'm not laughing," I said.

"Well, you should be. Because me saying I'm always right is bananas. That's the funniest thing I've heard all day. And don't forget I'm a cop, so hearing funny things is straight up part of my job," he said, looking over at me.

"Bananas," I said and let myself laugh, finally.

"You look beautiful, by the way," he said. I said thank you.

"Your laugh kills me. *Kills* me. You're light in a dark room, Cooper," he said, calling me by my last name.

It was snowing slow and sweet when Eamon kissed me for the first time in his kitchen. His mouth tasted like cinnamon and dark chocolate because we'd had cinnamon coffee and slutty triple-layered brownie cake.

"I'm a virgin. Well, practically. I'm not a nun or anything," I blurted out in between kisses.

He nodded, kept kissing me. It started snowing harder. We stayed up and watched movies. I picked *Pride & Prejudice*. He picked *Stand By Me*. He said I should stay over because the roads were getting bad and he told me to sleep in his bed. He took blankets and a pillow to the couch and when we woke up, the power was out.

We had no electricity for the entire next day. I put on two of his sweaters and three pairs of socks. We ate things that didn't have to be cooked. Sardines, crackers, apples and bananas. Peanut butter with handfuls of chocolate chips. Eamon lit a fire and we spent most of the day wrapped in blankets, sitting there watching the fire, telling stories. At night it was freakishly quiet and we could hear the tree branches snapping and breaking under the ice-weight.

"E told me that. About the branches cracking all night," Dalton says, nodding as he drinks.

"It was the creepiest, prettiest sound." I tuck my legs underneath me on the couch.

"You sit like a cat," he says.

"What?"

"You curl up like a cat. You always do it."

"I do?"

"You don't believe anything I say anymore. What happened?"

"I don't know," I shake my head and put my mug on a stack of magazines on the coffee table. "I guess I never thought you noticed stuff like that about me. Why would you?"

"I notice lots of things," he says. I wonder if I hurt his feelings again. I want to ask him what else he notices but I don't. He leans forward and puts his mug down too. He puts his head in his hands before he looks up again, over at me.

"I believe you. I'm sorry if I make it sound like I don't. It's not what I mean," I say.

"Do you feel shitty about last night?" he asks. It catches me off guard. I expected us to talk about it today. I wanted to. I *want* to. I didn't expect Dalton to use the word *shitty*. But the answer is no. *No, Dalton, I don't feel shitty about last night. I feel a lot of things but none of them are shitty. Let's see. I feel like the last person I kissed before you was Eamon.*

Six months ago. We kissed before he left for work. He kissed my mouth, my forehead. I told him I loved him and he told me he loved me too. He turned around and walked out. He turned around, walked right back in, kissed me again. I told him I loved seeing him in his uniform, never tired of it. He put his hand on my pregnant belly and told me he loved me again. I walked him to the door and smacked his butt and he turned to wink at me, to kiss my belly. He went to work. I made tea and called my friend Merit on the phone and went to bed early. While I was sleeping, Eamon was shot. I have dreams where I'm watching it happen and I wake up at the moment I hear the gunshots. I am always hot, like I'm on fire, burning and gasping for air.

"I don't feel shitty. That's not the right word." I tug at my sleeves.

"You're right. I'm sorry. I didn't mean it."

I ask him if he wants to smoke. Yes. So we both get up from the couch and go into the kitchen.

"I don't know how I feel." I tell him what I'm sure he already knows—I haven't kissed anyone since Eamon. "But tell me how you and Miss Indie Bike Mechanic ended up steaming up your truck windows," I say, as I sit cross-legged by the back door.

I take one of my slippers off and slide it out so the door will stay open a smidge. Dalton lights his cigarette and lets it dangle from his lips as he reaches up to prop the door open, using the hinge pin at the top. *Hinge: attach or join.* Fact: Dalton and I are *hinged*. I put my slipper back on and say *my hero* like I'm Olive Oyl and he's Popeye. He shrugs. I don't roll my eyes. We're both tender-hearted today. We're both tender-hearted every day.

Three days after Eamon was killed, Dalton sat down at the piano and played "Moon River." We'd inhabited the same space, quietly. No music, no TV. Our voices, silenced. The whole world, silenced, until Dalton played. Later that night he went out and got us sandwiches. He also bought a pack of cigarettes and I asked him why. He said he didn't know. He and Eamon would sometimes smoke cigars, but Dalton wasn't a smoker-smoker and neither was I. Dalton put the cigarettes in a drawer in the kitchen and we didn't smoke them until after I had Noah. Now we were different people. We were people who smoked for something to do when we ran out of words but still wanted to use our mouths. It was a ritual that made sense to us and helped us in some way even if we couldn't explain it. We didn't need to. Didn't want to. I would light up and think about how smoking killed people but so what? I needed to be here for Noah, but I wasn't afraid to die anymore. Part of me was already dead.

Dalton goes over to the kitchen table, grabs my red pompom snow hat and pulls it onto his head. He pushes it back so it isn't hanging over his eyes. I want to tell him how cute he is, but it seems trite. It's been so long and watching his quarterback body standing over me like this and seeing his lean, muscular arms reaching up to make sure the door stays open, it's making me feel things. He takes the cigarette from his mouth and hands it to me. He leaves the kitchen and returns wearing his hooded sweatshirt. I give him his cigarette back and he looks at me.

"Cassidy and I kiss sometimes," he says. It feels like forever since I asked the question. Usually I love how Dalton takes his time with things. Most of the time I love how laid-back he is. Like, even how he sits. He sits like he's never worried about anything in his life. So it's not just his personality, it's his body too. Everything about him.

But not now. Not when I want him to answer a question.

"Well, she called you D on the phone. I rolled my eyes," I admit, too jealous to remark on the kissing.

"You don't like her calling me D, even though my name is Dalton?"

I shake my head.

"You think she should call me A for Asshole?" he laughs.

I shake my head again and laugh. "So why isn't Cassidy your girlfriend?"

"Because of you."

"Seriously?"

"Seriously," he says.

"I'm jealous of her. But also it makes me feel special that you say she isn't your girlfriend because of me."

"Good. It should. You are."

"Who was the last girl you had sex with?" I ask. I'm surprised I came right out and asked it but let's just get it out there. I can't blame this on the Irish coffee; I've moved on to full-on nosy. I both do and don't want to know, but I also want to know if I'm right. I think it's his ex, Frances.

"This is the conversation we're having? I'd rather talk about something else. I thought we were going to talk about last night."

"It's all connected," I say, wiggling my fingers and twisting my hands in the air. I watch more snowflakes fall onto the deck and crook my neck to look up at the milky grey sky.

"I don't see what good will come out of it," Dalton says.

"We're friends, right? More than friends. We agree?"

He doesn't answer me because I don't need him to. He keeps his wide eyes on me, no expression. All country boy morning face.

"So we're talking as friends. As more than friends," I say. I make a little bet with myself. If I'm right and it was Frances, I'm going to put out my cigarette, get up, get a piece of dark chocolate and turn on the music. I'm going to turn on the Marshall Tucker Band and hippie dance to "Can't You See" until Dalton finishes his cigarette. That's what I'm going to have to do because I don't want to think about Dalton having sex with Frances, which of course never bothered me before.

Dalton smokes. I try to remember when Frances was in town. She lives in Austin, Texas, now. But I think she was in town right before Dalton moved in with Noah and me. I can't remember things as well as I used to. I'm sitting here watching him smoke. Watching the snowflakes fall. I already have the Marshall Tucker Band song in my head. The flutes at the beginning. I'm ready. I'm warm and dreamy-drunk from the sticky Irish cream in my coffee.

"Frances?" I say for him.

He nods. Takes a sip. I ask him if it was right before he moved in here. Right before his lease was up. He nods again. My eyes are welling with tears. I put out my cigarette and stand up. The room is already gently spinning before I lift my arms to the unseen sky.

Eamon

MY PARENTS LOVED EVANGELINE MORE THAN THEY'D EVER
loved any of my past girlfriends. Mom was a hard sell on anyone but
took to Evi as I knew she would. Evi was lovable—she was bright-
ness, warmth, a soothing presence. I loved Evangeline more than
I thought possible. What I felt for her made what Lisabeth and
I had feel like a flash, a glint—made what I'd felt for any other
woman feel like practically nothing. I had loved those women at
the time and in the beginning of those relationships, I'd even
argue that I'd loved them well. But something clearly faded away
with the others as the months wore on. Not with Evi. Everything
was brighter, more colorful, more alive. We'd been engaged for
a year, had a couple more months to go before the July wedding.
I'd wanted to get married sooner, quicker, but Evi wanted to plan
things, take our time and she had work. Ballet. She was Juliet in

the local production of *Romeo and Juliet.* Her ballet classes had their spring recitals. The following summer she was in *Giselle. The Nutcracker* in the winter. She wanted to have the spring to plan the fun wedding stuff. She wanted to have the summer as free as she could. She wasn't dancing in anything in the fall and would only be helping out with her smallest students once *Nutcracker* rolled back around.

Dalton and I always went together to the ballet to see Evangeline dance. Sometimes, Frances would go. My mom would join us sometimes too. I sat there in the hushed dark of the theatre, thrumming with pride watching Evi dance and make music with her body like that. No matter how many times I saw her perform, I was awestruck. My girl, up there turning her strong little body into a straight-backed column, a wilting flower. Spinning and leaping across the stage with the other dancers, completely in control of every movement. How the pink would peek through her cheeks on our rides home together, the big bouquet of flowers I'd given her wrapped in crinkling brown paper on her lap in my passenger seat.

I worked, passed my examinations—written, oral and physical— was promoted to sergeant after having been on the force for six years. The mayor held a ceremony, mine and Evi's family came. Fancy. Soon after, I had a scary night where some guy pulled a knife on me. Another cop shot and killed him. Mom still begged me to quit. Evi was surprisingly stoic about my job but I didn't tell her the scariest parts. I never told her the guy pulled a knife. She saw the story on the news but they didn't mention me at all. She asked me about it but I kept my answers vague, light. She and I both knew I kept the darkest parts from her. She knew when something was on my mind, but instead of obsessing over it, she offered comfort. She cooked for me, came over late and folded my clothes while I was sleeping. We were *together.* We were waiting to have sex which felt a little crazy to me, but she was worth it. And she wasn't a prude. I knew what was waiting for me on our wedding night. I'd smelled it, tasted it, worshipped it.

I still worked security at her church on Sundays. I slept better at night thinking Evi imagined me spending most of my days rescuing kittens from trees and helping elderly women cross the street with their groceries. She and I both knew better. I promised Mom I'd think about finding another career. I didn't lie to her. I thought about it a lot but nothing interested me. I wasn't a desk job kind of guy.

Evangeline's parents were good to me. Our families got along. Our moms traded pie recipes, our dads could sit together and have beers, shoot the shit. I was overwhelmed at the idea of marrying her and getting exactly what I wanted. I could see the beginnings of the rest of my life laid bare in front of me, my joy blooming like a rose. I knew it was too good to be true and last, but it didn't stop me from wanting it, from living for it. It's what got me out of bed in the morning. The *possibility*.

The night of my bachelor party, our only rule was no strippers. I'd promised Evi without argument. I'd seen enough strippers in my lifetime. We were hanging at Dalton's place, the two of us, waiting for the rest of our buddies to get there.

"You know our pact works both ways, right?" I said to him. The liquor made me want to discuss it. It broke the seal. I was a control freak and wanted to make sure Evi would be taken care of. But it wasn't as simple as having her taken care of, I wanted to choose who did it. I chose Dalton. It couldn't be anyone but Dalton. I trusted Dalton with my life. I trusted Dalton with my wife. We were close enough to feel like one person sometimes. He was my brother long before he was my brother. I didn't let people in often but I never had to let Dalton in because he was already there.

Plenty of people had wondered if we were lovers when we were in high school, college. Insecure, jealous kids wondered how we could be so close *without* being gay. Freshman year of high school I punched a guy who asked if Dalton was my boyfriend. And it wasn't even the fact that the guy was questioning my sexuality that offended me. I just didn't like how he said it. Like Dalton and I were freaks or gross because we were together all the time. Dalton wasn't really a brawler, not like I was. As he was sitting next to me while I waited outside the principal's office for our parents to show up—so I could be handed my suspension like a proper delinquent—Dalton calmly explained to me that I didn't have to punch the guy. I could've just told him we were brothers. I had my right knuckles packed in ice, told him my way *felt* better. But after that, I did it Dalton's way. *He's my brother,* I began saying real quick and easy whenever we got The Look.

Our entire family used to get The Look when my parents first adopted him. People would ask nosy questions. Dalton was clearly biracial but I would joke we'd adopted him from Africa. *White Africa.* I'd sometimes say I'd found him on our front porch on a dark and stormy night and my parents decided to keep him.

"Nope. We're not gay. It's gayer than gay. This transcends gay," Dalton would say when we were in college. Sometimes he'd throw his arm around me for added flair, kiss my cheek.

The girls we dated liked to tease *your boyfriend's here* when one of us would show up somewhere. Those sorts of things had the potential to drive a wedge between people and friendships, but for us? It made us closer. Dalton had felt like it was him against the world for most of his life—before Penelope killed herself and especially after. I willingly took some of the load off him, willingly stepped into his pain to suffer alongside him. I wanted to be the kind of friend and brother who would lay down his life for his friends and Dalton did too. We were intentional with one another. We didn't half-ass anything so we didn't half-ass our pact. The Pact was intense, like it needed us to bleed.

"The Pact," Dalton said in a deep movie trailer voice. "In a world where a pact has been made...can two brothers survive The Pact?" He laughed at himself. I laughed at his corny ass.

"That's right, little brother," I said, being six days older. "Our pact. It works both ways. With Frances or whoever you end up marrying. You know Frances kind of scares me but. If something were to happen to you, I'd take care of her, your kids. I'd make sure they were taken care of."

My parents did it for Penelope. Of course Dalton and I would do the same for one another if we ever needed to. But no, it wasn't like we had to talk about it all the time. I told him I wouldn't bring it up again until Evi got pregnant.

"And you and I both know I'm not marrying Frances," he said. I knew at one point in the not-so-distant-past Dalton had considered marrying Frances. He bought a ring and everything.

"You know what I mean," I said.

"I got your back. Always. You know this," he said.

"Same," I said.

The guys took me to the fancy steakhouse downtown. Dalton, Brian, my closest cop friend, two other cop buddies, couple guys from college and high school, couple of Evangeline's cousins, both of our dads, Detroit from the bike shop, couple of my cousins too. A giant table, fifteen of us total. We ate and drank and laughed and ended up at the driving range. I stepped aside, called Evangeline. Her voicemail picked up.

"Evangeline Maeve Cooper. *Bringer of good news. She who intoxicates. Barrel maker,*" I said, repeating her name meanings I'd memorized as soon as I Googled them. "Bless your French Irish great-grandmother's heart, your African great-grandfather. Your grandparents, your parents for creating you in all your splendor. Tomorrow I'll be your husband. Eamon means *guardian. Protector.* Tomorrow you will be a Royce. A *royal.* We're royals, you and me. Look. I love you. I can't wait to see you in your dress tomorrow. I won't be able to sleep. I won't be able to sleep. I love you. I won't be able to sleep. See you tomorrow."

I was a little drunk but still at the point where I could play it off with someone who didn't know me well. I didn't have to play it off with her voicemail. I leaned against the pole next to me, undid my top button. It was July, a blazing hot summer night. I felt the humid air, the muggy waves of Kentucky summer heat, all over me. Calefaction—the whiskey, the night, all of it. I couldn't *not* feel it. I felt frustratingly alive, overwhelmed. The usually cool, crisp cotton of my shirt was superheated against the skin of my back. I desired dulling. I hadn't lied to Evangeline. I wouldn't be able to sleep at all unless I calmed myself down. I undid all of my shirt buttons, slipped it off. A warm gust of wind cooled the sweat on the back of my neck. I watched the guys line up with their golf clubs. I spotted Dalton looking around for me. He found me, raised his hand. I raised mine and walked towards the guys again with my dress shirt gripped in my fist.

Evi and I got married in rainbow weather. It rained all morning, poured—but by evening it had cleared. I'd seen Evangeline in spectacular, jaw-dropping ensembles before because her ballerina costumes were anything but subtle—but seeing her step out and take her father's hand before coming down the aisle brought tears to my eyes. She looked unreal. *Not* real. A mirage. A chimera. I couldn't believe she was real until she got to me and accepted my arm after I offered it.

"You're okay?" she whispered as we turned towards the preacher.

"You look stunning. I'm literally stunned. I don't know if I'm okay or not actually," I said, forcing myself to laugh. I looked over at Dalton, my brother, my best man. He had tears in his eyes too.

"You're okay," she said. A gentle command from my bride. I was no fool. I did as I was told.

We saw the rainbow as we made our way to the reception. Evi snuggled against my shoulder as she pointed up at it.

"It's for us. It's good luck," she said.

⚓

We had an inside joke about "One More Night" by Phil Collins. Evi and I never broke up, never even came close. But once I told her I had this nightmare where we'd broken up and what got us back together was me, coming to her bedroom window Lloyd Dobler-style with a boombox over my head, blasting "One More Night." I'd grown up listening to Phil Collins, Billy Joel, Elton John, Sade. My mom loved her some adult contemporary soft rock. Mine and Evi's "One More Night" inside joke became our real first dance song. Hearing it felt like a secret.

We were at the reception, dancing to that song in front of everyone and I was praying not to lose it. Praying to keep it together. I leaned down and pulled her closer to me, pressed my nose against her neck.

"You smell so good," I whispered to her. I could smell her all over me—my hands, my fingers, the sleeve of my suit coat, my tie. We were one flesh already.

For a while, we sat and watched everyone drink and dance. Evi had slipped her shoes off, put her feet in my lap. She had Band-Aids on two of her left toes, the big one was bruised. Her right baby toe was bruised too. *I have ballerina feet* she'd told me the first time she took her shoes off at my place. She was shy, attempted to hide them underneath her. I held them one at a time, kissed the top of her foot, her toes.

On our wedding night, in that reception hall, in her reception dress, with her ballerina feet in my lap, her peacock-blue painted toenails, I lifted them again, one by one and kissed the tops. I loosened my tie. My suit coat was across the room, hanging on a chair I'd probably never sit in again. The crowd parted and I saw Dalton and Frances, pressed together, the swiveling spotlights made them look like they were underwater. My parents were out there too, Evi's parents, everyone we'd ever known. I knew I'd been waiting my whole life for something exactly like this, a feeling exactly like this. It was happening. The surreality of it was the hammer of my heart.

At the end of the night when we were in our suite, we made

love for the first time. I was terrified of hurting her. I kept double-checking. She worried the night wasn't living up to the picture I'd created in my mind. I assured her she couldn't have been more wrong. We woke up, made love again. *We'll get the hang of it,* I told her. Evi and I had amazing sex the next morning before we headed to North Carolina for our Blue Ridge Mountain honeymoon. *We got the hang of it,* she said from underneath me. With what little breath she had left.

After the honeymoon, Evi moved into my place. She had these little boxes of stuff. Books and DVDs and kitchenware. The rest of it was clothes, mostly leotards and dresses. And ballet shoes. So many ballet shoes. I called them her *ballerina boxes.* I had no clue how empty my house was until Evangeline moved herself and her little ballerina boxes in. A couple days after she was settled in, we made dinner and invited Dalton and Frances over. It was August. I'd been working a lot of overtime. The summer crime rate was always sky high.

"You been busy as shit?" Dalton asked me as he handed Evi a black glass bottle of red.

"Where's Frances?" Evi asked.

"Hmm?" Dalton said. Evi took the wine, set it on the counter.

"Been busy as shit, yeah," I said back to him, taking his hand. Bro hug.

"Dalton. Daltooon, my Huckleberry Friend. You heard me. Where's Francey-Pants?" Evi asked.

"We broke up after the reception." Dalton was smirking.

"What?" I said, laughing. This was laughable territory. I knew Dalton well enough to know he wasn't upset about this and in all likelihood, he and Frances would be back together (again) within the hour.

"We sat there and watched y'all cozied up on the dance floor, like grinding to Sade. In the swooping colored spotlights," Evi said. "Like, how even do you break up right after?" She giggled.

"So y'all are laughing at my pain? That's why y'all invited me over here?" Dalton asked, leaning against the kitchen counter. He was still smiling. He pulled his phone from his pocket, swiped it open and touched the screen before handing it to Evi. She gathered the hem of her dress in her hand, hopped up on the counter, read the text aloud.

Evi cleared her throat. Her wedding ring caught the summer sunlight. She had a zillion sundresses. Preferred them over shorts or jeans. This one was thin, breezy layers—a cream-colored garden lifting and falling again. She was Daisy Buchanan.

"Dalton, do you want to get back together? What are we doing? *What are we doing*?" Evi turned the phone towards us to prove the last part was written in all caps. She kept reading. "We don't know how to love each other the right way. You drive me crazy. You drive me fucking crazy." Evi bowed her head and shook it. She handed Dalton his phone back. I clapped, slow.

"That was poetic, D. Damn poetic," I said.

"Wait, gimme," Evi said, motioning her hand at Dalton. Her bracelets made a gentle click as they slid down her arm and back again once she was holding his phone. "What did you write her back?" She swiped his screen, clicked around.

"Nothing. I didn't write her back," he said. He got himself a glass. He got two more for us. He kept talking as he poured. "She sent that the morning after we broke up. So while y'all were packing up and heading out on your honeymoon, ol' Berkeley-Royce here was getting dumped."

"Oh please, *dumped*," Evi said. "You are not heartbroken and she'll probably text you during dinner. You'll go over there right after this." Dalton handed her a glass of wine.

"I don't look heartbroken?" Dalton asked, still smiling.

"What happened?" I asked.

"I don't know," Dalton said. "We were having a good time and I guess I said or did something to piss her off."

Evi came down from the counter, got the salad out of the fridge. I'd grilled steaks, some zucchini. Evi was only teaching ballet for the rest of the summer, not performing. It was nice having her home. The little domestic life we'd built together was only beginning. I occasionally thought about quitting the force but not enough to make any real changes and Evi didn't ask me to. This wasn't something I could be pressured into anyway. Not by Mom, not by Dalton. I had to figure it out on my own.

"Classic dude answer. So vague! What does that even mean?" Evi said.

"You've met Frances, right?" Dalton said, laughing.

"Okay I'll give you that much, but she *can* be fun and now it's me here with you two stinky boys," Evi said. She pouted. Dalton hugged her. He apologized for being alone and stinky. I watched him squeeze her, watched her beg for mercy.

"Okay! Okay! You smell good," she admitted when he let her go.

"Let's eat," I said.

Dalton ended up calling Frances after dinner. He put it on speaker so we could hear her.

"Dalton?" she said.

"Hey."

"What?"

Evi covered her mouth with her hand, tucked her feet underneath her on the couch.

"This is mean," Evi whispered to me. I was sitting right next to her, watching Dalton. She kept looking at me. I kissed her to keep her quiet.

"I was going to invite you over to Evi and Eamon's tonight for dinner but remembered we were broken up," he said.

"I'm on a date," she snapped.

"Really?" Dalton seemed genuinely surprised.

Evi pulled away from kissing me. Watched Dalton. I leaned back, put my arm around her.

"And I'm in Austin," Frances said from the other side of the phone.

"On a date with who?" Dalton asked.

"Some guy in Austin."

Dalton hung his head, kept looking at his phone.

"Evangeline and Eamon stay perfect and we fuck it all up over and over again," Frances said. She drew Evangeline's name out, made it super-annoying. Evangeline looked over at me, her mouth opened wide in feigned offense.

"Okay. Um," Dalton said. "Well call me when you get home if you want to." He looked up, winked at us.

"Are you seeing someone?" Frances asked. There was restaurant noise from her side of the line. I tried to picture her getting up from the table, in Texas, on a date with some dude, to answer Dalton's phone call. It was a very Frances thing to do.

"Nope," Dalton said.

"Are you asking me out when I get home?"

"I don't know."

"I'll call you next week, you fucking weirdo," she said.

"Okay. Have fun on your date. I guess," he said, laughing.

I'd seen some entertaining things that week. Got called to a house where an old guy was stuck in the bathroom window, trying to skip out because he was busted sleeping with his neighbor by the neighbor's husband. I'd broken up a fight at a grocery store between two disgruntled cashiers. But this? Listening in on the bizarre relationship between Dalton and Frances? It was right up there too, not going to lie.

So much of police work was uninteresting. Endless paperwork and responding to noise complaints. Directing traffic and waiting for tow trucks. Those small hours of the night when absolutely nothing happens. I never pictured my dad doing those boring things when I was growing up. I thought it was all adrenaline-spiked car chases and emergencies.

⚓

My first memory was of me standing next to my dad in full uniform in the kitchen. I reached for him and he picked me up. My mom was next to us, pregnant and showing. That night she started bleeding, lost the baby. A boy. My mom had called him Thomas. We buried him in a tiny casket and my mom couldn't have any more children. Those days when my mom was grieving and in their bedroom crying, my dad would take me out in his patrol car, let me turn the lights and sirens on if I wanted to. Sometimes we'd stop by Penelope's and pick up Dalton, go get ice cream.

Even though I was only four, I could feel the sadness waiting for us at home. Those escapes and adventures my dad took me on were important to me because I was sad too. For myself, for my mom, for him. It would be eight years until Penelope died, eight years until Dalton started living with us. There were tragedies, unbearably dark times, but we had one another and together we found the light. My mom was my hero, the way she held herself and all of us together even when she was hurting. My dad was my hero too because he was strong. Because he knew when to take me away, when to bring me back.

The sadness in the house lifted, only to drop down again after Penelope locked herself in her bedroom and took her entire bottle of sleeping pills while Dalton was spending the night with us. She'd left a note for him.

Dalton, I love you. This doesn't mean I don't love you. Loretta and Calvin and Eamon will take care of you. I'm sorry. I love you, I love you.

Penelope and Mom had an unspoken pact of their own. Family was a pact. Friendship was a pact. Love was a pact. Written in blood.

I didn't want to test the limits but also, I was a fatalist at heart. Wasn't my doom out there waiting to snare me whether I turned this way or that way or quit the force and decided to teach or work in an office? Attempts to outrun death were futile. Right? Right.

One day after roll call, I got in my patrol car and called Evi. Made a deal with God that if she mentioned anything about wanting me to quit I'd turn the car right back around, slap my badge on my superior's desk, turn in my gun, swap the patrol car for my truck and drive home to her. Leave all this behind.

Evi picked up and we talked about our plans to go apple picking with Dalton and Frances the next week since they were unsurprisingly back together again. She asked me to bring home bread and eggs. She told me she and Merit were going out for margaritas when her ballet class was over. She didn't mention one thing about my job outside of telling me to be safe. She told me she loved me. I told her I loved her. For the next eight hours I was Sergeant Royce.

Dalton

BETWEEN EAMON AND EVI'S ENGAGEMENT DINNER AND
their wedding, I bought an engagement ring for Frances. It was
Christmastime and she was pregnant. For real this time. She was
having my baby and this was something we were going to do together. Make a family. Frances and me, me and Frances. She'd
told me she was pregnant in such a chill, nonchalant way I didn't
believe her until she peed in front of me, showed me the two lines.

I had the ring in my bedside table drawer but I hadn't said
anything to her about it. We were going to a big Christmas party
at one of her friend's places in the city. I picked her up and like
always, she fussed about my truck.

"It's so old and you can afford a newer one, a better one," she
said, stepping up to sit next to me. She rolled her smoky brown
eyes so hard I thought she'd hurt herself.

"Yeah, but the new ones have an armrest here so you can't snuggle up against me while I drive," I said, putting my arm on the back of the seat, pulling her closer.

"Dalton," she said. A complete sentence.

Frances's friends were seemingly sorority-ish but the types of women who claimed to abhor that kind of thing. They were intellectuals, Type A's. Half of them had migrated from bigger cities to ours because of jobs or men. The other half were Kentucky Princesses, girls from Lexington, women who were PhD candidates at University of Kentucky, women whose fathers owned sprawling horse farms hedged with freshly painted white fencing.

Her closest friend Vox greeted us at the door decked out in a sparkly red Christmas dress with white fur around the neck. I'd never seen anything like it. I looked it up and down before looking her in the face.

"Franny! Dalton," she said, hugging us inside. Her place was dope and there must've been fifty people standing in the living room which wasn't big enough to hold fifty people, but there they stood and swayed and sparkled anyway. Vox handed Frances a Christmas martini glass, complete with clear liquid and three olives on a frilly red and green toothpick. Frances took it gleefully, pressed her lips against the rim and took a small sip.

"So…" I started, knowing she would fight me on it, knowing she would claim I was policing her. But she was pregnant and if she were going to drink when she was pregnant, this was something we needed to discuss and by discuss I meant nix.

Frances held her hand up at me. Her ring finger was bare, on her index there was a big glittery green Christmas tree.

"I'm not drinking the whole thing. I'm not drinking the whole thing!" she said. She took another small sip and handed it to me. I didn't want it either. If she wasn't drinking, I wasn't drinking. I found an empty spot on a table, and a coaster. I set it down. More of Frances's friends squealed when they saw her, threw their arms around her. I knew some of their boyfriends. I went to the kitchen for a glass of water and joined the men's circle. Most of them were wearing ridiculous Christmas sweaters. Frances had laid my clothes out for me the night before—grey wool pants, black shawl collar sweater—she'd told me the shawl collar part. The same brown boots I always wore, the boots Frances hated. She'd bought me a pair of black dress shoes and I'd put them on but didn't feel right in them. Figured everyone would've noticed the unease right away.

The boyfriends were holding cigarettes and cigars under a smoky cloud. They were drinking small batch whiskies and locally brewed beers. I put two lime slices in my water, bummed a cigarette from the guy next to me—Vox's new beau, a professor of something or other. I got that much from our conversation. When I finished my cigarette I took a breather, stepped outside to text Eamon and see what he was up to.

Are you working tonight? I'm at this Christmas party with F.

Working, yeah. Almost done. You give her the ring?

I'd told Eamon about the pregnancy, the ring. It'd taken me three days but I told him. Something about it embarrassed me. The pregnancy was a mistake. I felt too old to make mistakes like that. I thought about what the Royces would think, how they would seem and look as grandparents to the baby I had with Frances. Frances and Mom would have to learn to get along, there was no way around it. And regardless of whether they were a boy or a girl, when they were three they could join Aunt Evi's Littlest Sprouts dance class.

I allowed myself to think about the things that would be cute, the hopeful, joyful things about being a parent. I wasn't worried about the money. We had enough between the both of us. Also, Frances's parents were loaded. We'd have to find a bigger place but I was ready to get out of my lease anyway. I'd rented that house for two years—a change would be good. There would have to be a lot of changes. This was a solid. This was happening and I became more and more okay with it every day. So why hadn't I given her the ring?

Not yet.

What's up?
Nothing. I'm giving it to her tonight.
Ok. Gimme a call tmrw.
I will. Peace.
Peace, D.

I put my phone back in my pocket and went inside. Looked over the heads in the living room. Someone with taste had turned on the Diana Krall Christmas album, one of the few contemporary Christmas albums I didn't hate. I found Frances over by the window surrounded by women, some I knew, some I didn't. I watched her lift a glass of red wine to her mouth and drink. I excused myself through the sea of Christmas sweaters—Christmas dresses, tweed suit coats, shined shoes, pocket squares, afros, fades, slicked back, elbow patches, a dude in Christmas cowboy boots, a chick in an elf costume—and touched Frances's elbow. I asked her if I could talk to her for a second.

"I'll be right back," she said to her friends. She put the wine down.

We found an unoccupied bathroom upstairs. I locked the door behind us.

"What's up?" I asked her calmly. As calmly as Eamon had texted the same thing to me.

"Dalton, I may not keep the baby so it honestly does not matter if I have a drink," she said, crossing her arms.

"Wow. Wow," I said, turning my back to her. As I turned, I caught a glimpse of myself in the bathroom mirror. My hair was too long but I'd let it keep growing. Be a new me. Did this mean Frances and I were done? Was it time for me to think about other women, other things? The bike shop, maybe an expansion; I could look into getting a loan. Maybe sell the shop and open a surf shop on the beach? Eamon and I had taken one surfing lesson during spring break forever ago. Maybe I could ditch Kentucky, blow this joint. "Wow," I said again, staring at the back of the bathroom door. Frances put her hand on my shoulder.

"I'm sorry, Dalton. I don't know what I want to do yet," she said.

"I don't know how to do this," I said.

I turned to look at her. She was crying. Frances never cried. I put my arms around her. I didn't know what I wanted. Not having a baby with Frances was a relief—a fresh air, deep breath in. But as I stood there holding her, I also knew having a baby with Frances could be okay—a hot sigh.

Not a bone in my body alerted me to any falseness in my saying *I'll support your decision, either way.* So I said it. This was me, attempting to control half of the situation. I decided right then and there if she kept it, I'd ask her to marry me. If she got an abortion I'd take the ring back, wait until another time. Later. Eventually. See what happened.

We swayed and hugged in the bathroom. We peed. We kissed. We went downstairs and Frances finished her glass of wine. Just one. Inevitably someone heard Frances mention I was a pianist so I ended up at the one Vox had in her living room. People hollered out their requests. Some guy put a brandy snifter on top, dropped a crumpled twenty-dollar bill inside. I played for an hour. Made three hundred forty bucks. *Merry Christmas.*

I gave Frances that money plus four hundred more dollars even though she didn't want me to. She didn't want me taking her to the abortion clinic either. Her sister was doing it. Frances texted when she got home and I took her flowers. White ranunculuses. Afterwards, I thought the timing was better than ever to take the engagement ring back so I did. I told Eamon about it as soon as I returned it. Met him out for lunch, told him everything. He was working, but on break. I was going to buy his lunch but they gave it to him free anyway. Cops got everything for free. Perks. I asked him not to tell Evi and he told me he wouldn't. I regretted asking as soon as I did it. It felt immature. I'd never asked him to keep a secret from Evi before. I promised myself I'd never ask Eamon to keep anything a secret from Evi once they were married. That wasn't fair. Yes, he was my brother, but she was his wife.

I never told Frances about the ring. Not until the night Eamon and Evangeline got married.

It was a perfect night, I was happy for Eamon and Evangeline. I stood to give my best-man speech.

"Hey. I'm Dalton. Berkeley-Royce. I've known Eamon all my life. We've been best friends and brothers from conception. Our moms were best friends before we were even thoughts in their minds. I've seen every face he can make. Or so I thought. When he told me about Evangeline, the ballerina he met at church, he made a new face. It was kind of like this," I said, attempting to recreate the face. The room pulsed. Everyone was laughing and talking and eating and drinking. I thought about all of our heartbeats in that room, how the sound would drown me out if we could hear them all, thumping.

"He was like a jack-o'-lantern with a brand new candle inside on Halloween night, you know what I mean?" I said. "And I use that image specifically because one Halloween night we were like, what was it, ten?" I looked to Eamon for some help on our ages.

"Nine!" Mom laughed and whispered loudly from a couple seats over. Eamon nodded.

"Nine. Halloween night, Eamon and I are nine and we both end up in the emergency room after we'd snuck off and tried to carve a jack-o'-lantern ourselves. We both needed two stitches in our fingers. Our moms came to the rescue. And when Eamon needed a new face to make, Evangeline came to the rescue. I lost my mom…suddenly…when I was twelve. And Loretta stepped right in, day one. I never knew my father and Calvin took me in. He was my dad I'd never had. I didn't have a family like this until I did. And I definitely have the best brother a guy could ask for," I said. I looked over at Eamon. I was trying not to cry. My throat hurt from holding it in. I kept talking.

"Yes, he's the best brother, but no, he can't play piano. No matter how hard I try to teach him. Yes, he's faster than me. Yes, he's stronger than me. Yes, he's braver than me. And yes, he makes more money than me and yes, that's why he's paying me and threatening to arrest me if I don't stand up here and say all this stuff," I said, not able to hold back the tears any longer. I used my knuckle to wipe them away. I saw Eamon shake his head and laugh at me through his own tears.

"Eamon is truly the best guy I've ever known and my life would be severely lacking without him in it. I knew he'd marry a woman who was perfect for him. A woman who would keep him in line and bring out even better things in him. And that's Evangeline. Absolutely it is. I know this without a doubt. Dig. He's making the face. See!" I said, pointing over at Eamon and Evangeline, both of them so bright with smile.

"Damn. All right," I sniffed, "all of this to say, congrats to you, Eamon, and your beautiful bride Evangeline, who I'm lucky to now call my sister-in-law. I really love you guys. Thanks for letting me be a part of your life," I ended. Eamon stood to hug me.

"Fuck you," he said, his laughing-breath against my ear.

"Fuck you too," I said back.

We were dancing at the reception, Frances and I. I didn't hate to dance, especially if I'd had a couple drinks. "I Only Have Eyes For You." I loved that song. The colored lights were swinging down around us. We were both pleasantly buzzed. I was in love with her. I was in love with her. I only had eyes for her.

In the elevator on the way up to our hotel room I told her about the engagement ring. I told her I'd gotten one and took it back after she had the abortion. I don't know why I told her. I don't know what happened. One moment I was looking at myself in the elevator mirror, one moment we were in the elevator with other people, one moment the other people got off on another floor but we were still going up and up and up and the next moment I was telling her something I'd intended to keep a secret, possibly forever.

I loosened my tie, slipped it off, started wrapping it around my fist. Frances had made her fingers into hooks, had her shoes hanging from them. I had my suit coat hanging from my arm. We were coat racks, closets of all sorts of things we didn't want spilling out. I'd worn Eamon's cologne for no other reason than good luck. It was a smell I'd recently associated with him so whenever I was out in the world and smelled it on someone else, I instinctively looked around for Eamon.

I could smell it all over myself, my neck, my hands, my beard, my hair, which I'd recently trimmed but it was long enough for me to pull back and I kept it that length on purpose because Frances had said she liked how it made my face look. *You look like a Viking*, she'd said. I wanted to keep looking like a Viking for her. I thought of Eamon, realizing the woodsy scent was mine, was me. I wasn't buzzed. I was drunk. I was drunk and had accidentally told Frances I'd considered proposing to her, but changed my mind. Probably not the best thing to tell a woman.

"You are a *complete* asshole," she said to me after a moment of reflection, both literal and figurative. Her eyes, raccoon-rimmed with black in the mirror. She touched the tip of her finger to the glass, left a hot print.

"I'm sorry. It was unkind of me to tell you that. You don't have to be pregnant for me to want to marry you," I said. I apologized again. Reached out for her. She inched away.

"Maybe I don't want to marry *you*, Dalton. Maybe I don't want to be with you anymore," she said softly. Frances wasn't a *softly* kind of a woman. This was trouble and I knew it.

The elevator dinged and we got off. It took me four tries to get the key card slipped into our door the right way and even still, Frances snatched it out, slipped it back in until the little light glowed green.

"Do you want to break up?" I asked from the corner of the bed. I was toeing off my dress shoes. She was peeing with the door open.

"I guess," she said. I knew she was shrugging on the other side of that wall. "Don't you?"

I let out all of my air, fell back on the bed. I listened to Frances flush, wash her hands.

"Well, if you're pissed off at me, that's what we should do. But also, we can do whatever we want. We don't *have* to break up. We can find a way to stay together. Breaking up right after a wedding seems like bad luck, don't you think?" I said.

"I'm definitely pissed off at you. I'm fucking seething and I hate you," she said, her voice echoing off the tiled walls like some sort of truculent bathroom ghost.

I heard her walk out, stand over me. I opened my eyes to find her in her underwear, creamy lace everything. We had *let's break up sex* twice, slept *let's break up sleeps* next to one another, ordered *let's break up breakfast* in the morning and afterwards, I dropped her off at home.

One night I went over to Mom and Dad's for dinner. Eamon was working and Evi was working too, so it was just me. Mom had made meatloaf because she knew I loved her meatloaf and I was in the kitchen finishing the salad—chopping tomatoes, making raspberry vinaigrette.

"I want to talk to you about something but I don't want it to upset you," Mom said. She turned to face me. Dad wasn't there. He was out golfing with his buddies but he was supposed to be home soon in time for dinner.

"Okay," I said, nodding. I got a sick feeling in the pit of my stomach, like there was a small rodent in there, gnawing and gnawing like I'd been waiting for some bad shit to happen. I'd been feeling lonesome. I wanted to make sure I was giving Eamon and Evi their space to navigate the first months of being married. Frances and I were broken up. I wasn't seeing anyone else. I hung out with Detroit sometimes and stayed plenty busy at the bike shop, but sometimes at night I could feel the loneliness creeping up on me, like a rash. Hot. Itchy.

"Your biological father, Steve, contacted us. About you," she said. She was holding her hands in front of her, as if she were cupping a small invisible bird.

"What? What'd he say?" I asked. I stopped chopping, turned to look at the woman who had played such a huge part in raising me, who played such a huge part in my life and always would. *Miss Loretta. Penelope's best friend. Mom.* I loved her so ferociously, felt so protective of her. I didn't like the idea of my biological father contacting her at all. I didn't like the idea of her knowing my biological father at all.

"He asked a lot of questions about you," Mom said.

"Did you answer them?"

"No. But he left me his number. *If* you wanted to call him, contact him, whatever you wanted to do with it," she said, reaching across me to find the piece of paper. She pulled it out from underneath a catalog, some junk mail.

I took the paper. I didn't look at it but I took it.

"What did Dad say?"

"Your Dad doesn't like Steve. Never did," she said. "Your mother made a mistake getting involved with him, but she never regretted it because look at you. You are not like him. *Look* at *you.*" She shook her head. She started crying. Mom was always crying.

"Don't cry," I said. I shoved the paper in my pocket, put my arms around her.

"I didn't want to say anything to you because I didn't want you to get upset," she said into my shirt.

"*I'm* not upset. *You're* upset," I said, laughing lightly.

"You're allowed to be upset about this. You know that, right? And you know you can talk to me about it?" she said.

"Yes," I said and nodded.

"Do you think you'll call him? He really hurt your mother."

"I know he did."

We heard Dad's truck rumble in the driveway. Mom wiped her face, stepped away. "Your dad didn't want me to say anything."

"That's fine. We don't have to talk about it," I said.

Mom looked at me, really looked at me. "Are you sure?"

"I'm sure," I said.

"I want to make *sure* you're okay, Dalton."

"I'm okay. I promise."

Dad came in and we ate and didn't talk about Steve at all.

Steve. Penelope hadn't told me much about him. She told me they'd met when she was teaching piano at the performing arts high school. He was some sort of delivery man, came to the school a couple times a week. They went on one date, maybe two. She told him she was pregnant and he hung around for a while—until I was a couple months old—then he bolted. I knew he drank his coffee black because she'd mentioned it once. I knew his name was Steve Boone and it annoyed me, those two one-syllable names. Steve *Boo*, like he was a ghost. I couldn't even imagine myself as Dalton Boone if I tried. I hated thinking about it. Sure. Okay. I'd meet him out for coffee or dinner and then? Punch his fucking lights out.

Mom told Eamon about Steve before I did and Eamon asked me why I didn't tell him. Part of me was annoyed since it was my news to share, not Mom's. But it was Eamon, so my annoyance didn't last long.

"You know, this is why people think we're boyfriends," I said to him, laughing. "Do you tell me everything immediately?" It was Eamon and me at his place, watching the Cubs beat the shit out of the Pirates. It was September. He and Evi had been married for two bright months. Frances and I had somehow gotten back together. She'd gone to Austin to visit one of her sisters, gone on a date down there with some guy named Danny. *Danny.* I pictured him as Danny Zuko from *Grease,* calling Frances *Franny* like *Sandy.* A goofy dope calling her Franny. I wasn't threatened by Danny. *Franny and Danny.* Frances wasn't threatened by the one *duck* I'd gone on a date with. It wasn't worth mentioning, but I mentioned it anyway because that was how Frances and I operated.

"I *do* tell you everything immediately," Eamon said. He had to leave in an hour, was working the overnight shift so he wasn't drinking. I was on his couch, had drank one of his beers, was working on another.

"You do not," I said.

"Check it. I haven't even told Evi this yet. But I'm thinking about leaving the force," he said. Every time he talked about the force I liked to think of him as a mysteriously hooded Jedi Knight.

"No you aren't," I said.

"No shit. I mean, I'm thinking," he said, "but don't say anything to Mom."

"You know I won't," I said. I knew he was too stubborn to quit. He wouldn't do it. But I humored him all the same. I didn't want him to mention The Pact. I hated talking about The Pact. It made me feel sick.

"Don't say anything to Evi, either," he said.

"On what planet would I say something to her?"

"She likes you, she trusts you…she could get it out of you."

"She could not!"

"She could," he said. He nodded.

I shook my head, drank my beer.

"Are you calling Steve Boone?" Eamon asked, making Steve's name as annoying as it was.

I shrugged. "Yeah. Maybe to beat his no-good ass," I said.

"Do it. Then call me. I'd love to fill out that paperwork," he said.

Evi came home right as I was leaving. She'd taught a late class and had to run *Nutcracker* auditions afterwards. She asked if I was hungry, said even though Eamon was going to work, I could stay to eat if I wanted to. I kindly told her no thank you and left with Eamon.

"She gets lonely when I work nights," Eamon said.

"I understand," I said. Evi and I weren't all that different; I was lonely too.

I called Frances on my way home and within the hour we were sweating up my sheets.

This is why we got back together. This is why we're together. She does this thing with her tongue. She does this thing with her hips. She makes this certain sound, this kitten growl. This is why. No one takes us seriously, not even us. But I have my reasons for sticking around. So does she.

I wasn't lonely anymore.

Detroit and I went for a long bike ride all the way out of the county and through two more. Half-century. Fifty miles. The curving roads led us up the bluegrass-green Kentucky hills slowly, ambling towards the sky and back down again. We took our time. Couple times a year we went on rides like this. Couple more times a year I sponsored big group rides via the bike shop, got T-shirts made and everything. It was Labor Day weekend so the shop was closed. Detroit and I both had the day off. Detroit was Xavier from Michigan. I'd met him in college. First night, he got trashed and kept telling us he was from Detroit and kept forgetting he'd already told us. So we didn't call him Xavier anymore. We called him Detroit.

He was full-on tatted from neck to ankles—half black, half Mexican. Coolest dude I'd ever known. He played bass in a popular local band and knew just about everyone in town. We could hang out comfortably, talk when we needed to, be quiet when we needed to and I could trust him at work. We had a nice system, respected each other's space. It was nice to have another guy I knew I could count on. And he wasn't a Royce. He was outside of the circle. Proof I could branch out when I needed to. Proof I contained multitudes.

"Hey. What's up with your biological dad?" I asked him once we got to our halfway point. We took a break, had snacks and water. Some other bikers passed us, headed back down the hill. There was a swiftly running creek near our feet, a thick, brushy meadow to the right of us. The September chill hadn't made itself fully known yet but I could feel the whisper of it, even in full sun.

"Ol' Ozzie?" Detroit looked down at the chocolate-covered almonds in his hand, shook his head.

"Your dad's name is Ozzie? That's dope," I said.

"Oscar."

"That's dope too."

"Me and ol' Ozzie don't get along too well," Detroit said.

"Did you grow up with him?" I asked.

Detroit had told me about his dad walking out on him, his mom and his sister when he was five. He saw him occasionally off and on, growing up. Holidays, birthdays, funerals, church. He had a good relationship with his paternal grandparents, but his dad was never the kind of father he should've been.

Detroit had a kid. A boy, with his long-term girlfriend. The boy was four. He was about as cool as Detroit too. Detroit seemed like a good father to him, brought him up to the shop a lot, got along with and loved his girlfriend too. All the boxes that were important and checked off to pass the *Good Dad Test*. I paid him a little more than I should've for that very reason. Because I knew he was supporting a family. That mattered to me.

I wouldn't have bailed on Frances if she'd had our baby. I made up my mind from the moment she told me she was pregnant that I wouldn't bail on her, wouldn't bail on the baby. No matter what happened. I tried to put myself in Steve Boone's shoes but couldn't. How could a father willingly let another man raise his child and take no interest in that child's life? What kind of man could or would do that? Why was he attempting to contact me now? It was too late.

I told Detroit about Steve Boone, about having his phone number. I told him I didn't know what I was going to do.

"What is it with some dads? Like, why's it so easy for them to give up?" I wondered aloud.

It was an honest question and it made me feel childish. It was only us out there in the wild. I watched two brown-grey rabbits scurry past and flash their way through a cracked log, emerging on the other side, their white puff tails disappearing. The wind lifted the branches above us, lowed and shook off leaves, the colors, bold and raining—rust, mustard, orange. Breathtaking. I was moping up the place, thinking about Steve Boone.

"Not being there for my kid wasn't even an option for me, y'know? I never thought about it for one second. And with this, you've been given an option. Not everyone gets that. You can choose to have a relationship with Steve if you want to. He contacted your mom, reconnected and now *you* get to choose. When he left you and Penelope, *he* chose. But now the ball's in your court," Detroit said.

"Thanks for listening, man," I said. I worried I was wearing him out, talking about this heavy shit when this was technically supposed to be our day off, a day to chill.

"No worries. My main goal for the rest of my life is just not to mess up my kid. I'm not even claiming I know how to do that, but I'll die trying, right?" he said.

"Respect," I said and nodded. After a moment of quiet I started talking again.

"I grew up with a man who wasn't my biological dad, but he'd do anything for me. So there are also these guys out here doubling up. Pulling twice their load without complaining. And then there's lousy-ass men out here contacting their grown sons out of the blue. And for what?" I shook my head. Detroit took his fist, gently knocked it against my knee.

When we got back to the bike shop it was late. The sun was setting. Detroit left and I went to the office to finish filling out some restock order forms. Couple of minutes later I heard a soft tap at the front door and went to open it, to tell the woman we were closed but we'd be open again in the morning.

"Oh. I'm sorry. I was riding past and saw the light on. Both of my tires are flat. Both of them. Two flat tires," she said, holding up her fingers. I looked at her. Such a *goose*. Full-on *goose*.

She told me her name was Cassidy. I told her I'd fix her tires if she wanted me to.

"You're not a psycho murderer?" she asked, ticking her busted bike into the shop along with her.

"Not since last time I checked, but honestly, only do what feels comfortable. Or you can leave the bike here and I'll fix it. You can come pick it back up tomorrow," I said.

"I know how to fix it. I don't like have the shit and everywhere is closed and my apartment is like forever that way," she said, pointing. She corrected herself, pointed the other way. She had a million earrings in each ear and a diamond tattooed on the inside of her right upper arm, another said BAD in thick black text on the inside of her wrist. She was wearing short-shorts. I saw a rose bush tattoo way up on her thigh. I was trying not to stare and didn't want to make her uncomfortable. Anyway, I had a girl-friend. I had a Frances.

"It's no problem. It'll take me fifteen minutes," I said. She leaned against the register counter, started scrolling through her phone. The light illuminated her face, the diamond stud in her nose I hadn't seen before. I motioned for her to follow me to the back of the store.

"This is a nice bike," I said, after adjusting it up on the rack.

"I really appreciate you doing this," she said, putting her phone away.

"It's no problem," I said again. She smelled like vanilla, like cookies. "'Cassidy' is my favorite Grateful Dead song," I said. My attempt at making hippie conversation.

"My mom's too," she said, smiling.

"I'm Dalton." I hadn't told her. I'd forgotten.

"Thank you for not murdering me, Dalton. I like this place," she said, beginning to wander around the back room, touching things.

"Thanks."

Fifteen minutes of mostly quiet and I was done. I wouldn't let her pay me. I told her no at least three times.

"Well at least take my number. You can like, call me if you need something or want anything or whatever," she said. It was so clearly sexual. It was so purely innocent. I was dumb-struck. I watched her write down her number and slide the pad of paper back across the desk.

"Well, okay. Okay," I said.

She thanked me again, ticked her bike out of the store and I watched her put her helmet on and ride away. I turned off the lights, locked the door, headed to my truck.

I went home alone.

I didn't call Frances.

Didn't need to.

I decided not to be lonely anymore.

III.

Evangeline

EAMON AND I HAD SEX FOR THE FIRST TIME ON OUR
wedding night. The next day, we were honeymooning in the Blue
Ridge Mountains. We were lying out on the deck by the lake. It
was July. We got married in July, both of our birthdays are in July.
Dalton's too. Noah was born in July, late. Eamon was killed in July,
mid. There were fireworks when we were lying out on the deck. I
looked over at him and he reached out for my hand and closed
his eyes.

When I saw him in his casket, I thought about that moment.
How it looked just like when we were on our honeymoon at the
cabin on the lake and how he reached out for my hand and closed
his eyes. I thought about the fireworks and I thought about God.
How he allowed a random act of violence to take Eamon away
from us. A *kid*. And now the kid was dead too. I was sad for his
family, I couldn't get around that. I searched the darkest corners
of my spirit for forgiveness to offer them.

I believe in Heaven, I do. I know it. I know Eamon is there. I know he's there because he'd given his life to Christ. That's how you get to Heaven. And I know I will see Eamon again someday. I believe this, I do. But I don't want him to be in Heaven. I want him to be here with me so we can lie down together by the lake in the summer and watch the fireworks with Noah. Noah hasn't seen fireworks before. Colorful explosions in the sky don't look the same from the other side of it, I'm sure. *Eamon. I don't want this but this is what I have, so now what do I do?*

"I haven't had sex since July ninth," I say to Dalton, going into the pantry for the chocolate.

Dalton is quiet. July ninth was two days before Eamon was killed. July ninth was Eamon's birthday.

I find the Marshall Tucker Band song on my phone. I turn it up, but not too much. I unwrap the thin, gold paper and take a bite of the chocolate. I start dancing once the flutes kick in.

Dalton stands up and finishes his cigarette, stubs it out and drops it into a bottle on the deck. He closes the door to the cold and the kitchen begins to warm up again. He puts his hands into the kangaroo pocket of his hoodie. I'm dancing and eating my chocolate. Dalton tells me he likes it when I dance. I tell him I don't like thinking about him and Frances. I turn away from him and dance back over to the chocolate.

"I have no choice but to think about you and Eamon and he was my brother," Dalton says.

"It's not the same thing."

"What's different?"

"Eamon and I were married and he's the only person I've been with. You and Frances are or were...I don't know...different," I say, unwrapping more paper.

Dalton looks down at his feet. He says *were* and I echo him, add a question mark.

"It's not like I sleep around," he says as he looks up. He's holding his arm straight out to the side and the song is playing but I'm not dancing anymore.

"I didn't say you sleep around. I don't think that," I snap back, sounding angrier than I am. An accident.

"You act like it. Look. I feel like you're waiting for me to prove something to you and I can't. I can't prove it because I thought I already did."

"What's that supposed to mean?"

"We miss the same person. Don't act like you're in this alone because you're not. Even if you wanted to be, it doesn't matter because you're still not."

"I don't want to be," I say, quietly.

"I'm doing the best I can."

"Stop it. I know that. Look at me," I say, reaching out for him. I tug at his sleeve.

"You're giving me too much shit this weekend. And you don't want to talk about last night. What am I supposed to do?"

We stand there looking at each other. I turn the music off. Dalton pushes up his sleeves and goes to the sink. Starts washing a pancake plate.

"I *do* want to talk about last night. But I don't know what to say. Everything sounds stupid," I say. I could tell him he's an amazing kisser and I can't stop thinking about it. I could tell him I want him to kiss me again. I want him to take my hand and walk with me to my bedroom. I want him to kiss me and kiss me and kiss me and kiss me and put his fingers deep inside of me until I come and cry. If he did those things at least I'd be feeling something else. *Anything* else but this.

"It's not stupid," he says.

"I don't know how to do this."

Dalton turns around and says he doesn't either.

"Are you still in love with Frances?"

"Evi, my God. You don't get it," he says.

I clasp my hands together and bring them up to the middle of my chest. I can feel Dalton closing up. I don't want him to. I can see the elevator doors coming together and this is me putting out my hand to stop them. This is me saying, *Wait, there's one more.*

The water is still running. Dalton's back is to the sink and I'm standing in front of him saying nothing. I think about saying, *I don't know how to do this* again but Dalton starts to walk away.

"Where are you going?" I ask.

"To the garage. To work on my bike," he says without turning around to look at me.

He left the water running.

The water is still running.

Dalton and I cut our hair on a Sunday. It seemed appropriate. The first day of the week, the Lord's day, starting new. I awoke in the middle of the night to go pee because I was nine months pregnant. All I did was cry and pee and sleep and eat. Dalton had spent the night because he'd been here for dinner. My parents had stopped by. My friend, Merit, had been here too. Dalton, Merit and Merit's husband. They made spaghetti and meatballs for dinner but I barely ate. After they left, Dalton and I watched *Globe Trekker* on PBS. I asked him to stay the night and he said of course. I went to my bedroom and fell asleep. When I woke up and stood outside of the bathroom door, I heard the *swish swish* of a razor in a sink full of water. I said hey softly and pushed the door open. Dalton pulled it open the rest of the way.

He was using Eamon's blue and black razor. Seeing it in his hand made me dizzy. I stared at it and Dalton looked at it in his hand and asked if I cared that he was using it. I said no. I loved how close they were.

"Beard first, then my head," Dalton said.

"Then mine," I said, putting my hand flat on top of my head. My chin was quivering. My cheeks were burning hot. I scooted past Dalton so I could pee before I had an accident. Dalton put the razor down and turned his back to me so I could have my privacy.

I cut his hair and helped him shave his head. Cleaned up the back, made it even. I knelt down in front of the bathtub and Dalton cut mine. In the morning, Merit took me to her stylist to finish the rest and make it pretty. Afterwards, we went to Merit's and she made me tea, gave me a giant pair of dangly earrings. She said the shorter the hair, the bigger my earrings should be. She dropped me off at home with my earrings and my huge pregnant belly and I stood there in my kitchen—sad and small and dazed—touching my fuzzy head.

I've been helping Dalton cut his hair ever since. Sometimes he shaves it and sometimes he lets it grow out and I trim it when he asks, but I like it long. He doesn't shave his beard, though. It's back in full effect now. It's the beard of a flannel-wearing lumberjack. It's the beard of a winter mountain man. *Dear God, no matter what happens between us, I will always love that beard.* It looks so good on his face. Dalton has this wide-open face and these intense bright brown eyes. The beard wonderfully roughs them up. When I was with both of the boys together, I felt like I had everything. Even their names matched. *Eamon, Dalton.* Bookends.

I turn the water off and stand there staring into the sink. The soap bubbles and the plates, one orange, one yellow. I look out of the window in front of me. The ice and snow have turned the backyard into something from a sad, pretty movie. I don't want Dalton to be mad at me. I'm just jealous. How do I say, *Dalton, I feel guilty for having these feelings for you when Eamon's only been dead for six months. I shouldn't have feelings like this for at least a year, right? Aren't there rules for this?*

When I'm done with the dishes, I hear my phone ringing. Brian. He was one of Eamon's friends. When the kid shot Eamon, Brian put him down. He and his wife are really good about keeping up with me. I dry my hands on a clean dishrag and answer it.

"Evangeline. This is Brian. Lucy and I wanted to check in on you because of the storm. Make sure you have power. Do you need anything?" he says.

"Hi, Brian. I'm fine. Thank you. Tell Lucy thank you too. Dalton's here and we're good. We still have electricity. What about you guys?" I ask.

"Yeah, we do too. How have you been?"

We swap stories. I tell him Noah rolls over now and loves apples and pears, hates bananas. That Noah's at my parents for the weekend. I can hear Brian's kids in the background. One of them hollers something at Brian about sledding.

"Tell everyone I say hi," I tell him.

"I will. Promise you'll call if you need anything?"

"I promise."

Neither of us speaks and I get this cool, tingly feeling all over me. I clear my throat.

"Brian," I say.

"Yeah."

"Thank you for calling me. And for not forgetting about me. I mean, thank you for remembering me," I say.

"I could never forget about you and Noah over there. None of us will."

We get off the phone and I go to my bedroom and cry myself to sleep.

When I wake up, Dalton is sitting on the edge of the bed. I ask what time it is and he says lunchtime. He asks if I'm hungry. I say yes and sit up. He leans over slowly to kiss my mouth. *Thank God.* He kisses me once and I tell him my breath is stinky like Irish coffee and an hour's worth of sleep. He says it smells good. He says it smells like puppy breath. It makes me laugh. I notice it more when I laugh now. Mostly because I didn't think I'd laugh again. When it comes naturally and suddenly, without my knowing it, it's my favorite.

I look over at the water glass on my nightstand. It's empty, but it's been there for six months because Eamon drank out of it the last night we were in bed together. Sometimes I put my mouth on the rim of the glass and try to figure out where his was. So it can be like we're kissing. I pick up the glass and kiss the coolness of it. I put it back, lean over and kiss Dalton one more time. I tell him I'm sorry about earlier and he says it's okay and reaches for my hand. We walk out of the bedroom and down the stairs, back to the kitchen.

"Brian called," I say.

"Brian-Brian?" he asks. He's bending down to look at the bottom shelf of the fridge before he turns to me.

When our eyes meet, I nod.

"Checking in on you?"

I nod again.

"Are you okay?" Dalton stands up straight and puts his hand on top of the refrigerator door. "Do you want to talk about it?"

"No. I'm hungry. And hey. I'm sorry about asking if you love Frances. We don't have to talk about Frances. I'm too possessive of you. I don't own you. Even if it feels like it sometimes," I say, standing back.

"I don't think you're too possessive. Honestly," he says.

It's my turn at the fridge and I can't decide on anything. I close it and open the pantry door. I pick up a can of pumpkin puree and put it right back. I pick up a can of chicken noodle soup and do the same thing. Dalton steps next to me.

"That's not it," he says. He leans against the wall.

"What happened with you two? It's none of my business, but I do want to know," I say.

Frances had been in Dalton's life until recently. She was a wanderer, a drifter. She'd disappear for months and pop up again. She was nice enough. A worrisome beauty. To me, at least. I remember feeling so insecure around her the first couple times. She had thick, black hair that fell across her back like a curtain. She was always out doing something new. She'd come back with a new story and a new adventure and I felt silly talking about teaching ballet to babies. Even performing. Even when I was the lead. It never felt *enough* for Frances. To her, I was a bore. But Dalton was besotted.

"You've said Eamon never made you cry, but you guys fought sometimes, right?" Dalton says, reaching for two packages of ramen noodles.

"We have so much good food and we're eating ramen?"

"Fancy ramen with eggs and sriracha," he says. He closes the pantry and I sit up on the counter and tuck my hands into my sleeves. He gets two pots, fills them with water.

"Of course Eamon and I fought sometimes. Sometimes a lot. He just never made me cry. He didn't say mean things to me or try to hurt me on purpose. Every other guy I'd ever dated made me cry...like on purpose. I guess what I'm saying is that I dated a lot of assholes before him. He wasn't one," I say, watching Dalton click the stove on.

"Okay. That same night Frances and I hooked up? We had a huge fight afterwards," he says.

"The night before you moved in here?" My brain wheels are turning slowly. I didn't know about this latest fight. He hadn't told me anything about it.

"Yep," Dalton says.

"Because of me?"

"Because of a lot of things."

"Because you were moving in with us?"

"I haven't talked to her since," Dalton says, chopping scallions.

"She seriously won't talk to you because you moved in with Noah and me?" I ask. Now I'm angry. Forget possessive. Now I feel crazy. Frances is the worst. I hate thinking she's hurt him. He's had too much hurt in his life.

"I won't talk to her. She's called me a couple of times and sends me texts and emails but I don't want to deal with any of it right now," he says.

Dalton stops chopping and turns to me. Starts telling me the whole story.

⚓

Frances came back in town to visit her parents and Dalton knew she was coming. They had plans to go to dinner. He hadn't seen her in three months. They got sushi and went back to his place. He told her he was moving the next day and his place was all packed up. They had sex on the floor. Afterwards, she finally asked where he was moving. She hadn't bothered to ask before. Dalton said she was half-seeing a guy in Austin. He said sometimes it made him jealous even though he wasn't sure how he felt about her anymore. That's why he wanted to do dinner when she was in town. He hadn't been with anyone in a while. And he *did* miss her.

Dalton said he told her he was moving in with me and Noah. To help out. He didn't know for how long. Frances said maybe that wasn't the best idea. Dalton asked her why. Frances said because he can't take Eamon's place. He shouldn't need to. He shouldn't want to. She said Dalton was trying too hard to be like his dad. Trying too hard to be some phony hero-father swooping in. That he was better than his dad, that he was better than all of this. Dalton said he'd never been angrier at her. He told her to shut the fuck up.

For a moment when he's telling me, I think I might cry, but I don't. I sit on the counter, watching Dalton get two brown eggs from the fridge. When he turns back around to keep talking, I watch his mouth move.

"Was that it? Did she say anything else?" As if he hadn't told me enough.

Dalton looks out the window and tells me the snow is heavier, so I turn to look too.

"She apologized for the stuff about Dad. She's clearly not a fan of his. She just felt like it was too much. Extra. Me, moving in here. Plus, she's always been extremely jealous of you," he says.

"Jealous of *me?*" I say, probably a little too loudly.

"Because before, when you and E and me would be together all of the time. Then you and E got married and you were pregnant and happy. And now, you have Noah and me," he says.

I let it float there for a second. Dalton telling me I *have* him. It feels like something important I need to let in. Something I need to remember.

"Frances is a jealous person," he says.

"I am too," I say.

"No you're not."

"Dalton. I'm jealous of Cassidy because of you. I'm jealous of Frances because of you. I'm jealous of all the other wives of the cops in Eamon's department because it wasn't their husbands who got killed, it was mine," I say. My heart is racing like its got its arms up, heading for the finish line ribbon.

"She's jealous of strong people. You're a strong person. And you don't have to be jealous of her or Cassidy. Trust me. It's wasted energy. Save it for something else."

"So she, what, told you it was over for good if you moved in here?"

"Pretty much," he says.

The water is boiling now. He says Frances must've changed her mind because she left him voicemails saying she was sorry. She sent him an email asking if he wanted to get together when she was back in town. He hasn't responded.

"I...thank you. Just, thank you for...everything. For standing up for us and for basically being Noah's dad," I say. The tears come easy. I tuck my knees underneath my chin and close my eyes.

I cry at anything and everything now. It's one of my defining traits. Also, I'm easily confused. It started happening when I was around four months pregnant. I'd forget words and where I put things. It took me a whole day to remember the word *order* when I was trying to explain to the insurance company that the obstetrician wanted me to get some tests. But of course, the crying and confusion ramped up to its all-time-completely-fucking-insane-batshit-crazy level once Eamon was gone. I'd tear up anytime I'd see a cop car. I'd peek inside to see if I knew them. Every part of me would flu-ache because maybe I'd look in there and see Eamon and his big brown eyes looking back at me. Maybe I was more confused than I'd ever been. Maybe I'd made the whole shooting up in some sort of pregnancy psychosis.

Sometimes the cop would recognize me and wave. Once, Brian pulled me over. Turned his lights on and everything, but not his siren. He said he didn't want to scare Noah. He just wanted to see him, to see how I was. We were in a mostly empty parking lot. I got out and hugged Brian around his neck. When I pulled away I could tell he was trying hard not to cry. It's the same face he made at the funeral. I took a deep breath in and we stood there staring at each other, holding hands before he reached inside the car to softly touch the top of Noah's head. He told me to call him and Lucy anytime, day or night.

There are a lot of pauses whenever Brian and I talk—slick pockets of silence we slip into. I don't have to say anything and neither does he. Brian was with Eamon when he took his last breaths, so I think some of Eamon is with Brian still. Maybe some of his breath got inside of him and Brian carries that around and that's why we're quiet so often when we're together or when we're on the phone.

So we can hear Eamon.

Sometimes I'd leave the house without shoes and not realize it until I was a mile away. When I did remember my shoes, sometimes I'd put on two different ones. One time I went to the bookstore wearing one of Eamon's blue flip-flops and one of my black ones. It'd taken me ten minutes to nurse Noah and quiet him down in the car, so I wasn't about to turn around and go back home to change one flip-flop. I wandered around with Noah strapped to me, sleeping. I bought four different casserole cookbooks. That was two months after, when all I did was cook. I made Chinese chicken casserole with mushrooms. Cheesy casserole with seasoned textured vegetable protein instead of hamburger. I made black bean enchilada casserole. I made everything.

I labeled and stacked them. I ran out of room in the freezer. One day Dalton ordered a new deep freezer and had it delivered. He came over, took the casseroles out to the garage and put them in there. He was standing in front of me wearing a navy blue T-shirt and his old jeans and a brown ball cap. He took off his ball cap and put it on my head. He asked me if it was okay for him to ask someone at our church about the hospitality ministry and Eamon's mom about the one at her church too because new moms needed meals delivered. Once or twice a week I'd take some casseroles over to those churches. I made stickers that said MADE WITH LOVE BY EVANGELINE & NOAH ROYCE and put them on top of the dishes. It was something. I was doing something.

"Like I said before, remember our new rule. No more thanking me," Dalton says, shaking his head.

"I don't think I've ever said it aloud that you're basically Noah's dad, have I? It sounds weird, doesn't it? It shouldn't but it does," I say, wiping my eyes with my sleeves.

"Evi, it is my honor. And blessing. I know what it's like, being adopted. The root of it is love, plain and simple. Big love," he says. He stretches his arms out wide and I just keep crying. "Shh. Shh. Come 'ere, come 'ere," he says, helping me down off the counter. The steam from our boiling pots of noodles is swirling up towards the ceiling. He pats the piano bench and sits down next to me and says he'll play anything I ask him to. I tell him and "Carry On Wayward Son" drifts up from the piano.

I watch his fingers on the keys. I love his fingers, I love his hands. I love how he walks. I love how he smells. This is my life and this is where God has put me in this moment—this hazy sadness, encircled by light. I'm here with Dalton right now. On this piano bench, watching his fingers and listening to him play; the gentle *plink-plunk* sounds like falling snow. I have the urge to get rip-roaring drunk even though it's the middle of the day. It's just us and there's nothing else to do. I feel like I've earned it by still breathing and being here. If Jesus were here with us I would ask him to turn the faucet water into wine.

I go into Dalton's pocket for the lighter. I flick it and hold it up.

He's being so cute this afternoon, I'd have to be crazy not to have a crush on him. There it is. A banner trailing across the sky: I have an actual *crush* on Dalton Berkeley-Royce. Another one behind it reads: I don't know how to do this. I know my feelings are bigger and more important than a crush, but that's part of it. I wouldn't let myself think it before because I felt too guilty and it felt too weird and wrong and uncomfortable. I like him and obviously love him but now I have what amounts to a schoolgirl crush on him too. I let that thought settle slowly like a feather falling to the floor.

"Let's eat, then get drunk and talk," I say after a bit. Dalton's still playing. He's moved onto another Fleetwood Mac song. I lean my elbow on the piano and rest my head against my hand.

"Well dammit, what the lady wants, the lady gets," he says. He smiles and nods his head towards the kitchen. His face lights up. Someone might say mine does too.

Dalton and I eat our soup. We sit across from each other at the kitchen table. I tell him he's a really good kisser. I tell him I feel silly for saying it aloud.

"I'm shy about it. I was going to wait until I was drunk to tell you," I say, covering my face with my hands.

"You don't have to get drunk to tell me stuff. Quit it," he says. "I loved kissing you."

"You always tell me to *quit it.*"

"Because I'm trying to stop you from going too much into some…thing," he says, leaning forward to take a bite.

"I go too much into things sometimes. I know I'm doing it. But I don't know how to stop it," I say, sitting back in my chair.

"That's okay," he says.

"How are you not scared of everything all the time?" I ask him. I've been wanting to ask him for a while.

He asks me what makes me think he's not. I want to say, *look at how you're sitting there and how you have this thing about you* but I don't know what that thing is. I can't explain it so I don't try.

"Well I *am* scared of a lot of things but sitting around thinking about them doesn't matter because that doesn't stop them from happening. It hasn't in the past," he says.

The truth of it makes my eyes sting.

One night in September I asked Dalton to tell me something about Eamon that I didn't know. I was searching for anything. Anything that would make me feel closer to him. I'd been wearing one of Eamon's shirts for two days—a red and black buffalo plaid. I was sweating in it. It wasn't autumn yet. The seasons hadn't clicked over.

"Damn," Dalton said, turning the baseball game down. He was over and we were watching the Red Sox catch up with the Yankees. Noah was asleep in his bouncy seat. I watched him breathing in and out, glad he was doing it. Glad the world was still turning and we were both still breathing.

"It can be anything," I said.

"Give me a sec," he said. His voice was sleepy. Mine was too.

Dalton told me that after our first date, Eamon said he was going to marry me.

"Our *first* date?" I asked.

"Legit. But I already knew it. Eamon had never been like that about a girl before," Dalton said. We took turns looking at the TV screen. We took turns watching Noah sleep.

"Have you ever been like that about a girl before?"

Dalton shook his head and then he said no.

"Okay, I want to talk about why I'm so conflicted and why I feel so weird about everything," I say when we finish eating. Dalton puts his bowl in the sink with a clink and I move the faucet to wash mine out.

"Didn't you say we were supposed to get drunk for this?" he asks.

"Last night you said we *shouldn't* talk about this stuff when we're drinking."

"I changed my mind, I think. It probably doesn't matter," he says.

I'd like to think that we would open up more if we have a drink to loosen us, but in reality, Dalton and I can get down to it without any liquid courage. Drinking makes me less self-conscious, sure, but it never lasts. Regardless, it's cold and there's snow. Also, I want to have a glass of whiskey by the fire. Since Noah's at my parents' for one more night, I may as well take advantage.

"Fine. Get the whiskey," I say to Dalton. I grab my phone so I can call my mom to check on Noah. I miss holding his little warm body in my arms and how he smells.

While I'm talking to her, I can hear Noah fussing. My mom says she's about to put him down for his nap. She says Noah and my dad are watching ESPN, having dude time. When I get off the phone, I'm reset. Relaxed again because I'm reminded Noah is safe, warm and okay. Dalton hands me a short glass of whiskey and we cheers. *To whiskey and ribbons.* Dalton says it. I say it. We walk towards the fireplace. I double-check my memories to make sure I can hear Eamon saying *to whiskey and ribbons* in my head. The specific cadence of his deep voice. I used to tell him he sounded like Superman. His voice was commanding, but kind and he'd soften it when he talked to me. *Look at you*, he'd say and put his hands on both sides of my face. *Look at you*, I'd say back to him. I'd give anything to be able to look at him again. *Please, God.* I put my fingers on my neck to check my pulse because I'm still alive. But how? Dalton sets his glass of whiskey on the table and bends down to start the fire.

After one whiskey and another, Dalton and I are sitting in front of the fire, watching it and talking. I want to ask him a question I've never asked before. Partly because I don't want to know the answer. Partly because I already do.

"Dalton?"

"What's up?"

I cross my legs, sit up straight and put my glass down between us. My face is hot, from the whiskey and the fire. I scoot back from it. "Did you promise Eamon you'd take care of me if something happened to him?"

Dalton takes my glass and lifts it to his lips, but it's empty. He puts it back down.

"Not like you think," he says.

"I want to know what you think I think."

"That's confusing."

"You know what I mean."

Dalton shrugs. "It's hard for both of us to accept things, so you probably think the only reason I moved in here and the only reason I'm with you like this and with Noah like this is because I owe it to Eamon."

"That's not so crazy, though," I say. I find the thought comforting and frustrating. I don't want Dalton doing all of this out of obligation. But also, there are worse things in this world than someone keeping a promise.

"Back before...everything...did you think Eamon's parents adopted me, took me in, gave me everything they gave me out of obligation to Penelope or because they wanted to? Does it matter? Honestly? Does it make a difference? Aren't they both love? Don't they have the same results?" Dalton says. He's had most of his life to think about these things. All these little flicks of truth, leaving bruises. We both sat under the silent weight of secrets, the heaviness of keeping them, of having them kept from us.

"I'm not accusing you of anything," I say. I'm lying. I'm passive-aggressively accusing him of moving in out of pity. I want extra-reassurance that he didn't.

"Did Eamon ask me to be there for you and Noah if something were to happen to him? Yes. That's true, Evi. I'm not going to lie to you. But would I have done it even if he hadn't? Yes. That's true too. But you knew he asked me. You had to. You knew he couldn't have slept at night if he didn't feel like you'd be taken care of. Don't try to talk yourself out of what you deserve," he says.

I look into the fire. Dalton's phone starts ringing. He sits there next to me and lets it ring.

"You can tell me things. Anything. It's like we need to come up with *rules* about our relationship or this isn't going to work," I say.

"What isn't going to work?" Dalton asks.

"This, Dalton. This," I say, pointing back and forth between us.

"You need to know...in my mind? Failure is not an option when it comes to this, when it comes to us," he says. He is straight-faced serious and it is intimidating.

"But what if we just fuck it up?"

"Not an option," he says, shaking his head.

"But it's an actual thing that could happen."

"No. It isn't," he says, confidently. He stands up, crosses his arms.

"So what happens if you meet someone or I meet someone?"

Right on cue, Dalton's phone rings again. He lifts it from the floor, makes it stop ringing.

"See. Exactly what I'm talking about. Cassidy is hunting you down. She's obsessed with you," I say. He doesn't immediately defend Cassidy being obsessed with him so I don't know what else to say.

"She's...she is in love with me," he says. My stomach dives.

"And you?"

"Me? *I'm* in love with you," he says.

"You're not," I say.

"Are you kidding me?"

I look up at him, standing there. I feel like nothing. We've been drinking and drinking but I'm not drunk. I'm not even buzzed. I would welcome it, but I'm not, although clearly there is alcohol in my bloodstream, clearly I feel a little lighter, a little more disconnected, a little more Super-Evangeline.

Dalton bends his knees, crouches next to me.

"You know I love you. Let's stop playing games," he says.

"I'm not playing games."

"And those piano kisses—" he says. *Piano kisses.* "Those kisses weren't about me. You and I both know it. You know I love you, so stop it."

My eyes fill with tears. Dalton is usually over-the-top gentle with me but he's not being gentle now. He matches the fire snapping next to us. I've gotten good at reading his emotions but find myself confused. His words. *You know I love you. You know I love you.* I hear him. But his face is twisted. Angry? Frustrated? I can't read him. I can't figure him out. He's a fuzzy station that won't come in clearly. *Let's stop playing games. So stop it.* It's bossy and weird and I'm sensitive to it, to him, to everything. Usually when I cry, Dalton comforts me immediately. Puts his arms around me, hugs me or offers me tea or tissue. He doesn't do that this time. This time he stands back up, turns away from me.

"I love you," he says, looking out of the window. The never-ending snow. Everything is white white white white white white white white. My life used to have color. Now it's monochromatic. I don't wear bright colors anymore. I haven't performed since Eamon was killed. I haven't sewn the elastic and slick pink ribbons to my pointe shoes, haven't wrapped the ribbons around my ankles, toed into the gritty-soft crunch of the rosin box.

I was one person before all of this and now that person is gone.

Grief is horrifyingly personal. Grief is horrifyingly generic.

I wipe my eyes, stand up.

Dalton and I tell each other we love one another all the time. It's easy for us, easy and true. But this is different. He said it differently.

"I kissed you because I wanted to kiss you. *You,*" I say.

"You wanted to kiss Eamon. You *should* want to kiss him. He should be here," he says, turning towards me.

"But he's not," I say.

"I am more than willing to be that man for you. That's all I'm saying."

"I love you too. In the way you don't think I do," I say, tucking my hands into the sleeves of Eamon's sweater.

"Part of me wants to ask you how you can know that already when it's only been six months and your heart is still breaking. So is mine. And part of me wants to tell you I'll try my best to accept it. You don't know how much I want that to be true," he says.

I think of our breaking hearts sounding like the snow—so quiet we can barely hear them, but after the right amount of time we can look around and see how everything is changed. Covered.

"I know how I feel. I'm not confused," I say.

"And you think I am?"

"You tell me. Where do your feelings for Cassidy fit into all of this?" I ask, boldly. I know he won't want to talk about it. I don't care. However, I do wish I were drunk for this. I walk to the kitchen, find the whiskey. Pour. Drink. I am still crying, kind of. I've never been more tired of anything than I am of crying.

I hear Dalton walking towards me.

"I don't love her like this if that's what you're asking. No. I don't love Cassidy like this and I don't love Frances anymore," he says.

"But Cassidy...you like her?" I say, giving in to the fifth grade girl in my heart. *You like her.*

"I like her. She's kind to me. I like her enough to hire her," he says.

"You like her enough to kiss her."

"I like her enough to have kissed her a lot in the past, yes."

"Yeah, I'm getting that," I say. I am horribly jealous, so jealous I want to throw this glass at him. "And?" I say. He's standing in front of me and I am pouring more whiskey.

"Easy," he says, putting his hand on mine.

"I'm fine," I say, pouring.

Dalton takes the glass, so some of the whiskey spills on the counter.

"Stop it," I say.

"Stop drinking. Stop. Talk to me," he says, holding the glass away from me.

I reach for it. He's like a foot taller than me. This is ridiculous and it's pissing me off.

Dalton's phone rings again. I thought he'd turned it off. Cassidy must be calling and calling, blowing up his phone to profess her love. I'm still reaching for the glass and Dalton steps back, downs it. He slides the glass across the counter and it clinks against the olive oil bottle, the pitcher I keep the wooden spoons in.

I calmly reach for a dishrag and wet it, wipe up the counter where the whiskey spilled.

"You answer your phone and go be with Cassidy and I'll do whatever," I say, shaking my head.

"This is our first real fight? I mean it was bound to happen but you're not listening to me. You *refuse* to listen to me. You're acting crazy and I'll allow you that. You've been through a lot of shit you shouldn't have had to go through. So have I. You can act crazy. It's okay. But I don't have to stand here and listen to it," he says. He goes into the drawer for the cigarettes. The ritual of opening the door, propping it, lighting the cigarette, inhaling. The way he always holds his arm out, touches the doorframe. He's doing all of those things.

"Well where are you going? It's a blizzard," I say. So stupid. I'm embarrassed that is all I can come up with. I am an embarrassing person and I want to disappear. I check the clock on the oven, wonder what Noah is doing. Probably having his bottle. Probably making his little noises. I can hear them, even when he's not here.

"I'll walk out into this I guess," he says, half-laughing.

"I don't want to fight. I'm jealous. I'm embarrassed about how jealous I am," I say.

"You don't need to be jealous."

"Why does she keep calling you?"

Dalton smokes.

"Did you have sex with her?"

"You're obsessed with that so you won't believe me when I tell you no anyway," he says.

"I'm not obsessed with it!" I am.

"No. Evi. I haven't had sex with her. I'm not going to have sex with her. I told you earlier Frances was the last girl I had sex with. We've had this conversation. I haven't lied to you," he says. He lets the cigarette dangle from his mouth, goes to the living room floor to retrieve his phone. He comes back over to the door, smokes, taps around on his phone and sets it down on the counter, playing a voicemail from Cassidy through the speakers.

"Hey, D. I don't want anything just saying hi. And this place we talked about going to dinner...this place downtown...looks like they're closed on Wednesdays so maybe we could pick another day? I'll let you pick! I'm excited about this by the way. As if you couldn't tell. Okay. I'll talk to you later."

Dalton smokes, leans over to click the other voicemail. Lets it play.

"D, it's me again. Obviously. I don't know if you're too snowed in or whatever. Maybe it's crazy to even ask but if you wanted to stop by tonight that would be cool too. I'm here by my lonesome, doing nothing. Trying to find something to marathon on Netflix. So...you could call me back, brave the awful weather like some kind of superhero and we could be snowed in together. Just an offer. No worries. I don't want you to think this is too much or something. Just an offer. Merely that. Okay. Okay. Sorry, bye!"

Dalton's phone makes a soft clicking sound as he turns off the screen.

"We both listened to those at the same time. You heard the same thing I heard," he says.

I go to him, he hands me the cigarette.

"Is our fight over?" I ask.

Dalton shrugs.

"I want our fight to be over," I say.

Eamon

THERE WERE TIMES WHEN EVI AND I WOULD BE SUPER-careful so she wouldn't get pregnant and there were times when we weren't careful at all and I found myself hoping we'd be surprised. I also found myself praying we wouldn't. I changed my mind about it a lot but I'd made up my mind about one thing: I'd turn in my badge when she had a baby. I'd surprise Evi and keep it a secret from her until then. I'd talked to Brian about it. I'd talked to Dalton about it. I didn't tell my dad about it. I didn't tell Mom. I didn't need grandbaby pressure on top of work pressure. My mom had supported me in everything I'd done. She had cried happy proud tears when I graduated from the academy even though I knew it broke her heart. I didn't want to break her heart. I inherited the desire to serve from my dad and violence had never scared me. If it weren't the force it would've been the military. My uncles were Marines, one on each side. There were a lot of ways to break a mother's heart and unfortunately I found several. My mom was a woman I never wanted to hurt. Ever. Evangeline was another.

I saw Evi as this precious thing, this delicate petal. But out in the world, she was a hard-ass when she needed to be. She was tough and a strict ballet teacher with a spoonful of sugar. Sometimes when she taught her tiny little dancers they'd warm-up to "A Spoonful of Sugar" from *Mary Poppins*. I visited the studio at times to watch her work. I'd pop in, bring her coffee or food. She wore one pair of the countless ballet shoes she owned, pale pink and black leotards, white tights, grey legwarmers, her long hair pulled up in a bun, diamond stud earrings I'd gotten her for her birthday, the gold cross necklace she always wore. Truth was, she was a whole flower, not a petal. Resilient, honest. Every woman I'd ever known felt like a copy of a copy of a copy when I met Evangeline. I'd heard men say things like that, heard actors say things like that in movies—that everything-was-black-and-white-until-he-met-her moment, then suddenly ultralight, vivid, eye-popping color. Evangeline was my Technicolor moment, the big reveal, the screaming colors so bright it felt as if I should hold my ears.

Although rare, we had fights, but never did they worry me. We tended to lean towards one another when we disagreed. Neither of us pulled away. We didn't fight when she told me she didn't want to be super-safe at all anymore about pregnancy. She wanted to barrel ahead and make a point of it. Evi had a plan and Evi with a plan was like a tornado spinning its way across the Oklahoma plains.

I had to work an overnight but we'd had the day off together, napped and fooled around and gotten pizza from our favorite joint up the road. We got garlic knots and the biggest pizza with absolutely everything on it—banana peppers, sausage, ham, Canadian bacon, pepperonis, onions, black olives, green olives, green peppers, tomatoes, mushrooms. Evi had demanded I order that one since she was ovulating and ravenous.

We were both in bed with our laptops. Evi closed hers, smoothed it towards her feet, the end of the bed. It was seven. October. The lemon-orange sunset light, glowing our bedroom window. We'd been married for two years, three months. We'd both been comfortable being child-free so far. Two years, three months was a nice amount of time to have to ourselves.

"It's time to make a baby," she said. Her eyes focused on me intently—a kitten who'd just seen a bird's shadow. She was wearing one of my T-shirts, so big it hung off her shoulder. She was always wearing my clothes which made her seem smaller, more fragile than she was. She never wore a bra in the house. Her smallish breasts hung heavy, her nipples hard in the October chill. I could see down her shirt, didn't try to hide it. She swatted at me and smiled, readjusted herself against the headboard.

"We're supposed to try to have a baby but I'm not allowed to look down your shirt? This is going to be a tough one," I said.

She lifted the hem up, flashing me like she was some young drunk girl desiring Mardi Gras beads. I nodded at her, gave her breasts my full attention—the attention they deserved.

"It's time. I'm ovulating," she said.

"I've got an hour until I have to leave," I said, lifting my eyebrow.

"I want to have a baby now. I don't want to use anything anymore," she said.

"Then let's not use anything," I said, meaning it. Although part of me wanted to ask aloud, *but what if we just fuck it up?* This wasn't going to be something for me to decide. I wanted her to make the decision and when she made it, it was done. If she got pregnant I'd find another job when she had the baby. I'd tell our child I used to be a police officer. *Daddy used to be a cop. Before we had you. Daddy loved you so much he didn't want anything bad to happen so he quit. Just like that.*

"Let's see what happens," I said, kissing her. A question.

Her answer was sex. No protection, no regrets.
Let's see what happens.
She came twice and we called it good luck.

Twice a year, once in October and once in May, Dad, Dalton and I went up to the Two Hearted River and stayed with my Dad's brother, James. Fished for coho and pink salmon in the fall. Fly fished for steelhead in the spring. James was three years older than my dad. He'd been a Marine, served in Vietnam. He never talked about it. When I was a kid, my dad would tell Dalton and me not to ask him about it when James would come and visit or when we'd go up to Michigan. It made me nervous when I was younger, fearing my uncle would suddenly have a flashback or a breakdown. My dad told me James was always quiet, but came back from Vietnam even quieter. Dad had told me my uncle had won some medals, had been a sniper. I obsessed over it when I was a kid, picturing James as a kick-ass video game superhero. But as I got older when we'd go up to Michigan and I'd see James stare off at the river as we sat there and drank beer and waited—how he'd smoke and smoke—it was like he wasn't there with us. Like he wasn't anywhere at all. I'd feel sorry for him, sorry for everyone, sorry about everything. I knew how to use deadly force if I needed to and so far I hadn't. I wondered if the time ever came when I had to do it, if afterwards I'd feel how James felt when he'd smoke and watch the Two Hearted River rushing by.

That October, Dalton and my dad and I all drove up in Dad's truck. It was about an eleven-hour drive. We left Kentucky and kept driving up, up, up until we got to the top of Michigan, then we kept going. Mom and Evi had packed us some food. We ate it and stopped for more. Delicious junk. Diner burgers and fries, warm fruit pie and black coffee. When we finally made it to James's place, he had another pot of coffee waiting for us.

"Glad you boys made it up safe," he said after pouring our

coffees. He sat down at the table wearing his USMC cap, like always. I was sure he'd be buried in it someday.

"Coho biting?" my dad asked.

"Was out there the other morning and got one about this big." James held his hands two feet apart. "Two more, a little smaller."

"Fried them up already, I bet?" Dad said, looking around the kitchen.

"Vivian cooked them over the fire out back," James said. My Aunt Viv was Finnish and legend had it my Uncle James fell in love with her at first sight. He'd moved to the Upper Peninsula, became a game warden, met Viv his first day on the job. *That was all she wrote,* he liked to add at the end of the story. James was recently retired but still taught fly fishing lessons.

Viv made herself scarce the weekends we came up. It was as much a part of our tradition as the fishing. She and her sisters went on trips to New York City to catch shows on Broadway or to an Arizona spa for sauna treatments and massages. This time they'd gone to Disney World. So it was just James up there in that house by the river until we showed up—Uncle James and their old coon dog Betsy because of course Uncle James had an old coon dog with floppy ears who wasn't much good for anything outside of sleeping and eating and getting her belly rubbed. I held my hand down for her and she came over, sniffed it. I pet behind her ears, the top of her head.

My dad and James were my grandparents' only children and I liked the symmetry there. My dad and James, Dalton and me. *Two by two.* I knew how to operate around them and James loved Dalton. Ever since we were kids, James had gotten us to work with our hands tying flies, hooking worms, sorting the hooks in his tackle box. He used to call us The Twins when we were boys which made us laugh because Dalton and I couldn't have looked more different. *Twin spirits,* my Uncle would say when pressed for more.

⚓

"Evi's trying to get pregnant. Maybe she already is, I don't know," I said to Dalton the next morning as we were getting ready to head out to the river. Imagined my sperm in the dark of her womb, squiggling their ways to her egg as we drove away from Kentucky, away from her and everything down there. I ached, missing her. My dad and James were inside, packing up. We'd already hitched both fishing boats to the backs of the trucks. Dalton and I were next to them, sharing coffee from a green Stanley thermos. We always smoked when we came up to the Two Hearted. Cigarettes and black coffee. The early morning sky was a slit, an eye half-opened.

"All right. Good for y'all, man. Good for y'all," Dalton said, smoking. The steam from his coffee was waving up. It was chilly, fifty-some-odd degrees. I was hoping it would warm up. I blew into my cold fist.

"Does it make you uncomfortable, talking about this?" I asked him. I knew Frances had gotten an abortion a while back and Dalton seemed on the fence about it. I didn't want to unnecessarily trudge up unpleasant memories.

"About Evi being pregnant? Why would that make me uncomfortable?" Dalton seemed bewildered. "I'm so excited for y'all. Are you kidding me?"

"I mean...Frances...*not* having a baby. I don't want it to be awkward," I said.

"I'm happy for you. That's it." Dalton patted me on the back.

"You and Frances...still together?"

"It's complicated," he said, laughing. I knew he'd been hanging out with a *goose* called Cassidy sometimes. I'd stopped by the bike shop a couple times, seen her in there talking him up. She seemed a little punk rock for Dalton's taste, but he only had good things to say about her. I didn't know what was up with her and didn't usually press him. Dalton was always open with me, told me things. I rarely had to ask, but sometimes I did, just for the fun of it.

"And Cassidy?" I asked, smoking. I raised an eyebrow.

"Nope," Dalton said. He poured himself more coffee.

"Let me know when you do."

"I know I *could*. She's made that more than clear."

I heard my dad and James making their way towards us. Heard the door slam, turned to see them walking with their tackle boxes and poles. James was about an inch taller than my dad although they were both tall, grey-haired, sturdy but lithe men. My dad could be the boisterous one when he wanted to, the sparking electric next to James's old-timey quietness. My dad would tell me stories of bullies attempting to pick on him in the neighborhood and how James would suddenly appear and the bullies would scatter—his big brother stepping in to save the day. My dad would tell me the kids respected James because he was the quiet one, kept to himself. They didn't know what to expect of him. My dad's mouth could get him into trouble but James was always there, his protector.

Besides people thinking Dalton and I were gay and teasing us from time to time, we didn't have to deal with a lot of bullies in school. Dalton was a super-talented kid but also one of those people who could fly under the radar when he needed to and he was good at that. I had a natural ability to be able to hold my own. I wasn't one to back down from anything and although that alone had the potential to cause me problems, for the most part it did me all right. Who knew what mine and Evangeline's kid would be like. More like me? More like Evi? Maybe he'd be a lot of me with some of my dad and James thrown in for good measure—a quiet, scrappy brawler with a heart of gold.

I took the tackle box from my dad, set it in the back of the truck next to mine and Dalton's. Dalton grabbed the poles from James, followed suit.

"Y'all talking about women?" Dad asked.

"A little," Dalton said as Dad walked around to the driver's side, opened the door. I put out my cigarette.

"You and Frances done?" Dad asked.

"That same girl you're always with? She's something else," James chimed in before climbing into his own truck. James had met Frances at least once or twice at my parents' Christmas parties.

"Frances, yes. But there's also someone else," Dalton said.

"Someone else could mean trouble if you got another woman in the picture," James warned. He might not have said much, but when he did, it was always some sort of attempt at being helpful. Advice or a quip.

"Ain't that the truth?" Dad added.

"Wow, Dad, I never knew you rolled like that back in the day. I'm impressed," I said.

"Just making conversation." Dad winked at me.

"It's all good," Dalton assured us. I wanted to ask more about Cassidy but saved it for later when Dad and James couldn't nose in. Dalton got into the truck with James. I was riding with Dad. I'd been in charge of the coolers and turned around to look in the back for them. Double-checked they were still there. Success. We had beer, plenty of food and all of our fishing supplies.

I thought about Evangeline, wondered what she was doing. I thought about what our baby would look like and whether it would be a boy or a girl. I'd always liked the name Noah. *Noah Royce.* I wanted a boy. I'd bring him here with us to fish the Two Hearted as soon as he could hold his head up. Maybe next October we'd have a son and he'd be here in his car seat in the back of my dad's truck. I held that thought as long as I could, felt like holding my breath. And then, like a candle blown out, it was gone.

We fished and drank and smoked and Uncle James didn't stare off too much. James and Dad in one boat, Dalton and me in another. Caught plenty and talked to the other fishermen we passed by who had gotten up early, come out like us. We docked. Enjoyed the view. I sat back down after packing my last fish in ice. Opened another beer, texted Evi. *I miss you. Are you pregnant yet?*

The afternoon sun was almost directly above us, pouring down. It'd warmed to fifty-three degrees and we all knew that was the highest it would get. I pulled my snow hat over my ears. I watched Dalton and Dad packing their fish. James was lighting his cigarette; James loved smoking and it was weirdly inspiring, that love and obsession.

He always made a point of asking me things about being a police officer, felt kinship with my dad, with me, the three of us serving the people. It was a source of pride for him, to feel like he wasn't being selfish, to feel like he'd added something to this society, this country, this world instead of just taking and taking and taking. I felt those same things too, untangled them from my heart when I decided to follow in my father's footsteps, no matter how generic and unoriginal it made me feel at first. There was so much truth to it. Fighting for the good, fighting for something I believed in. My heart was a sinking ship when I thought about leaving the force when Evi had a baby, even though I'd promised myself that's what I would do. I knew part of me would feel like a quitter, like I was letting more people down than just me. But I realized I was getting ahead of myself.

Who knew how long it would take Evi to get pregnant or if we could the natural way? It could take months, years. If we couldn't do it the old-fashioned way I'd be willing to do whatever Evangeline wanted. Tests, drugs, whatever. I was fully committed. Nothing about it felt wrong. I'd never wanted to marry another woman before Evi. I'd never wanted to have a child with another woman before Evi. Those things meant something to me. I didn't ignore them. This could potentially be something we would have to be patient about. Mom lost Thomas. And I remembered Brian's wife had a miscarriage and how heartbroken she'd been. For about a year afterwards, anytime I saw her she looked like she'd been crying. I hated thinking about something like that happening to us, happening to Evi. But maybe it wouldn't. I was thinking too much. Dalton went into the cooler for another beer. A light beer. I wasn't drunk at all, but I could feel them. I was on my fourth. I drank it faster, waited for Evi to text me back.

It was Saturday afternoon so I knew she'd finished teaching her ballet classes. She usually got lunch afterwards. Later, I knew she and her mom were going to a movie and out for dinner. I imagined her leaving the ballet studio in the October sun but I felt suddenly anxious about it which wasn't normal for me. I worried something had happened to her. Why hadn't she texted me? I unlocked my phone to text her again and saw the grey blinking bubbles, meaning she was writing me back. I waited. And waited.

I ACTUALLY AM. EAMON I AM PREGNANT. CAN I CALL YOU?

My heart, a sinking ship. My heart, a bottle rocket. My hands started to shake and I was usually Steady Freddy, with my gun, with anything, with everything.

But.

CALL ME

I told the guys I was stepping aside to talk to Evi on the phone. I'd be right back. I looked down and saw her face on my screen. I tried my best to casually jog away so I could have privacy but I was sure I looked ridiculous and didn't care. I was glad I was wearing my sunglasses because my eyes were tearing up.

"I am!" Evi said into the phone as soon as we connected. She was very Evi when she said it, calm but sparkly. She was so cute I couldn't stand it. My wife. We were having a baby. We, three. It was happening.

"I love you so much," I spilled out. The emotion I thought was creeping up on me slowly hit me like a hammer. And kept hitting me. There were probably cartoon bluebirds and stars and all kinds of symbols rotating over my head. I looked back at my dad and Dalton and James and it was business as usual. I half-expected at least one of them to give me shit for calling Evi during our Guys' Weekend but then I remembered Dalton had been talking to either Frances or Cassidy on the phone the night before and both my dad and James called their wives before bed. I was the last holdout. We were all pussy-whipped suckers and okay with it.

"I love you too. I didn't want to say anything until I knew for sure but this morning in between classes Merit came and brought me coffee and I told her and she went back out to Walgreens and bought me a test and we went to the bathroom together and I took it and I felt guilty because you're all the way up there and I didn't want to have to tell you on the phone and I'd been feeling crappy but didn't want to say anything but now I'm telling you because I had to tell you. We're having a baby," Evi said, finally stopping to take a break.

"I'm so happy. I'm crying. I'm standing next to the Two Hearted, crying. But I've got my sunglasses on so the guys don't know. I have to keep my man card," I said, slipping my finger behind my sunglasses to wipe away a couple manly tears.

"I'm two hearted right now as we speak. Well *almost*. I think the heartbeat is there at five or six weeks and technically I'm about four. I'll call and make an appointment with my gyno on Monday," she said.

"You're *two* hearted," I said, softly.

"Are you having a good time?"

"Who cares?" I laughed. "Yes. We are. But I wish I was with you."

"You will be soon. Are you going to tell the guys? I don't care if you do. Or we could keep it secret for a little bit longer," she said.

"I'll tell Dalton. He won't say anything. We can tell our parents together later. Sound good?"

"Yes. I wouldn't expect you to keep anything from your boyfriend anyway," Evi said.

When I made my way back over, Dalton came and stood by me.

"Evi's on the nest?" he said quietly before I could say anything. His favorite movie was *It's a Wonderful Life* and that's what George Bailey says to Mary when he realizes she's pregnant with their first baby.

"That's right," I said in my best Jimmy Stewart voice.

Dalton hugged me and I hugged him back. Dad and James were turned around.

"Don't say anything. We'll tell everyone else later," I said to him.

"Absolutely. Congrats, bro. Congrats," he said so passionately I had to wipe away a couple more tears. I realized Dalton was crying too. We hugged again and pulled ourselves together before Dad or James got suspicious. We hid behind our sunglasses. Finished our beers. I texted Evi again.

I cannot contain the joy I feel at this moment. These words mean nothing on this screen. I bet you can feel my heart all the way down there. There is nothing I want more than this and you.

She wrote me back. Five words.

Yes! I can feel it.

Later, we came back to James's place, cleaned and cooked and ate our fish. I called Evi again to check in. After I showered and the sun had gone down and Dad and James had gone to bed, Dalton and I were hell-bent on getting all the way drunk. We planned on sleeping it off in the morning, when Dad and James went down to the river. We'd catch up with them later. We got properly trashed at least once whenever we came up to Michigan. Tradition, rituals, it's what made us who we were, who we were to one another. We made a fire out back, sat there in the cold passing the bottle of whiskey back and forth.

"To whiskey and ribbons. This is to you, man. To you and Evi and the new little one," Dalton said, lifting the bottle to the air before downing some.

"Blowing my mind right now, honestly. Having a little family," I said, lighting a cigarette. Drinking to get drunk, smoking. We needed *what happens in the Upper Peninsula stays in the Upper Peninsula* T-shirts. In two days' time I'd be back at work, writing tickets, breaking up bar fights, talking to the news, confronting rowdy skateboarding teenagers at the mall.

"I was kidding myself when I thought I wanted that with Frances. I didn't feel the way you feel right now," Dalton said. He was smoking too, drinking. It wouldn't take us long to get drunk at this rate. We'd been drinking all day sitting under the sun. We'd feasted on fresh salmon with lemon and buttery hot sauce. Crispy potatoes and pie. Aunt Vivian had made four apple pies before she left. One for each of us. God bless Aunt Viv.

"You know this means The Pact takes on a whole new level, right? You ready to level up The Pact, Dalton? Are you ready?!" I said, laughing. He knew I was serious, but it made me laugh too, the drama of it all. If something were to happen to me in the line of duty before the baby was born, Evi would get a sweet payout via my department's life insurance. Two years' salary, federal benefits and state benefits. Morbid as hell to consider but it was part of my job, part of my life to consider it. Evi would be taken care of, that was what mattered. The financial aspect was done. She'd have almost a million dollars. I was worried about her being taken advantage of. I didn't want her to be or feel vulnerable. She was gorgeous and she'd have money. I didn't want some asshole dude swooping in and hurting her. I knew Dalton would never let that happen. He'd take care of her because it's who he was. He was always taking care of the neighborhood's wounded animals when we were growing up—fallen nests full of baby birds, boxes of baby bunnies—Dalton was a natural nurturer.

"I don't want to talk about The Pact. Let's enjoy tonight. You're having a kid! We're up here! This is perfect," Dalton said, drinking and looking up at the cold witch-black Michigan sky, glittered with pinprick stars. At least a billion of them.

"I'm not going to tell her I'm quitting until later. I was thinking of writing her a letter and giving it to her right after she has the baby, y'know? Some flowers and the letter because I'm smooth like that," I said, leaning over to get the whiskey bottle back.

"That's dope," Dalton said, fist bumping me. He was a beautiful drunk bastard. I looked up at the stars again.

My heart a shooting star, my heart blazing.

I loved being up at the cabin but I missed Evi and couldn't wait to get home. I made Dad and Dalton stop when we were almost back to my place, remembering something Evi had told me. She'd read once that to some, pomegranates represented fertility. Abundance. They also represented something spiritual, untouchable. She told me about her art history classes in college, referenced paintings of baby Jesus holding a pomegranate, in Mary's lap or nursing. She said some thought it was the forbidden fruit. The idea of the red, ripe apple? Nope. They got it wrong. It was a pink-purple pomegranate. A whole tree full of them, the fruit hanging low on their branches in the midst. She said if she thought about it hard enough, she could see them in the cool Garden of Eden evening. The times when God would come down and go for His walk with Adam.

"I wish I had a pomegranate right now," she'd said randomly some days before I left.

Although God had already done the fertility work for us, I didn't want to go home empty-handed. Dad pulled up at the grocery store and I went in and came back out with a plastic bag of pomegranates for Evangeline.

When I opened our front door, I saw her sitting on the couch. I went to her, put the pomegranates in her lap and kissed her like I'd been gone for one hundred years.

"I have been praying for pomegranates, but was too lazy to go get them myself. How did you know?" she asked, kissing me again.

I told her how much I loved the name Noah if it were a boy and I promised her I'd think of a girl name I liked too. She looked overwhelmingly radiant to me and I didn't know if it was because I hadn't seen her in days or because the pregnancy hormones were already at work, glowing her from the inside out. She was going to paint her toenails but I did it for her and I'd gotten better at it since last time. She got sad when she talked about how she wouldn't be teaching ballet once she got super-pregnant but I assured her it wasn't forever. She could go back to work if she wanted to. Our parents could watch the baby, we'd work it out. Everything was going to be perfect. Everything was going to be fine. *Everything was going to be just fine.*

Dalton

CASSIDY STARTED COMING IN THE BIKE SHOP A LOT. A LOT. I'd gotten used to her smell. Vanilla, but not too powdery or sweet. Like, fresh vanilla. A thin vanilla bean slipped into a thick glass jar. She was pursuing me and didn't make a secret of it. It was alluring, being chased. She, the lioness. Me, a leaping gazelle. I considered letting her sink her sharp teeth into the weak of my neck, letting her carry me home, slack and bleeding. However, I was still mildly involved with Frances. There were bits of us all over one another and we couldn't rinse it off. Oil and feathers. I'd just gotten off the phone with her when Cassidy walked in. I'd half-heartedly invited Frances over later. She was considering moving to Austin to be closer to her sister. It was likely that soon she'd be gone. She'd come over, we'd watch Netflix, get a pizza, tangle and untangle ourselves like we did so often. She'd been seeing at least one other guy I knew of. He sounded all right. I was mildly jealous and kept expecting to feel it more. Like waiting for a late bus, checking my watch, squinting down the road.

Cassidy would find one reason or another to stop in. Bike parts, new wheels. Once she stopped in for a new bike lock because she said hers had gotten stolen but she conveniently found it the next week, came back and told me so. This time she came in and said she was looking for an entirely new bike. Was ready to make a change.

"I've had this one for a couple years. My ex-boyfriend moved to Costa Rica, left it in my garage. It was never mine to begin with," she said.

She was on the other side of the counter. I'd just pulled my hair back, tucked the strays behind my ears. I was craving a cigarette. Cassidy's vanilla smell made me ache for the dead heat of summer but it was early spring. By the dead heat of summer, Evangeline would have her baby and Eamon would be a father. I'd be an uncle. I was almost embarrassed about how stoked it made me. It wasn't *my* kid so why should I be so excited? But yet, there it was. A new room of the family unit roofed over us. I didn't have to step into it. I was already there. We all were. And that *we* included me alongside everyone else. Not as adopted brother, but as uncle. Uncle Dalton waiting for a new baby Royce. A tiny Royal baby. I had thoughts of my own non-relationship with my biological father and whether I should finally go ahead and call him. I shook my head to clear it. Asked Cassidy if she had a cigarette.

"Not that you seem like a smoker. You don't smell like smoke. You smell like...vanilla," I said. I'd gone too far to turn back now. Now she knew I knew what she smelled like. I needed to make sure this worked in my favor. I didn't mind her knowing I'd sleep with her. I would've. Might've. Could've.

"I have cigarettes. I smoke sometimes. It's awful. I use this vanilla hand lotion," she said, reaching into her bag to show me things. A yellow pack of American Spirits. A small tube of vanilla hand lotion.

"Your secrets are safe with me. Let's go out back," I said. Detroit was there in the front of the store helping a customer. I led Cassidy past the office, out the back door. She handed the box of cigarettes out for me and I took one, so did she. She got a lighter from her pack and lit mine, then hers.

"I would've been a gentleman about it…lit yours first but I don't have a lighter," I confessed.

"Forgiven." She winked. "Okay so, I'm going to come out and ask if you have a girlfriend," she said.

I smoked. The air was warm. A hedge of azalea bushes had bloomed across the parking lot. The birds were singing. A bee buzzed too close to Cassidy and she fanned it away. The world, the sky, the grass, the trees—teeming with possibility, fecund with promise and hope and new beginnings. None of it was lost on me. I found myself thanking God in that moment, for all I was able to experience and feel and think and see. I wanted to sit down at the piano and write a song about it. Something in a minor key at first, changing shade to something happier, expectant. Something that sounded like a colorful heart blooming and blooming, over-ripe. Drooping heavy from the stem. Exploding, popping up and out and then falling slowly like spring snow.

"No I don't have a girlfriend. Although she may beg to differ," I said, smiling after I blew smoke.

"So you do," Cassidy nodded.

"No really, I don't."

"Well you obviously have *something*," she said. She smoked. I watched her. I took my phone from my pocket and snapped a picture of her. Before she could object, I told her she looked pretty.

"Plus you come in here smelling good. I notice," I said. I looked down at the photo I'd taken. Cassidy in her sunglasses, four sparkly earrings in each ear. Her volcanic red matte lips. She had all of her hair piled on top of her head. Her hair was golden-brown, the tips dipped a Valentine's Day pink. She was wearing cut-off jean shorts, a *Star Wars* T-shirt, tube socks pulled up to her knees, black Vans high tops. She was basically a Suicide Girl.

A Suicide *Goose*. The complete and total and everything and all of it opposite of Frances. Cassidy: screeching guitar feedback to Frances's echoing cello strings.

"I come in here to see you," Cassidy said, looking down at her feet.

"I would make a *very* terrible boyfriend right now," I said. As hot as she was, as much as I didn't want to say no, I knew my heart wouldn't be in it and something about that made me sad. How the timing could be so awful. If I'd met her a year from now, maybe.

"I'm not looking for a boyfriend."

But what if we just fuck it up? I thought.

She gently knocked her shoulder against mine.

"We could hang out," I said.

"When?"

"Tomorrow."

"Okay."

Frances came over later in her pajamas. I finally told her about Steve Boone contacting Mom.

"When?" she asked, licking butter from her finger. I'd made popcorn on the stove. We hadn't turned the TV on yet. We sat on my couch, facing each other.

"A while ago," I said.

"Why'd you keep it a secret?"

"I didn't."

"You didn't tell me. You told Eamon? Evangeline?" Frances asked, digging back into the popcorn bowl.

"Nope. I didn't tell Eamon. Mom did."

"Wow, really? I mean I'm pissed you didn't tell *me*, but I'm *more* pissed your mom told Eamon before you could. It's rude," she said.

I shrugged. "It doesn't bother me."

"Maybe it should, Dalton! You keep everything—" Frances

made her body smaller. Hunched her shoulders and clawed up her hands. "—inside. You act like things don't bother you when I know they do."

"Okay," I said, not fully giving her the satisfaction of telling her she was right.

"What are you going to do?"

"I don't know. I haven't called him. Don't know if I want to," I said.

"Will you tell me what you decide or is that a secret too?" she asked.

I reached into the bowl, grabbed a handful of popcorn, shook some into my mouth.

"Depends," I told her. Honestly. If I was in the mood to hear her opinion on my choice to call or not call Steve Boone, I'd tell her. If I wanted quiet, I wouldn't. Or I'd wait.

"Should I keep my secrets from you?"

"Depends," I repeated. Honestly. If she wanted to tell me specific details about what she did with other men, she could keep those to herself. If she wanted a listening ear about work or her family, I was all hers.

"Danny asked me to marry him," Frances said. Danny from Austin. When she was there, she had Danny. When she was here, she had me.

I was aroused by her on my couch, in her pajamas, the familiarity of her femininity. Her breasts and eyelashes. Her hands and soft thighs, the magical warmth waiting between them. It clouded my thinking, like always. Confused me. Yes, Cassidy and I had sat next to each other, had cigarettes, but Frances *was* smoke. An enveloping darkness pressed against me when I was in her presence. Emotional chains. I wasn't free around her. When I locked my heart away from her, she jimmied it. Found a way in. I wasn't jealous of Danny because I didn't own her. Frances didn't belong to me and I didn't belong to her. I knew she would never belong to Danny either. She would never belong to anyone. I sat there thinking about it, finally figuring out why I'd never become the right amount of jealous when she was with someone else. It was because I knew she'd come back to me, no matter what, if I wanted her to.

I watched her lick butter from her bottom lip. She took a big drink of water before sipping wine from the glass on the table next to us. We hadn't had sex in two weeks. I hadn't been with anyone else. I wanted to. Both: have sex with Frances, be with someone else.

Danny asked me to marry him.

"And, are you?" I asked.

"I'm not going to marry Danny."

I felt something almost like relief. Like I'd won something practical in a contest I hadn't entered. Something I would try and put to good use so it wouldn't be a waste.

"Did you tell him that?"

"Not yet."

"Want to watch something?" I asked, turning the TV on.

She shook her head no.

"I'm horny," she said.

I turned the TV off.

In the morning, Frances left, was going back to Austin. She worked for an interior design company that had an office here in town, one near Austin too. She always had something to do, somewhere to go, someone to meet. We decided we'd talk later, when she got back in town, not before. She said she wanted to know what it felt like not to talk to me, to be in Austin detached from me. She told me she was pretty sure she was moving down there and no she wasn't going to marry Danny but at least he'd asked her. I hadn't asked her. She said there was an invisible force field keeping me from asking her. That I'd never asked her because I didn't want to. It was as simple as that.

When she was gone, I made a turkey and tomato sandwich. I played piano with the window open so my neighbor Miss Margaret could hear. I closed the window when I jerked off and thought about Cassidy. I took a nap on the couch. I had a beer and another sandwich and went down to the shop to pick up some paperwork. I called Mom and told her I was calling Steve Boone. I told her to tell Dad. I called Eamon and told him I was calling Steve Boone. When I got back to my place, I called Steve Boone. When he picked up I told him who I was.

"Dalton!" he said, cheerfully enough to create suspicion. I didn't know what he wanted and only half of me cared.

"Loretta gave me your number forever ago. I didn't know what was up," I said, trying to keep my voice even. For a moment I wished I had a dog, a pet, something's head I could reach down and touch when I was feeling how I was feeling. I thought of Uncle James's old coon dog Betsy. Betsy was getting up there in years. I wished she were there with me in my kitchen so I could scratch behind her ears and tell her she was a good girl.

"I didn't know how you'd feel about me trying to contact you. I didn't know if you'd ever call," he said.

I was talking to my father and I'd never talked to my father before. Never met him. Never heard his voice. I'd seen one picture, an old faded one before my mom burned it. All of it began sinking in and my chest warmed. I thought I might cry. I was standing there, concentrating on breathing. Taking slow, deep breaths. I got a tall glass from my cabinet and filled it with water but didn't drink it. I wet my index finger, smoothed it around and around the rim of the glass, attempting to make it sing.

"I know how awkward this is. But I'd like it if you told me a little about yourself. I'd love to hear what you're up to," he said.

"Oh. Okay. I, um...I own a bike shop. Called B's. It's by the railroad tracks over on—"

"I've seen it. I know exactly where it is," Steve said.

"Do you ride?" I asked.

"I used to when I was younger. Mostly road bikes. That was before everyone started riding mountain bikes all over the place." Steve laughed a little.

"Yeah. We get a lot of people in the shop who still ride the roads.

It's scarier and scarier out there, though, because everyone behind the wheel is just staring at their phones all the time," I said.

"And that's a damn shame," Steve said.

We both got quiet. I cleared my throat.

"So, yeah. This is pretty weird for me since we've never met," I said.

"Not that you remember, no. I was there for a couple months with your mother when you were a baby," he said. *Your mother.* Penelope was my mother. Loretta was Mom.

"But then you left," I said.

He was quiet on the line.

"Why'd you want me to call you?"

"I don't know."

"Seems like you should," I said. I took a drink of the water. I wanted to make sure I didn't take things like fresh, cool water for granted. Made a mental note of it.

"My own father passed and it got me to thinking about...every-thing. And I would've done a whole lot more but...I never knew for *sure* if you were mine," Steve said.

My blood went as cool as the water. My legs quivered. I leaned against the counter, steadied myself. The sadness I'd felt earlier quicksilvered into anger.

"What the fuck?"

"Listen. Calvin and Loretta could fill you in. They knew a lot more than I did about Penelope."

"I'm not Calvin's or Loretta's or yours. I'm nobody's," I said. I ended the call.

I drank the rest of my water.

I stood in my kitchen alone and cried out of frustration. Anger. I had absolutely zero feelings for the recently deceased biological grandfather I'd never met.

When I was done I called Eamon to see if he was working, if he wanted to do something. He was finished with his shift, invited me over. I went.

⚶

I sat in Eamon's driveway, texting him that I didn't want to talk about Steve Boone in front of Evangeline. I didn't feel like it. I hadn't told Eamon about what Steve Boone said yet, kept it generic. Told Eamon I'd talked to him for a minute. The key change again, my life, lowering. This time the key change was Steve Boone. I didn't want to think about him.

I got you, brother. No worries. It's a chill night, Eamon wrote me.

Thank you, I wrote him back.

I got a text from Cassidy.

Hey. I'm at the shop but you aren't. ;)

I checked the time. The shop would be closing in half an hour. I was going to eat dinner with Eamon and Evi and I wouldn't mind having dessert with Cassidy. Whatever dessert was. Whatever dessert could be.

Having dinner with my brother and his wife. Text you later?

I'd forgotten I told her we could hang out tonight. Between Frances and Steve Boone, my brain was slop.

I haven't forgotten about hanging out tonight, I texted, for insurance. *Drinks later? On me?* I wrote her back.

Okay! Text later, she wrote, with a pink heart emoji.

I got out of my truck and let myself into Eamon and Evangeline's like I always did.

I turned it over and over in my head, inspected it. Steve Boone's voice telling me he never knew for sure if I was his. I was having a hard time processing my feelings about it. It's not like it would matter if Steve Boone weren't my father. I didn't know the guy, had just grown up hearing his name. I knew Dad didn't like him, but he'd never given specifics. Dad had only said he wasn't a good guy. I knew he ran off on Penelope. That was it. It wouldn't be a crushing blow if Steve Boone weren't blood-related to me. But if not him, who? And who knew? Mom would surely know. Dad too. It wasn't like them to keep secrets from me, but then again maybe there was a loop I was outside of and never knew it. Eamon was their biological son, I wasn't. For as much as they never made me feel like an outsider, maybe there was nothing they could do about some parts of it. I didn't have their blood. Period. *I'm nobody's.* No attachments, no family. Maybe I could start new. Find a wife, start our own brood. Begin again. Do things right. *I'm nobody's.* But was there anything sadder than not being able to biologically tie yourself to anyone? No one at all?

I was in a foul mood and glad I was in a place where I didn't have to pretend to be anything else. There Evi was in a maternity dress that made her look like a flower. In a good way. She said hi and told me she was making spicy shrimp and cauliflower grits. I had no idea what cauliflower grits were but I trusted her.

"Want a beer? Whiskey?" Eamon asked me after we hugged. He pointed to the fridge, to the cabinet.

"Whiskey," I said. Beer wasn't strong enough for my shitty attitude.

"What's up?" Evi asked. She looked over at me and back to the shrimp skillet. There was a sharp sizzle. She added a small amount of water, some Old Bay and hot sauce.

"Nothing much. I told you Frances was moving to Austin, right?" I said to both of them. Eamon slid my glass of whiskey down the counter to me and I caught it. Told him thank you.

"For sure?" Evi asked.

"Yeah. Pretty much. She also told me ol' Danny Zuko asked her to marry him," I said.

Evi gasped.

"For real?" Eamon said, smiling. He took a sip of his beer, leaned against the counter.

"Yep," I nodded.

"And?!" Evi said. She turned the burner down, moved the skillet off it. She turned to both of us and put one of her hands on her pregnant belly.

"She said no," I said.

"Dalton, come here, feel this," Evi said, motioning to me. I walked towards her and she took my hand, placed it on her belly.

"Feel that? Baby Noah hears his Uncle Dalton talking. He got excited when you walked through the door," Evi said. I felt underwatery movement against my hand. A hard thump, two softer ones.

"My boy knows what's up," Eamon said.

"This is amazing," I said, standing there, still touching her. Evi widened her eyes and mouth at me.

"Oof. That one hurt," she said. I left my hand there a moment more before taking it away.

Evi reached for my hand and held it against her again.

"Feel that too? He just keeps going. He's been sleeping all afternoon and evening and now he's wilding out!" She kept her hand pressed on top of mine, moving it slightly so I could catch the kicks. "And I can never tell if this is his butt or his head. This right here," she said, moving my hand to a harder part and pressing down gently. "This is either butt...or head." She moved my hand to both sides of her belly and eventually took my other hand so I was standing there with both of my hands, feeling for the baby.

"Dalton, this is your nephew Noah and one day you're going to teach him to play the piano and you'll build him a custom bike to make all the cool kids jealous," she said.

"Absolutely, I will," I said.

"Talk to him," Evi said, pointing. I bent my head down.

"Hey, Noah. Um, I'm your Uncle Dalton and usually something like this would make me feel ridiculous. I know you're nice and warm in there and I'm stoked to meet you when the time is right. You've got some like, over-the-top tremendous parental units out here by the way," I said. I felt three deep thumps against my hand.

"He's obsessed with you. He keeps kicking!" Evi said, giggling.

Eamon came over and bent down to Evi's belly.

"Okay, little man. Stay in there until July and you'll have plenty of time to hang with your Uncle Dalton," he said.

Uncle Dalton. I let my arms fall back to my side.

"Okay. Food's ready," Evi said, turning back to the stove and counter. There was a big bowl of fluffy white stuff. Cauliflower grits, I assumed.

We ate. It was delicious. We sat down in the living room afterwards and watched baseball. It wasn't long until Evi was asleep on the couch next to Eamon.

"She's out like a light every night at nine," Eamon said quietly.

"Growing a whole new person makes you sleepy," I said. I'd finished my whiskey, opted out of anything else since I was leaving soon, meeting Cassidy. I told Eamon.

"The Suicide Goose," he said. We'd only called her that a couple times but it seemed to stick. The word *suicide* used in such a ridiculous way didn't ring my Penelope bell. Evi hadn't met Cassidy yet and I'd only mentioned her in passing. Eamon had met her on accident when they were both in the shop at the same time.

"That's a ridiculous nickname and we should probably stop," I said.

Eamon shrugged.

"She is like... *after* me," I said.

"So let her have what she wants," he said, plainly. Eamon was good at detaching extra emotions from things. I envied that.

"Steve Boone told me he was never sure I was his," I confessed.

"That bastard," Eamon said, his angry face brimmed then disappeared.

"Technically it makes *me* the bastard when you think about it," I said. I asked Eamon if Mom or Dad ever said anything to him about anyone else potentially being my father.

"Not to me. No way. I would've said something. You know I would've. He's just being an asshole," Eamon said.

"Maybe."

Maybe Steve Boone *was* just being an asshole. I hadn't hung around on the phone with him long enough to find out. Part of me felt bad about that. Maybe I should've heard him out. Maybe I should've called Mom or Dad and told them immediately. Mined them for clues. I felt suddenly distrustful of everyone and couldn't shake it, like a lingering headache. A distrust hangover.

"I think I'm going to head out," I said softly. Evi readjusted herself on the couch but was clearly sleeping like the dead.

"You good?" Eamon asked.

"Yeah. Yeah, I'm good."

"You're lying."

"I don't really want to talk about it, though."

"But maybe you *should*. It's a big deal. You're allowed to have feelings about it."

"I know," I said, nodding quickly. I heard all of them. Mom, Frances and now Eamon, telling me it was okay to feel things. I knew that. I got it. They meant well. All of this thinking was wearing me out.

"I hear you. You don't want to talk about it now but maybe you'll want to talk about it later and I'll be all ears." Eamon held his hands behind his ears to show me.

"Okay," I said, flicking one of them before telling him thanks.

He was pushing me but not shoving.

Cassidy showed up at the bar in a B's Bike Shop shirt. The ones Detroit had designed—wheel and spoke with a playing card, the address and website info on the back. Cassidy was wearing the purple one with white writing. My favorite.

"Hey you," she said, lightly punching my shoulder after we'd hugged. "Did you have a good day?"

"Actually, no," I said.

"Do you want to talk about it?"

"Nope."

"Then it's settled. What should we drink?"

"Something strong so I can forget about my day," I said.

"Let's do it," she said.

I followed her to the bartender.

She ordered us two Tennessee whiskey Manhattans. I paid for them, left a tip. I took a couple sips of my drink, followed her to a small table at the back of the bar. It was something I found myself doing with women often: following them.

Cassidy put the end of her red and white stirrer stick in her mouth, looked at me.

"I think I know what bike I want," she said.

I drank. She talked.

She wanted the Surly Cross-Check. A pavement bike. We had a couple of them in stock. The orange one was my favorite. It was called *Dream Tangerine* and reminded me of a popsicle. Cassidy always made her way over to it when she was in the shop. The bike was a lot like her. Good-looking but sturdy. Funky but classic. Tough.

"The 2x10 or the single speed?" I asked her.

"The 2x10," she said.

"It's a fucking sexy bike," I said, smiling.

"It should be for eleven hundred dollars," she said. She took a drink.

"You want the complete or you want to build it?"

"Or you could build it for me?"

"It would be an honor," I said, lowering my head.

"I also need the drivetrain replaced on my old one. And then I'll have *two* sexy bikes," she said.

"You don't need it replaced, just cleaned," I said.

"You guys do that?"

"We do everything."

"I want to learn how to do that stuff," she said. Pouted. Cute cute cute.

"Detroit and I are starting more classes at the shop in a couple weeks. Bike Mechanics 101. Then there's a professional repair class. Advance certification seminar—" I stopped when her eyes got wide.

"I would *love* to take a class. I never thought about it, which sounds dumb now that I say it."

"It doesn't sound dumb. This is my job. It's the only reason I know about this stuff."

"Okay. Thank you! I'm excited," she said.

I drank my Manhattan and listened to her talk. I went to the bar and got us two more drinks. I was buzzed. Buzzed and finally, feeling good. *Praise.*

We talked for hours. A good chunk of that time was spent talking about bikes. My doubts about her maybe not loving the mechanics side of it slowly slid away. Cassidy was a straight-up bike dork. She talked about flat bars vs. riser bars and monkey nuts, cassettes, triple cranksets—things I didn't usually talk to anyone about besides Detroit or the random nerd customer. I was drunk when we were finished, knew I couldn't drive home.

"Did you drive here?" I asked her once we were outside. We stood leaning against the brick wall, sharing a cigarette.

"Nope. I rode my bike," she said, pointing to it chained to the lamp post down the sidewalk.

"I can't drive. I came in my truck, but I can't drive it home," I said. The bike shop was close enough. We could walk there. I could sleep it off, walk back to my truck in the morning. I looked at my watch. It was exactly midnight.

"Are you drunk?" I asked her. I couldn't tell. We'd both had three Manhattans when I should've stopped at two. I hadn't eaten or drank any water since leaving Eamon's. That was my bad. So what? *I'm nobody's.* I could do whatever I wanted.

"Enough," she said.

"Same," I said, laughing. I pulled my phone from my pocket. Saw a text from Frances.

I know we said we wouldn't talk when I was in Austin but I'm not leaving for Austin until tomorrow so I wanted to say hi. I think about you even when I try not to.

She'd attached a picture of her ass in a pair of black lace underwear I'd given her. It was a picture of her reflection in her bathroom mirror. She took it over her shoulder. Her long black hair pulled to the side, her tiny tank top, the color of dried blood.

"Just a sec," I said to Cassidy. I was drunk enough to play this game with Frances. I texted her back while Cassidy finished our cigarette.

I'm drunk. Out with Cassidy. But here I am writing you back, thinking about you and now, your ass.

She wrote me back. *You like her?*

We were adults in a sometimes-relationship and she was texting me things like *you like her* like we were in elementary school.

A little.

Good for you. She wrote me back.

I like you too, I wrote her.

I know you do, She wrote me, attached a picture of herself in bed, holding up her middle finger.

Talk when you get back from Austin, I wrote before sliding my phone back into my pocket.

"I feel like that was rude and I want to apologize," I said to Cassidy. While I was texting Frances, Cassidy had gone over to the lamp post, retrieved her bike.

"No worries. Good thing you're cute, though," she said, stepping off the curb, rolling her bike next to her.

"Let's go to the shop. To the shop we go," I said. Too loud. Loud enough to make her laugh. She put her head down, shook it.

I liked being with Cassidy. There was a certain wildness there I looked for in a woman, which always had the potential to get me in trouble. Cassidy didn't know much about me. There were no expectations there. Everyone else I hung out with knew me inside and out. This was something new and I could relax into it, stretch out. I'd barely told her anything personal. It made the boring bits of me seem interesting, kept things fresh. I tried to maintain that so I only told her snippets of personal things and let her do most of the talking.

She knew I'd been adopted by the Royces. I told her that after she met Eamon at the shop once. She knew Eamon and Evi were soon to have a baby. I'd told her that too. She knew I played piano but she'd never heard me and I wondered if she imagined me being as good as I actually was. What she'd think about that. Once I realized I was imagining her imagining me, I knew I was in trouble.

We got to the shop. I opened the door, locked it behind us. I leaned on the counter. She let herself fall against me. I turned my head and kissed her for the first time. She pressed her hand against the cool buckle of my belt.

IV.

Evangeline

I DIDN'T HAVE TO TELL ANYONE HOW EAMON DIED because everyone knew. It made the national news. I got cards from girls I knew in high school. I got cards from my dentist, my doctor and people I'd forgotten I used to work with in college. The parents of the little girls in my ballet class and some of their grandparents. The picture of Eamon they showed on TV and printed in the newspaper was a picture of him I love, even still. He's standing and smiling in his police uniform and his hands are in front of him, one of them holding his wrist. His head is tilted back. Noah looks so much like him. I can't imagine being in this world without Eamon's little boy here with me, so I can look into his big syrupy-brown eyes and see him every day, all over again.

One night I asked Dalton to help me go through Eamon's stuff, but only some of it. There are things still hanging in the closet because I'm not ready to put them away yet. Dalton helped me clean out one of Eamon's drawers. The drawer was mostly socks and underwear. I asked Dalton to put everything in a box and to put that box in the garage, behind the file cabinet so I don't have to see it every time I go out there.

There's a secret box that Brian gave me. I know it's stuff from Eamon's locker at work but I haven't been able to bring myself to go through it yet. I know whatever is in there is some of the last stuff he touched. I asked Brian if it was anything important. He said he didn't think so. Someone else had cleaned out Eamon's locker, not Brian. He said it was probably just a T-shirt, maybe some socks. I hid it at the top of the bathroom closet behind a pack of extra ice scrapers and light bulbs, put it away for a day when I could open it. I put Eamon's toothbrush in a plastic bag and I put it at the top of the bathroom closet too. I didn't want to throw it away. I wear a lot of his sweaters and I left his running shoes by the door for a long time until one day they were gone. I knew Dalton had hidden those in the garage for me. I put Eamon's wedding ring in a small wooden box and I keep it next to my bed. Right there with the empty water glass and my Bible and the countless black bobby pins I need since I'm growing my hair back out.

There were so many quiet nights before Dalton moved in when I'd hear his truck engine rumble to a stop in the driveway and I'd hear his knuckle tap on the door. We'd hug and he'd hold Noah while I'd ask him questions about the bike shop or anything so we wouldn't have to talk about sad things. I'd tell him any new thing Noah was doing.

I liked how Dalton saw the world. I liked how he chose his words so carefully. He made me want to choose my words more carefully too. And I tried, when I suggested he move in here with Noah and me. Because I meant indefinitely, but I didn't know how to say it.

The night I invited him to move in, I'd just put Noah down to bed, fully expecting him to fuss an hour later, but I was relieved to be able to sit on the couch and have my hands to myself. I heard Dalton's truck. I went out on the porch to meet him.

"A modest proposal," I said as he made his way up the steps. It was cold and although I hadn't done much Christmas decorating, I'd strung a strand of multi-colored lights around the wrought-iron banister on the porch, mostly because it was Noah's first Christmas and I figured he should at least have *something*. Twinkle lights were something.

Dalton and his brown boots stood in front of me. "Yeah?"

"Stay here as much as you want. You don't have to leave, like ever. I hate taking out the garbage and I'm scared to kill bugs. And...I don't know. I'd be more than okay with you being here all the time," I said, disappointed in myself for not being more eloquent. So much for choosing my words carefully. But he was a smart guy. He knew what I meant.

"I was thinking the same thing but I didn't want to be weird about it," he said. We both stepped into the house. I closed the door and Dalton's smell mixed with the smell of the hot chocolate I'd made on the stove. The smell of the fire I'd started in the fireplace. The smell of my coconut shampoo. Dalton's smell was so familiar to me already, but even more so now. That night? Soap and clean cotton with the hint of piney Christmas and snow.

We hugged and talked details. We sat on the couch and I turned on a college basketball game neither one of us watched. It was comforting, hearing the squeaks of the sneakers and the commentary and although we didn't mention it then, I knew we were both excited about doing something together. It was a relief. Doing something together made us feel like Eamon was still with us. And he was. And he is.

A week before Dalton and I kissed for the first time I asked him if he watched porn. I assumed he did like I assumed all men did and probably most women too. Maybe that wasn't true but I didn't know what Dalton did about stuff like that. I assumed there were secrets he kept from me. Everyone had a secret life, right? Both of us knew that. I wanted to know Dalton's dirty secrets but didn't want to snoop around to find them out. I wanted him to tell me.

"So like, if you looked at porn what kind of porn would you look at?" I asked him. It was a Monday night. We cracked open beers and turned on football, both of us in our pajamas on the couch. I'd ordered Dalton, Noah and myself matching pajama pants. It felt appropriate because we were a *tiny tribe*, so we should obviously dress alike.

Dalton widened his eyes and pretended like he was going to spit out his beer. He always went overboard for comedic effect. It was endearing.

"Where is this coming from?"

"I looked on your laptop. Your search history," I lied. Yes, I'd thought about it but reprimanded myself for the idea. It was none of my business to find anything out that way. He wasn't my boyfriend or husband. I had no right. But I still wanted to know. I didn't have the guts yet to ask him straight out who he'd been sleeping with, if anyone, but breaching the topic of sex in general would maybe help me get there.

"Okay, so you looked at my search history?" he asked, raising an eyebrow. He put his beer on the table, glanced at the kickoff as it slid across the TV screen. I couldn't read his feelings about my revelation and usually I could read his face. I kept watching him but he didn't look over at me.

Noah made a fussy-ish sound from the bedroom so I cocked my ear to the side like a puppy to see if he would stop or keep going. Dalton grabbed the remote, turned the volume down a couple notches. We both got real quiet and listened. Noah fussed loudly one more time then gave a soft whimper, which meant he was asleep again. Dalton left the volume down.

"I did. And I mean *hot black chicks with big boobs* seems immature for someone like you. You need to step it up. *Boobs*, Dalton? *Tits* sounds way more porno if you ask me," I laughed.

"Evi, shit I thought you were serious for a second," Dalton said, laughing and shaking his head.

"I could've been, right? Read your mind?" I said.

"No. I wouldn't search for boobs," he said, glancing at me and back at the TV. We both watched a running back make his way to the goal line as if the guys on the opposing team were wearing magnets that wouldn't let them get too close.

"Are those guys even *trying* to catch him?" I spat out, annoyed.

"He's too fast. He's the best running back in the NFL," Dalton said. He lifted his beer and sipped it. When he was finished, I slipped it from his fingers and chugged it. I only felt a little guilty, knowing Noah would wake up in a couple hours or so, wanting to nurse. Either way I had a good stock of backup milk in the fridge and freezer if I wanted to drink more beer. I liked sharing drinks with Dalton. It made me feel closer to him.

"So you're an ass man?" I asked him, steering us back to the porn conversation because the football was boring me. I was weirdly horny and sad at the same time, which could've been the title of my memoirs for the past month or so. I made a mental note of it.

"I'm an ass man, a tit man, a *leg* man. I love it all, I want it all," Dalton said. His voice was deep and sleepy. Sexy. My stomach did a slingshot thing and then again. I recognized sexiness. Still. I wasn't broken. I'd recognized Eamon's sexiness the first time I saw him in his uniform at church.

I slapped his arm and he smiled over at me.

"Are *you* an ass man, Evi?" Dalton asked.

"I want it all," I said, teasing him.

"I don't like this fancy new porn anyway. I like seventies porn. Afros, armpit hair, creepy mustaches, yellow shag carpets and weird, orange lamps. That's what I'm talking about," he said. He leaned back more, drank more. "I'm getting another one. You want one or you just want to keep saying no and drinking mine instead?" he asked. I nodded. He handed his bottle of beer to me. I didn't watch him walk into the kitchen because I loved how he walked too much. I didn't want to start doing stuff like that because once I started doing stuff like that it was over.

"Do you really watch seventies porn?" I asked, loud enough for him to hear me. The football game went to commercial. I heard Dalton go into the fridge. I heard him slide open the kitchen drawer with the bottle opener in it, heard the *clink* of him rooting around for it in there and the *tap-click-shh* of him opening it. The chunk of him tossing the bottle opener inside and sliding the drawer back closed. My senses were super-heightened when I was pregnant, but those skills had hung around after I had Noah like I was trying to hold onto everything, even the tiniest things because Eamon wasn't around anymore to notice them with me or for me.

Dalton walked back into the living room, shrugging and swigging from the green glass bottle.

"Sometimes, but not like all the time," he admitted.

The commercials were over, the game came back on. The commentators were talking. Dalton leaned over and grabbed the remote, turned it up.

"Do you?" he asked after the refs blew a whistle and there was a break in between plays.

"Do I what?"

"Look at it. Look at porn," he said. He was watching the flat screen, peeling back the sticky wet-paper corner of his beer label.

"Eamon said he stopped when we got serious," I said, mentioning him as if his spirit weren't sitting there between us, always.

"I know he did. But what about *you*?"

"No. I don't look at porn. I feel sorry for the women—like they're trapped. It feels wrong. And anyway, what do you mean you know he did?"

"I mean, he told me. We'd talked about it," Dalton said, finally meeting my eyes.

"Oh."

Dalton continued. He did that a lot after Eamon was killed. Cleaned up after everything he said, swept it all up for me so he could present it neatly. He was hyper-aware of my sensitivities and so gentle with me—my glass bones, my glass heart—never stomping in the kitchen of my feelings so he wouldn't cause my heart cake to fall.

"We'd talked about it. Both of us were looking at it too much before he met you. Right around the time he and Lisabeth broke up. We were trying to hold ourselves accountable. Something like that," Dalton said.

Lisabeth came to the funeral and sat near the back. I recognized her from pictures. She reached out her hand for me as I was walking out. I took her hand and she squeezed mine. She sent me a card and flowers, after—the pale-pink rose petals almost numbing my fingers with their softness. The card simply read *I know how much Eamon loved you. That man could love. Truly, Lisabeth.* I thought about her huge, deer eyes crying at the funeral.

My eyes teared up thinking about those indescribably tender days after the funeral when I was walking around with my heart outside of my body. A feeling that was recreated and made more intense when Noah was born. Grief made me want to give up. Other people had prayed for me to be strong but that wasn't the prayer I prayed. The prayer I prayed was *Jesus Christ, take it take it take it.*

Dalton put his arm around me and I leaned into him. He put his hand on my shoulder. The warmth was so comforting, soothing. The urge to cry passed over me and I was grateful.

"You good?" Dalton asked. I could feel his tender heart peeking out, reaching for mine.

I kept my eyes on the football game.

"What I'm saying is that I know for a fact he wasn't looking at it once you two had locked it down. He told me," he said.

"Don't worry. I know he wasn't perfect," I said.

"Damn close, though," Dalton laughed.

"Yeah," I said. What I didn't say: *and that's probably why he had to die.*

At halftime I went to check on Noah to make sure he was still sleeping. Dalton put a frozen pizza in the oven. When I came back, Dalton asked if Noah was fine and I said yes.

I had a sex dream about Dalton once. A couple of months before the kiss. The dream was not a lie. I *did* want Dalton like that. I felt awful, gross and guilty about it, but it was true. Thinking about Dalton like that now was an escape. I didn't need to think about it when Eamon was alive and it wasn't hard because I truly loved Eamon and didn't feel like I needed to look anywhere else because I didn't. But Dalton was attractive and always has been. He was different in a perfect kind of way. As if I had only two types of men who interested me and Eamon and Dalton were those two types. In the past month leading up to the kiss, I wouldn't force myself to stop when those thoughts about Dalton trembled like smoke and ribbons in front of me.

In the dream, there was candlelight and incense. I joked to Dalton that it was overkill. *What's next? Zuzu's petals?* I mimed like I was gagging myself. He laughed and handed me a glass of lemonade that turned into a plate of spaghetti. We ate and whined about how much we ate, how we ate too much. He took off my shirt to rub my belly. I was insecure about my belly because I'd only just had Noah. I told him I wanted to take my bra off because my breasts were swollen and hard with so much milk. He said he could help me with that and he drank milk from me. Afterwards, we kissed and he was wearing the same pajama pants I got for him, our tiny tribe pajama pants. We had sex and I was holding on to the couch saying his name over and over again. Sometimes I would say Dalton. Sometimes I would say Eamon. Sometimes I would say Damon. A powerful, wavy, warm orgasm woke me up and Dalton was standing at the foot of the bed, holding Noah, shushing him and feeding him a small bottle of breast milk which meant I'd missed Noah's breakfast entirely. He'd moved on to his mid-morning snack. I glanced at my watch, saw it was after eleven.

"You were making noises. Are you sick?" Dalton asked. He was using a different voice with me and I worried I'd said his name aloud or that he'd stood there watching me writhe around. I was embarrassed and felt my cheeks blush hot.

"No. I'm not sick," I said, holding my arms out for my baby.

He handed Noah to me. Dalton set the bottle on the dresser and lifted his shirt to scratch at his stomach. My panties were wet and I wanted him out of there, so I told him I wanted to see if Noah would nurse. That was Dalton's cue to go for his run in the cold rain. He always left the room or looked away when I nursed Noah.

I know Dalton drinks his coffee black most of the time, but every once in a while he'll say, *make mine how you make yours* and I add soy milk or almond milk and sweetness and he always says, *sometimes I like it like this too.* He knows if he puts the toilet paper on the holder the wrong way, I'll switch it and flip it over. Dalton has stopped by on his way home from work before he moved in, found me weeping in the kitchen listening to "One More Night" on repeat. He's come to me, turned the music off, lifted me from the floor, put me to bed. Made me hibiscus tea the color of communion wine, only to bring it to the nightstand and let it go cold. We've stood at the bathroom sink and brushed our teeth together. I've cut his hair. He's cut mine. We do each other's laundry and dishes. I got over my shyness about him seeing and touching my dirty underwear. I've watched him toss my undies into the washing machine. The stained, flowery bloomers I wear when I'm on my period. The pretty, pink underwear I paid a lot of money for. We've seen each other first thing in the morning. Last thing at night.

Dalton's short hair sticks straight up from his head when he wakes up, no matter how he sleeps. It makes him look like a little boy. He knows it takes me a while to wake up. I don't talk much in the mornings. I prefer a hug first thing, before I have my coffee.

We've been up in the middle of the night, passing a fussy baby back and forth in the blued moonlight. I make Dalton's bed when he leaves it unmade in the morning. I buy his favorite peanut butter cereal when I go to the grocery. He buys three avocados for me when it's his turn to go.

We've had our lives here, separate and together. I'm taking care of Noah and myself and letting Dalton love us both. What matters is that I remember to take deep breaths when I'm in the kitchen making dinner while Dalton and Noah are at the piano, sending layered chords of sound into the air. On bad days when Dalton is at the bike shop until late, I can see the whole day alone with Noah stretched out in front of me like a long, thin, lonely desert highway.

"The fight is over." Dalton stumps out the cigarette in the snow-filled ashtray on the deck. The snow is still falling. He closes the door again. Wraps his arms around me.

I tell him our neighbors across the street probably think I'm the Whore of Babylon. He denies it at first but ends up laughing because he knows it's true.

"In their defense, you say you're a dancer but I don't think they ever believed you were a ballerina," Dalton says. The word *ballerina*, soft and light in his handsome hearty mouth.

"Is that what I should do? Strip?" I tease.

"I'd pay for that," he says and lifts his eyebrow. Dalton, flirting with me. Something I have to get used to—my heart, beating lavender blooms, spilling out into my bloodstream. His flirting calms me, makes me feel safe.

"Naturally, people think living together means sleeping together," I say. Buzzed, not drunk. It happened between the stolen shot of whiskey and the cigarette.

"Well, we *are* living in sin," Dalton says.

"Except fornication isn't our sin," I say. At least it's not mine.

If Frances appeared in front of us right now, Dalton would

probably have sex with her. It isn't like I know everything about his relationship with her, but I've seen them together plenty of times and their sexual chemistry is off the charts. But to be fair, Frances seems to be the kind of woman who can have sexual chemistry with a house plant.

"I heard you fornicate with Frances the night Eamon and I got engaged," I admit.

"What?" Dalton says, making an adorable face. He shakes his head, scratches at his beard. He squints at me. "You didn't."

"I did. I got up to pee and heard you two," I say. My face warms. I press my fingers to my cheeks.

"What did you hear?" Dalton asks, lifting his chin. We have swung through every human emotion possible in the past twenty minutes.

"I heard Frances making kitten growls and you um…making noises too," I say.

"So let me get this straight. I put my shirt on when you come home and make sure I lock the door when I shower so you don't have to accidentally walk in and see my pale ass, but you've heard me having sex…so now all bets are off," he says, smiling at me.

"It's not like I peeked. It's not like I was watching you two," I say, covering my face.

Dalton steps over to me, starts to pry my fingers away.

"I'm sorry you had to hear it. Is that the appropriate response to this? For me to apologize?" he asks. His hands are warm. I am grateful he is touching me. I love it when he touches me.

I peek at him from between my fingers.

"You sounded like…heavy breathing…and then, this long sigh. I don't know how else to explain it," I say. It's embarrassing but I *want* to talk about it. Talking about it feels like turning a corner, shifting gears, all the fitting driving analogies to represent change, newness, excitement.

"Oh so you heard like…the end of it?" Dalton asks, genuinely intrigued.

"I guess. Unless you had two rounds of it," I say, still peeking.

Dalton makes a face, closes his eyes.

I take my hands away.

"Are you serious? Is that like the *only* thing you two did?" I ask. Jealous, borderline irritated.

"It was the only thing we did *well*, yes," he says.

"I'm so jealous. Frances is this sex kitten and I'm like..." I hold my arms out. My hands disappear into the sleeves of Eamon's sweater again.

"Please. There's nothing for you to be jealous of," Dalton says.

We are talking in circles.

"Oh you wouldn't be jealous if you heard Eamon and me having sex?"

"I've heard you and Eamon having sex," Dalton says.

"What?" I squeal.

We are *definitely* talking in circles.

"First New Year's Eve you two were married. Frances and I stayed over here. I heard you. I heard both of you obviously because you were together. It was right after the ball dropped," he says.

"It was not!" I say.

"Was," he smiles over at me.

My mind flashes back to that night. Even though I don't like New Year's Eve, we had fun. All confetti and my sparkly dress. The champagne. I was a little drunk. I remember the sex. I remember the sex being loud. I cover my mouth with my hand.

"You remember," Dalton says.

I start laughing. More. Harder.

"You remember," he says again.

I decide not to analyze this moment and just let myself laugh. Dalton joins in.

"I am so embarrassed. Why didn't you tell me?" I squeal.

"I love that you think there was some way for me to approach the topic. You give me far too much credit, Leeny," he says. The nickname is sweet. We are on good terms, not a fight in sight if he's using *Leeny*.

"Okay. We've got all that out of our systems. Did Eamon know you heard us? Did you tell him?" I ask.

"Of course I told him."

"Of course?"

"I told him everything. *Almost* everything. And even when I didn't tell him something immediately I could only keep things from him for like a couple weeks, tops. I've always been that way. My whole life. Whenever something would happen to me it almost felt like it hadn't happened until I told E about it," Dalton says.

"He was so good to me. He knew when to keep things from me which is a very important part of marriage. I am so thankful for the stuff he kept from me. Which may sound weird to hear, but it's true," I say.

Dalton looks at me. His phone beeps.

"You can get it. It's fine," I say.

"Nah. I'd rather talk to you."

"I'm interrogating you," I say, instantly aware of how police-language grips my heart and saddens me. "I'm asking you a lot of questions."

"Nah. It's just stuff we've actively been *not* talking about since the summer."

I pull my wool socks up. Dalton sits, leans with his back against the couch and stretches out his legs. He folds his hands across his stomach.

"Can I say you're stunning?" he asks.

I make a face at him.

"No. *Listen* to me. You're beautiful," he says.

I shake my head at him, but find the words to say thank you.

"Will you go out with me?" he asks.

I laugh and put my hand over my mouth. Dalton tilts his head and smiles. I watch every move he makes. He rubs one of his eyes and touches his beard before folding his hands across his stomach again.

"Like on a date?"

Dalton nods. "Tonight. I'll make you dinner. We'll go on a date in the kitchen. Let's stop bullshitting," he says.

"Are we bullshitting?" I ask.

Dalton sits up straight and says he thinks we are.

"Well I straddled you and kissed you last night. So we both have me to thank for the non-bullshit of that moment," I say, proud of myself. It was bad ass. I wanted to do something and I did it.

"It was my pleasure," he says, looking down, "I loved kissing you. Are you kidding me?"

"But it's going to be weird, I know," I say, before he needs to. Dalton is ferociously loyal about Eamon. I don't think he'll ever be able to get the fact that I was Eamon's girl out of his mind. Neither will I. What Dalton and I have is irradiant. We're a country song they play over and over on the radio, the one that makes everyone cry. He reaches out for me and I crawl into his lap.

Once I asked Eamon what was so important about being a cop and he told me. "Because there's all this shit, right?" he said, fanning his hand in front of his face and then, extending his arm into the air. We were sharing a bottle of red wine in this house not long after we married. "There's a lot of it. Bad shit over here and horrible shit up here and awful shit down here," he continued. He was buzzed. He lifted both arms up into the air and smiled across the table at me. He shook both of his hands like tambourines.

"Do it. It feels good, don't it?" he said. I lifted my hands up with him and shook mine too.

"You're a loon," I said, shaking my hands. Shake shake shake shake.

"In the middle of all of this shit, there has to be some good. There has to. *Has* to," he said, lowering his arms. I put my elbows on the table and leaned forward. He poured more wine into his glass. More into mine. He leaned back and winked at me. "Gots to be the good, baby. Gotta be the good," he said.

I put my feet in his lap. He put his hands underneath the table and grabbed them and told me he loved me.

"I love you too," I said. He never had to ask me to hand myself over to him. It was done.

His smile. Sudden. Disarming. There's a picture of Eamon in

the bathroom, hanging next to the light switch. He's grinning. One of those huge shit-eating grins too, showing all of his teeth. He has a dimple in his right cheek. He's holding a fish—its silver-blue scales, glinting and catching the sunlight like a thousand little mirrors. I miss that smile. What's most confusing and heartbreaking is that his smile and his presence are the things that could fix all of this. I'd *feel* better if he were here. I don't like that God decided Noah and I have to live underneath the weight of his absence. It feels like drowning and dying of thirst at the same time. But God is the one who gave Eamon to me in the first place. And me to him. And Noah to both of us. And maybe now it's my turn to be the good.

I suggest to Dalton that we dress up, this being our first date and all. I have a breezy, ruffly melted-butter yellow dress I haven't worn yet. Merit got it for me for my birthday but I never put it on because it felt garish and disrespectful for a widow with a newborn to wear something so bright and happy. And although the color and style don't necessarily reflect how I'm feeling inside now, it feels way more like a possible-possibility now than it did back in July.

"I'll put on my suit after I get dinner started," Dalton says, "I have a grey one."

I look at him, relieved. I didn't want him coming down here in the black suit he wore to Eamon's funeral. There are things I simply cannot do.

We don't say anything else. We don't need to. Another way I know for sure this whole thing has the potential to last forever. It's the way I am with my parents, with Merit. It's how Eamon and I were. And now, Dalton. We can be quiet together. It's important to know when we don't need to say anything.

Eamon

I MISSED THE ULTRASOUND APPOINTMENT WHEN EVI found out our baby was a boy. I'd never missed an appointment before. I had my alarm set but turned my phone off, not thinking. I was sitting in my patrol car writing letters. One for Evi, one for our baby. Just in case. I'd worked three homicides that week alone. One was a baby. I was used to a lot of things but would never get used to that. It'd been a rough week and I felt overloaded, worn out. Thin as mist. I'd finished my shift and sat in the car, writing.

> *Dear Evangeline,*
> *It's been a rough week but what keeps me going is coming home to you and our little bud growing inside of you. I wish I could always play it cool like I wasn't worried about something happening to me, like I wasn't worried about leaving you a widow with a baby to*

raise on your own. And it's not like I don't think you could handle it. I know how tough you are. I know what you're capable of. But I want to protect you from every awful thing I possibly can. I carry the weight of these things although I obviously can't control everything that happens. I realize some of these feelings are irrational. That's why I'm not even saying them aloud. I'm writing them here, saving them for you. I waffle back and forth between thinking my life would be safer and easier if I had another job and feeling like things like that don't matter. God is in the details, yes, but in ALL the details big and small. And He knows the course He has set for me. And I would do anything for you. I love you so much. That love is a fire that always always always keeps me warm.

Dear Baby _____,

Hi there. You are so incredibly loved. More than you can even process in your still-forming precious little brain. We couldn't be happier about you making your way into the world and there is so much to see and do here. So much for you to learn and soak in. I tell your mom you're my little buddy already. My forever little buddy. Our little mystery. From where I'm sitting I can feel the sunlight on my face and it's very warm. It's warm where you are right now too. And I'll do everything in my power to make sure you always have everything you need. I can't wait to talk to you about God and wonder.

At times I wanted the letters to be proof of something. Proof I had something worth saying and leaving behind, something for my wife and baby to remember me by. Proof that although I wasn't always the best at getting my emotions from my head and heart out of my mouth, I had a whole world inside I could put down on paper if I sat down long enough. The letters transformed from an *if something happens to me* experiment to a study of *here's proof everything's going to be just fine.* A lesson in *this is how your dad used to be and this is who he's becoming.* A live feed of growth, of growing.

I poured my guts into those letters and my mood darkened, then lifted when I was finished. I turned on my phone and saw that Evi had blown it up with texts reminding me of the appointment. I texted her how sorry I was. Told her I was on the way. Tried to call her at least three times but couldn't get her on the phone. I swung by the doctor's office first, in case she was still there. She wasn't. I went home and found her on the couch, reading.

"Evi, I am so sorry. *So* sorry. I turned my phone off and it completely slipped my mind. How pissed are you at me?" I asked her. For me, arguing with Evi was like a sprained ankle—uncomfortable until we got everything all settled again. I wanted the uncomfortableness over. I was dreading it already. I was exhausted and needed to sleep. My brain was warm and fuzzy. I'd been up all night.

"Where were you?" she asked.

"My shift was over but I was at work and I'm sorry," I said. I was embarrassed about writing the letters and didn't want to tell her. It all felt too *something*. I was letting the anxiety get the best of me. I wanted to be a good dad, a good husband, a good man. *Gotta be the good, good, good.* All that good set me up to fail and I didn't want to fail.

"Everything's fine. The heartbeat and measurements and everything," she said, looking away from me. She'd found a small thread in the hem of her shirt, started gently tugging at it.

"Good, good. Do you feel okay?" I asked. I was sitting next to her, reluctant to reach out and touch her.

"I'm fine. But promise him you won't let it happen again," she said.

"Who?" I asked, like a dumb-dumb.

She rolled her eyes.

"My boy? A boy?" I said, putting my hand on her belly. She laid back for me.

"Hopefully he'll be better at being on time than you are," she said, smirking.

"You're pissed at me and we're having a boy," I said, my eyes hot and watery.

"Noah," she said.

"Noah," I repeated.

"You're sleeping on the couch," she said.

"Okay," I said.

It was the morning and I sometimes slept on the couch after my night shift anyway. She was trying to punish me, but sweetly. It was fine. I went to the bedroom, took off my gun, my duty belt, my uniform. Got in the shower. When I got out I found that she'd made the couch up for me with a sheet, a blanket, my pillow.

"You weren't with some girl?" she asked me after I'd tucked up, closed my eyes.

"Are you serious? Look at me," I opened my eyes, sat up.

"No."

"Evi. Never in a million years. Don't even joke around," I said, readjusting myself. I was so tired, my eyes closed again on their own. "It's been a rough week. I can't get out of my brain but I'm trying. I promise."

I felt her warmth and presence leaning over me. She kissed my forehead.

Two days later, to make it up to her, I painted the nursery. We already had a blue guest bedroom so for Noah's room we went with a green color called *electric pickle juice*. I turned up Prince's *Greatest Hits* and got to work. Evi was out for the day, shopping and getting a pedicure with her mom. I was surprising her even though she hated surprises. I knew she'd like this one.

I was halfway finished and decided to take a break, took a walk to the coffee shop about a mile away to get some fresh air and a cup. I saw Lisabeth as I was crossing the street. I hadn't seen her since we'd broken up. I never saw Lisabeth, I never accidentally ran into Lisabeth. And yet, there she was.

"E," Lisabeth said—her term of endearment for me. I hadn't expected her to use it. I wasn't exactly sure where we stood but I wouldn't have guessed it was kind or solid ground. Not as solid as the concrete sidewalk we were standing on. There was a tele-phone pole next to me, covered in band posters, dog and cat posters for both the missing and the found, new staples and old staples and rusted staples and the ghosts of staples' past.

"Check you out," I said. I never said things like *check you out* but I had on a shirt with green paint on it, an old pair of running shoes and shorts I never wore although it wasn't warm enough for shorts yet. I was also wearing a pair of sunglasses I'd grabbed off the counter on my way out. I'd worn them once and lost them. Evi had recently discovered them behind the couch. I felt like a different person in all that stuff. The sun was spring-afternoon-bright and bumping into Lisabeth gave me a dreamy feeling, like I was on cold medicine.

"What are you up to?" she asked, her voice as familiar to me as it was when we were dating. People moved on, yes, but our minds and hearts remembered things we didn't realize and when brought to our attention again, there they were. Clawing. Leaving scratches.

"Evangeline is pregnant. My wife. It's a boy. I'm painting the nursery today. Hence the *electric pickle juice* on my shirt," I said. I didn't know whether she'd heard about Evangeline and me through the grapevine, maybe she'd heard about the baby too. We still had friends in common.

"And on your face," she said, pointing at me. She took a sip of whatever was in her coffee cup.

I put my hand to my cheek, wiped.

"Let's call it good luck," I said. I wasn't sure where the paint was on my face and it didn't matter although it was very Lisabeth of her to tell me about it.

"Congrats! A wife and a baby, huh?" she said.

"Thanks. What about you?"

"No. I don't have a wife or a baby," she said.

I nodded.

"I do have a girlfriend though," she said.

"A girlfriend, really?" I asked. I always thought Lisabeth would've made a great lesbian. Had maybe even told her that once so felt like I could take a little credit for this new lane she'd turned down. Her girlfriend owed me one, big time.

"I'm bisexual. Didn't realize it until after we broke up," she said, sipping from her drink again. Although she was familiar to me, our relationship felt a galaxy away—like I'd have to be put to sleep in a spaceship going full speed for eighty years until I could reach it.

"You're happy? You seem happy," I said.

"You know me," she said. I wasn't sure what she meant but I left it alone.

I was leaning against the pole with my arms crossed.

"You will be a great dad, asshole," Lisabeth said, punching my forearm lightly.

"Ah, I do miss you giving me shit."

"Well whenever you need it, come find me. Me and my girlfriend," she said, slipping her sunglasses from her purse, sliding them on.

"All right."

"See you later, E."

"See you later."

She turned and walked across the street towards the parking lot.

I went inside the coffee shop, stopped by the bathroom to get the slip of green paint off my face. The baristas gave me a cup for free when I was in uniform but today I was a civilian. I got a large Americano and a copy of *The New York Times*. Sat myself down for a half an hour. Drank. Read. Imagined Lisabeth and her girlfriend in bed together for a couple minutes before stopping completely and drinking and reading some more.

By the time I was finished painting the nursery, Evangeline was back home.

"Ta-da!" I said when I saw her face after I'd hollered down and told her I was upstairs.

"Look what you did!" Evi said, her mouth open in sweet surprise.

"To make sure you weren't still mad at me *and* because it was time to do it," I said. "Now we have a *boat blue* room, an *electric pickle juice* room and a *hot chocolate* bedroom."

I remembered the color we'd decided on for our bedroom

when Evi moved in. *Hot chocolate.* Before she moved in, the walls in all of the rooms upstairs were white. Evi filled my life with color.

I didn't get anxious often. It hadn't been much of an issue in my personal life or my work life. It hadn't been an issue in my relationships with women. But everything with Evi was different. Even before the baby. Magnified now. I worried constantly about something happening to her, the baby. I worried about something happening to me. I worried about leaving her alone in this world.

I still felt guilty about missing the OB/GYN appointment. I apologized again.

"Stop it," she said, kissing my mouth.

I kissed her back. Grabbed her ass. I loved her ass. I recognized sexiness and respected it.

We kissed and kissed and ended up on the floor. Christened it for the first time in all its new *electric pickle juice* glory. The Prince album was turned down low, both of us sweaty and panting, coming to "Let's Go Crazy." Afterwards, Evi's toes were sprinkled with green paint. I watched her wiggling them, imagining our baby boy in the darkness of her womb doing the same thing.

Dalton and I were out for beers one night after he'd talked to Steve Boone on the phone. I was worried about him lately. Didn't seem like he was sleeping well. Maybe he was drinking too much. He wasn't That Guy, but I didn't say anything about it. Figured he was sorting out his shit. Frances was in Austin a lot and he'd been hanging with Cassidy, the bike shop girl. Mom was worried about him and I promised her I'd talk to him. It was something I was planning on doing anyway. It was what we did. We were all set to leave out for the Two Hearted the following weekend for our May fishing trip. Last time we were there was when I'd found out Evi was pregnant. Now our unborn baby was the size of a pineapple.

"What would you do?" Dalton asked.

"Me? What would I do if my biological dad were Steve Fucking Boone?" I asked him.

"About him saying he didn't know for sure if I was his," Dalton said plainly. Usually he would've laughed but obviously wasn't in the mood.

"Call him back, call him on it. Ask him what he meant by it," I said, surprising even myself. It's truly what I thought Dalton should do. I could tell he wouldn't be able to let it go and he shouldn't. He had the right to those answers. For as much as I'd had my moments of worrying Dalton would be pulled away from our family, I also understood something now more than ever— the bond between a father and son, a parent and a child. Noah wasn't even born yet but I could feel it. I could feel it all over me. And whatever Dalton felt like he needed to do was the right thing.

I finished my beer. Turned my head when I heard rising voices in the back corner of the bar. I wanted a chill, peaceful night. I wasn't working. I didn't want to have to break up a bar fight. From what I could tell, it was all good. Some guys having fun. I motioned to the waiter for another beer because I'd been feeling so high-strung lately and the alcohol helped. I'd only be having two, though. I'd met Dalton at his house, we'd walked over. I was being a hypocrite telling Mom I'd talk to Dalton about how he'd been feeling lately when I hadn't been telling anyone how I'd been feeling. Not even saying it aloud to Evi. I didn't want to worry her.

But I was still writing her letters in my black leather Moleskine notebook. I continued confessing my anxiety and fear about impending fatherhood, being able to make her and the baby happy, to provide for them. I kept it at the top of my locker next to my tube of ChapStick, my backup water bottle.

"Look, I'm not in your shoes, but I get it. I feel you," I said to Dalton. "You have every right to want to know what he meant by it. But I know you may not want to find out bad things about Penelope... *if* there are bad things to find out."

"She had terrible taste in men, obviously," Dalton said. The waiter came to the table with a new beer for me. Dalton ordered his second. He was quiet, looking out the window next to us. It was deep dusk, the navy blue of night slowly inking its way across the sky.

"I don't know if I want to find out who it is if it's not him. My whole life I've had this ghost of a biological dad who didn't want me...and I had Calvin, who did, who took care of me, who did everything a bio dad would do," he said. Dalton never called my dad Calvin. I knew he was making a point. My dad had been transformed from Calvin to Dad and was only Calvin to Dalton when he held him up against his biological father—the truth made truer when next to a lie.

I let him be quiet. He said he'd keep me posted if he talked back to Steve, if Steve talked back to him. I asked him about Cassidy.

"We're not boning," Dalton said.

"All right," I said, nodding.

"Not that I wouldn't."

"Bad timing." I kept nodding. Drank.

"Something like that. She's taking these bike mechanic classes and when she's certified I'll probably hire her. That'll complicate things," Dalton said. The waiter came back with his beer. Dalton put it to his lips.

"You and Detroit and Little Miss Indie Bike Mechanic all up in B's," I said.

"B for Berkeley. B for Bastard," Dalton smiled. Barely.

The way he said it made me sad. I felt for him. I could try and try to put myself in his position, but I knew that could only go so far. He knew his world and I knew mine. I had Dad, he had Calvin. I didn't feel like I could do anything to help besides sit there and let him talk when he needed to, drink a beer with him when he needed to. Let him be quiet when he needed to. My brother.

Evi made us sandwiches and snacks for our drive to the Upper Peninsula like always.

"You promise promise promise you don't care I'm going and you don't want to come with us?" I asked. I was double-checking the pockets of my fly fishing vest, my rod and reels were by the door. I began packing up my tools and fishing knives—my favorite Tanto, the multi-tool Evi had given me for our second wedding anniversary the year before, the fillet.

"There's no room for us," she said, smiling and pointing at her big belly. I loved that belly. I walked over to her, touched it.

I felt okay with her being there alone because I was leaving my patrol car in the driveway. Dalton's truck was staying too. Merit was coming over to stay the night. My mom and her parents were close if she needed anything.

But.

I still felt a deep ache as my dad drove us away from the house in his truck. I almost wanted to cry. I had visions of her going into early labor alone, being scared, me not being there for her or our baby. Dad must've felt the fear and anxiety pulsing from me because he put his hand on my knee and said, "Hey. She'll be fine. It's all right," like he'd read my mind. Dalton reached up from the back seat and put his hand on my head, the same way we used to do one another when we were little, the same way Dad used to. It was an easy intimacy we'd always had. The three of us smushed together in Dad's truck when Dalton and I were little, Dad and Mom up front and the two of us sitting in the truck bed with our drippy ice creams in the summer.

"My boys," Dad had said to us, the same way he'd said to us almost our whole lives. "I'm proud of my boys."

Dad drove the first couple of hours and when we stopped for food, I took over behind the wheel.

"My boys," I said in my best Dad voice. "I'm proud of my boys." And Dalton put his hand on Dad's head.

"Steelhead was biting something fierce yesterday." Uncle James had lived in the Upper Peninsula for over forty years and his Yooper accent was thick and amazing. Aunt Viv had made us four pies before she and her sisters headed off to New York to see *Hamilton* on Broadway. She'd written MUSTIKKAPIIRAKKA: FINNISH BLUEBERRY PIE on an index card for us, drawn a bowl of blueberries. Viv still treated Dalton and me like we were twelve and I loved her so much for it. I was looking forward to feeling like a kid up there at Uncle James's place. A kid, but I could drink, smoke, cuss, have phone sex with Evi before I went to bed if I wanted to. I wanted to go back in time and tell twelve-year-old me this stuff so I could blow my own mind.

James's coon dog ol' Betsy had finally been put down and now he had a new coon puppy, Buster. I picked him up and carried him around with me. He pressed his cool wet nose to my cheek, licked my face. I was stoked to get out on the river first thing in the morning. I texted Evi on the first night and checked in to make sure she was okay.

Merit and I are eating ice cream and doing Noah's baby laundry. We are fine.

I loved that Evangeline knew about things like washing the baby's clothes before we brought him home. I didn't know that was a thing, but of course she did.

You're a gift. I love you.

I love you too. Call me tomorrow. Tell Dalton goodnight for me.

I looked up from my phone and Dalton was on the twin bed next to me, looking at his.

We'd come upstairs, unpacked our stuff. Like always, we shared a room when we came up to the cabin, even though we could've had our own. Tradition.

"Who dat?" I asked him.

"Cass," he said.

"Cass?"

"Cassidy," he said, still typing.

"Yeah. I know. I've never heard you call her Cass before."

"We're still not boning."

"You've made that clear."

"We'll see."

"Evi says goodnight," I told him. Motioning to the phone in my hand.

"Goodnight, Evi and Baby Noah," Dalton said into the emptiness of the room, made even emptier because I missed Evi so much. The ache and anxiety super-heated my bones. I went downstairs to get a beer in order to cool them off.

Dad and James were in the kitchen, eating peanuts, talking shit. I'd heard their stories a million times but I still liked listening to them. I scooped up Buster, re-warmed by there being a new puppy in the house. In a couple years, Buster and Noah could play all day when we came up here together. I sat down at the table and let them finish. When I heard the shower turn on upstairs, heard Dalton close the bathroom door, I knew what I wanted to ask.

"Dad, do you know of anyone else who could be Dalton's father? He says Steve Boone told him he wasn't sure if he was his dad. Did he always go around saying that?" I asked.

My dad lifted his beer to his lips and I drank mine too. James told us he was going out back to smoke. Told us Viv wouldn't let him smoke in his own damn house anymore and made a grumpy face. He winked at me when he said it. I held out the puppy for James and he reached with both hands for him. I scratched behind the puppy's ears one more time, told him how good he was. Yes he was.

"No boy wants to hear how his mama got around, Eamon," Dad said after he'd swallowed.

"Wow. Forreal? Penelope got around? She seemed so...quiet," I said, remembering her sweet smile. How even when she was smiling, she still looked sad.

"I'm going to tell him. Don't you tell him," he said.

"So you *do* know?" I asked. My blood flashed with surprise.

I looked at my dad and decided he was drunk. He looked it. His eyes were all glassy and bloodshot, but not like he was simply tired. I'd only seen him drunk once before and that was when I was so young. After my mom lost my baby brother. It was weird for my dad to be drunk so quickly, especially on beer. I turned and saw a half-bottle of whiskey on the kitchen counter. He must've chugged it as soon as Dalton and I went upstairs to unpack. Strange. He never drank like that.

"Your mother doesn't know," he said. He was drunk-mumbling so I asked him to say it again. He did. His eyes were sad and for a quick moment, soulless. I'd never seen him like this. Not even when Thomas died. Everything was crooked and upside down.

"Your mama lost Thomas and Penelope. I can't hurt her anymore," he said.

"Wait, what?"

I wasn't sure why he was getting his stories mixed up.

"Hold on. Dalton's dad *isn't* Steve Boone?" I asked.

"He's not."

"What does that have to do with Mom or Thomas?" I asked. A wrinkle of sadness folded itself into a paper bird and flapped around in my gut whenever I thought about my mom losing that baby. My little brother. When I thought about how I would feel if Evi lost Noah, that paper bird burst into flames.

Something about how my dad looked over at me. Something about how the lights above us seemed to flicker. Something about how I could smell Uncle James's cigarette through the slip of open window and how the cool air ribboned its way into their cozy warmed kitchen. Something about how my father's face turn down at that moment, the same way Dalton's face had turned down when he was talking about Steve Boone the week before at the bar.

Suddenly after all this time, I knew.

I'd been absolutely fucking blind to it before. Something right in front of me, in front of all of us. Hiding in plain sight.

How could I not have known?

My heart split—equal parts anger and happiness.

My parents had adopted Dalton because Dalton was my father's *biological* son.

I didn't remember standing. I didn't remember cutting my hand on my bottle of beer. I didn't remember going up the steps or taking my clothes off or getting in bed. But in the morning, that's where I was with my hand dried-blood-sticky, my eyes burning.

It was still dark out. I heard Uncle James and Dad moving

around already downstairs. We always headed down to the river at the crack. I couldn't decide if I'd keep my mouth shut or if I'd be able to. Why would my father keep a secret like this for so long? Treat Dalton like his son but never admit he *actually* was? Lead Dalton to believe he'd been abandoned by a biological father who didn't give a shit? That shaped who he was, who he'd become. Those kinds of things weren't so easy to erase. How could he do that to my mom? With her best friend? It gutted me, my mom not knowing. Sickened me. I got up out of bed, went to the bathroom. Puked up the beer from the night before, streaked with blueberries from Aunt Vivian's pie.

I got back in bed, looked over at Dalton sleeping. My father's son. My actual biological half-brother and he didn't even know. I had a flash of remembrance from the night before. My father standing when I cut my hand, touching my arm, telling me he was going to tell Dalton himself. Telling me Evi being pregnant with Noah convinced him more. The family was growing and he didn't want to keep the secret anymore. Not from Dalton. He never wanted my mom to know, but Dalton needed to know. He'd tell him. *Don't you tell him. I'll tell him myself,* he'd said. It dawned on me that my Uncle James knew. Of course he knew. He and my dad were super-close and looking back, in his gentle way, James was letting me know he knew. By always telling Dalton and me we were *twin spirits.* By the way he never favored me over Dalton. By the way he got up from the table last night and went outside to smoke before I figured it out. Like he'd been waiting thirty-one years for the conversation to finally happen.

I would never do this to Noah. I would never keep secrets from him. I'd never let him live his entire life believing one thing when I knew the truth. I made that promise to him in the dark of the guest bedroom I'd been sleeping in for two weekends a year for my entire life. I made that promise to God and to Evi. I hadn't told Evi. I wouldn't be able to keep it for long but I hadn't told her yet. I'd tell her when I got back to Kentucky. I'd look in her eyes and tell her the truth and my voice would carry to Noah's dark, wet ears.

The cut on my hand was small, not deep, but it burned. Everything burned. I was scalded. My heart was on fire. Tears stung in my eyes and I pressed my fists against them. I could already feel the weight of the secret clawing me from the inside out. Could hear the blood-breath of it rushing through my head. My dad had taken Dalton in, given him his last name, raised him as his own alongside me. Right under my mother's nose—the son of her closest friend. Her closest friend who had betrayed her in the worst way.

My mind raced up and down rows and rows and rows of memories from my childhood, coincidences, certain looks. The way Dalton and my dad both drove the same kind of truck and used the same fly reels. Infinitesimal, meaningless things. Dalton looked a *lot* like Penelope. *A lot.* As if he had no father, no one else to resemble. I thought about everything, couldn't stop. How Dalton had the same brown-gold tint of his hair my paternal grandmother had when she was younger. How Dalton had lived this far in his life thinking he didn't have a biological family when he'd been hidden inside his very own for so long. How all those times I thought I was imagining it when Dalton sounded like my dad on the phone, I wasn't imagining it at all. It was real. *Our dad.* We were six days apart. *My brother.* As a police officer, I made a living listening to people lie to me. All day long, every day. I usually knew when someone was lying and trusted almost no one, but my father? I trusted him. And now I was burdened with a secret that was never mine. A secret on loan. A ghost, haunting the wrong house.

Dalton

I KEPT TELLING EAMON THAT CASSIDY AND I WEREN'T boning and I didn't lie. But I hadn't told him everything. Not yet. Not about Cassidy, not about Steve Boone. And that wasn't like me. I didn't keep things from Eamon, period. But he was married now. Things were different. Between that and work, I didn't want to bug him. He had his own life, I had mine. Yes, we were two separate people although there had been times when it felt like we were the same, operated the same, lived lives resembling one another's. And just like anything, the more I did it, the easier it became; keeping things from Eamon became easier, even when I hadn't meant for it to. I met Steve out for coffee and food but I didn't tell Eamon about it at first. Instead, I opened up to Cassidy.

Cassidy and I had gotten into the habit of making out at the bike shop after we were closed. Most of the time we kissed against my desk in the back or the register counter out front. She'd invited me to her place twice but I wiggled out of it without hurting her feelings. It became ritualistic the way we'd wait until Detroit left, if he was there. Wait until the last customer had made their purchase or decided they didn't want anything at all anyway. I'd finished building her bike already and she loved it. We'd taken a couple long rides together, stopping for lunch and picnicking wherever we could find.

Some nights I'd count out the register and Cassidy would sit on the floor, flipping through her phone. I'd look up to see her pale brown skin and the little white lights wrapped around the bike rack next to her, the rose bush tattoo on the outside of her right upper thigh. How the thorns wrapped and disappeared—lost in the mystery between her legs. I'd tried to remain as gentlemanly as possible. I hadn't slept with anyone but Frances in so long and sleeping with Cassidy would be making a promise I wasn't sure I could or wanted to keep. Although I knew Eamon would understand because he understood me, I still didn't want to talk to him about it yet. Cassidy and I were who we were to one another and I wasn't going to use her just to get off. I knew better.

It was beyond hard, both literally and figuratively—turning down a blow job from a woman I was attracted to, but I wouldn't have felt good about it and I didn't have to be a prophet to know that. Cassidy and I were on the floor of my office and she was slowly moving her head down my stomach. Lifted my shirt, kissed the clip of my navel.

"Hey. Come here," I said, gently wrapping my hand around the back of her neck.

I looked down at her looking up at me. Her brown eyes in the almost-dark of the room. She made her way back up to my mouth. We kissed and kissed, her mouth—melted dark chocolate in gold foil. Unwrapping.

"You don't want to do anything else?" she asked quietly. She put her hand between my legs and I let her. "It feels like you want to do something else." She bit her bottom lip, destroying me.

"I was in a weird, complicated relationship for a really long time. *Too* long," I said.

I imagined Frances in the room with us, sitting on the corner of my desk in one of her expensive black dresses with her arms crossed, clicking her tongue at me. Her amaranth mouth slowly rising at the corners. Our entire relationship was summed up in my vision. Frances as queen in a crooked jeweled crown, mocking me. Me, being willingly mocked. Frances had written me a note the night after we had sex for the first time. Quoted Liz Phair and kissed it with her sticky lipstick mouth. Mercy. I hadn't talked to Frances in two weeks, which was donkey's years for us.

"So I can help you forget it," Cassidy said.

"You are. You are helping," I said.

I was feeling confessional. The pulsing white-hot electricity of lust blazing through my veins like Joni Mitchell's holy wine. I heard the piano music for "Case of You" in my head. The headlights from the hilly street behind the bike shop swung low into my office, lighting it up. But only for a moment. Our eyes, quick to adjust and readjust to the darkness. I pushed myself up so I was sitting with my back against the desk. Cassidy laid her head on my thigh. I told her about meeting Steve Boone for the first time. I told her I didn't know why I was keeping it from Eamon. He was being weird ever since we got back from the Upper Peninsula the week before. Distant. I figured he probably had work on his mind. He'd recently been called to the scene of a brutal murder of a small child, arrested the monster who did it. I knew he'd been through a counseling program at the police department back when he first started. It was optional, but he felt like he wanted to do it, wanted to give himself the best chance at protecting his mental health. I wondered if he'd consider counseling again. He oscillated between wanting to find another career and sticking it out as an officer. Mom had gotten off his back about it for the most part but I knew Evi being pregnant kept it in his head, even when he didn't want it there. And I was trying really hard to give him room to get his head straight, although he hadn't asked for it. I didn't want him to worry about my feelings about my biological father. I used the weirdness Eamon and I were having—that steely cold space—to go ahead and meet up with Steve, see what he had to say.

I told Cassidy all of this in the dark, the warmth of her body heating mine.

I told her upon seeing Steve's face, I knew I didn't hate him. As much as I could've or maybe even should've, I didn't. He looked old and sad, his eyes watery and greyed by cataracts. He was kind to me, had nothing but kind things to say about Penelope. His eyes teared up when he talked about her suicide. There he was sitting across from me, crying about my mother and I was being strong for him. Nodding and listening.

"So he was like in love with her?" Cassidy asked.

"At least he was up until he found out she had another boyfriend," I said.

I told Cassidy he said Penelope had more than one boyfriend when she got pregnant with me. I didn't know that. He told me he waited to see what I looked like when I was born. If I'd look like him or not. He kept waiting to be able to tell, but he couldn't. He said his father thought I looked like him but his mother didn't. He said he waited four months and he and Penelope got into an argument and she told him I could've been someone else's. That was the last time he saw me.

I told Cassidy that I said Steve and I should get a paternity test and he said he'd take one. I regretted telling him it as soon as the words left my mouth. Calvin was the only dad I'd ever known and he'd raised me, taken care of me, loved me as if I were his own. I told Steve I'd call him later and we could set up the paternity testing or whatever. I asked him if he weren't my father then who else could it be. He said he didn't know. Penelope had never mentioned any of her other boyfriends by name and he'd never met them. He apologized and cried. I felt guilty for hating him so much for so long. Felt sorry for myself for being eerily right when I'd said, *I'm nobody's.*

Cassidy listened. She sat up, put her head on my shoulder.

"So did you set up the paternity test?" she asked. Quiet. Vanilla.

I liked her. I liked how she talked to me and how she kissed. She had a deep dimple in her left cheek and I liked that too. Sometimes she wore a sparkly stud in her nose, sometimes a little silver hoop. I liked both of those. I liked her tattoos and how much she loved talking bikes and riding. She seemed hungry for me.

"Not yet. I will," I said. She kissed my cheek. My mouth. We sat like that for a while and she said she was heading home. I locked the door behind us, drove home. Jerked off and slept.

Was awakened by Frances texting me because I'd forgotten to turn my phone off.

Are you sleeping?

I looked at it, stared at it. Turned my phone off without replying.

Eamon and Evi invited me over for dinner but I asked them if I could have them over to my place instead. They were always feeding me and it was my turn. I was both stoked and anxious to reconnect with them and had missed the comfort of our closeness, even though not much had changed. Eamon and I were simply being a little quieter. We made plans, I went to the store and got good steaks to grill out, a big bag full of green, red, yellow and orange peppers, corn, zucchini. Got some French bread, fancy cheese, a little raspberry chocolate cake from the bakery.

When I got home, Frances was sitting on my stoop. She'd cut her hair but it was still long and I wondered what was the point in doing a small thing that didn't make much difference. But then I thought that a small thing could be a big thing to someone and who was I to judge? Seeing Frances on my stoop convinced me. Of what, I didn't know. I felt odd. Prickly, as if I were getting sick although I didn't actually feel sick. It was the only way I could describe it to myself. Frances's eyes were rimmed with smoke-grey pencil, her mouth a hot purple. Desire flashed and dripped, my own.

We fucked fast on the kitchen floor. The peppers fell from the counter, the hush and heavy of the plastic bag next to my ears. I bit her neck, pulled her hair. Turned her over, kissed her warm breasts. I had to bite the inside of my cheek to keep from accidentally calling her *Cassidy*. I thought about Cassidy when I came. I didn't mean to, but I did. I thought about Frances too.

"I need to start dinner," I said, looking at her.

"Quick shower, start dinner," she said. I knew she was referring to both of us. She was surprise-back, like she'd never left. We took a shower like we always did. She put her panties in her purse like she always did. She put her dress back on, her hair wet.

I went outside and fired up the grill.

Frances had made me feel better.

Cassidy texted me. *Hey! What are you up to tonight?*

I'd write her back in the morning, tell her none of this. This was tonight. Tomorrow was tomorrow.

Frances helped me grill the veggies, the colors popping like fireworks against the black and grey ash. I put the steaks on when Eamon and Evangeline showed up. When it was Eamon and me in the kitchen alone I told him Frances was on my stoop when I came home from the store.

"She still lives in Austin?"

"Yeah. I guess she'll always be back up here for one reason or another," I said, opening the fridge, handing him a beer. I got one for myself.

"One reason or another," he said, pointing at me the whole time.

I shrugged.

Eamon was still being weird. I asked him what was up.

"Ah, nothing. Got a lot of shit on my mind," he said, looking over at the back door. Evi was standing there, full pregnant and glowing. Her dress, blowing in the backyard breeze. She'd hugged me extra-tight when she first saw me, not an easy feat when she was working with so much belly. She'd gotten tears in her eyes when she took my hand and wanted me to feel Noah kicking this time. She'd touched my shoulder when she called me Uncle Dalton. She'd brought me a big pot of flowers for the deck and was standing in front of them, talking to Frances, who was taking the veggies off the grill, flipping the steaks for me.

"You don't want to talk about it?" I asked, leaning. Drinking.

"Nah. But Dad wanted us all to go out tomorrow for lunch. Just the guys. For pizza. I have to work in the morning but when I get off. You down?" he asked.

Everything was going to be fine. *Everything was going to be just fine.*

Frances was sunshine that night during dinner and afterwards. I found myself wondering why I hadn't ever asked her to marry me, why she wasn't enough for me. Or maybe I wasn't enough for her. Or maybe it was both.

"Do you feel like you're harboring an alien life force?" Frances smiled, asked Evangeline. Frances took a sip of her red wine from one of the huge wide-mouthed glasses she'd bought me a set of years ago. She'd done it a lot during our relationship—passive-aggressively brought stuff into my house that she needed and wanted when she stayed over, under the guise of gifting. I'd gotten my fancy coffee maker that way, those wine glasses, twelve pairs of wool socks.

Evangeline laughed. It made me love her even more. How easily amused she was, always. Lighthearted, free-spirited.

"Kind of, but Noah's a good boy," Evi said, putting her hand on her belly.

I could smell the flowers in the pot she'd given me. It was spring. *La primavera.* The world was new. I heard Vivaldi in the curtain breezes again, the blooms blowing. Penelope, straight-backed at our piano, playing it with her eyes closed, the windows open. The trees in my backyard had begun to show green. I'd cut my grass the day before. The trees in my neighbors' backyards, blowing swirling whirling dervish storms of helicopter seeds across their lawns and mine. The whole world—fecund and humming, buzzing with lawn mowers and bees and children and life. New life. Evi, growing new life inside of her. Spring was overwhelming to the senses in a way the other seasons were not. Fall and winter were sleepy and summer was unabashedly on fire, but spring was both expected and unexpected depending on us—a chance to begin again if we were willing to take it.

I put my nose in the air like a puppy, sniffed the flowers, the spring air, opportunity and second chances and wasn't embarrassed by how ridiculous I may have looked because what I was smelling and feeling and thinking and doing was being alive. Being *aware* of being alive. Being thankful and opening my heart, then opening it more. My heart, a piano. My heart, a thousand violins. The music soaring. I looked at Frances and thought of how she'd roll her eyes at me if she knew how full my heart was at that moment. If she knew I could hear music when there was none.

"And you're due in what…two more months?" Frances asked Evangeline.

If Frances hadn't gotten the abortion our baby would've been two years old. Thinking of that dropped my mood, swung it low—plumbed the depths. My heart, a mournful organ. My moods didn't usually swing back and forth like this. It worried me for a moment. I prayed about it and let it go.

Evangeline and Frances continued their conversation about babies and pregnancy. Eamon had been quiet, had finished his second beer. He reached and put his arm around me, let his hand rest on my head.

"Uncle Dalton," he said before asking if I had any cigars.

I did. I went inside and got them. I poured us whiskies.

We parked ourselves off the deck so the girls wouldn't have to sit in our smoke. We put our chairs in the grass and smoked our cigars and drank our whiskies. *To whiskey and ribbons.* I could feel a scattered darkness pouring from Eamon, like something I'd never felt from him before. It wasn't sadness. It was anger. But it wasn't aimed at me. It wasn't aimed at Evangeline. I didn't know who or what it was for and I didn't ask. I sat there next to him and we were quiet for several minutes.

"E, you can be pretty pushy with me when I don't tell you shit," I finally said to him.

"True," he said.

"You don't want to talk about whatever it is?"

"I'm good."

I was glad to be next to him. I was glad to be in his presence. I hoped that by simply being close to him, I could take some of whatever burden he was carrying, hoped he could feel the lifting.

Evi got sleepy soon after we had dessert so she and Eamon left. Frances spent the night. She was going to be in town staying with her parents for a week before going back to Austin. When she left after breakfast in the morning, I texted Cassidy and invited her over to my place later, after I had pizza with Dad and Eamon. I'd never invited her over to my place before and to plan on having her over the night after I'd had surprise-not-surprise sex with Frances felt like a real fuckboy thing to do, but I allowed myself that. I allowed it. Maybe it was in my genes and I couldn't shake it. Maybe Steve Boone or not-Steve Boone or Penelope left fuckboy fingerprints on my DNA.

When I got to the pizza place, Dad and Eamon were already inside in the corner booth we usually sat in. When Eamon was in full uniform, he was intimidatingly authoritative. He was handsome, tall, commanding, had all the badges, patches and shit around his duty belt—his gun, taser, radio, two pairs of handcuffs, flashlight and more. We pretended to be cops when we were kids and there he was, a real live one. I lifted my chin at him. *What's up?*

Dad had a look on his face I'd never seen before. Scared. He looked like a child. As soon as I sat down, Eamon held his hand up to Dad and started talking.

"Hey, man," Eamon said. "I just want to say I knew this. Since being up at James's I knew. I was letting him get his shit together to tell you himself. That's the only reason I didn't tell you." Eamon rarely cursed in front of Dad. I felt like I needed to go to the bathroom. I felt hot.

"Dalton, Steve Boone is not your biological father. I am," Dad said quickly. The words tumbling out as if he couldn't slow or stop them. His voice was rickety and he looked me right in the eyes before looking down and unnecessarily readjusting his fork, his napkin. He cleared his throat. He sat there blinking at the table.

"What?" I asked. The waitress brought drinks to our table for Eamon and Dad. I heard Eamon tell her I'd like a water. I heard the clock ticking across the restaurant and some inane pop song pouring from the kitchen speakers.

"Darth Vader, Luke Skywalker shit," Eamon mumbled, putting both of his palms on the table.

"What?" I asked again. I searched his face, Eamon's. I searched Dad's face again for any truth.

"I slept with Penelope once and I know you're mine. You're ... my boy," Dad said, looking back at me.

"What?" I asked again.

What what what what what what what. It was all I could hear and nothing felt real. I felt half-awake and the part of me that was awake, was panicked.

"Dalton, I'm sorry. I'm asking you to forgive me. And I'm begging you not to say anything to Loretta. Ever. She doesn't know," Dad said.

I shook my head. "What?" I asked again.

"I raised you as my own because you *are* my own. You're my son," Dad said.

I looked over at Eamon. His eyes were brimming with tears. I began to cry, used my knuckles to wipe my eyes. I felt like I was choking. I got up from the booth and walked outside.

I put my hands on my waist and looked up at the sky and sobbed with my mouth wide open, crying in the blazing yellow-white high noon sun. I walked behind the pizza place, back by the dumpsters. There were two guys from the kitchen out there, smoking.

They turned to look at me and I saw Eamon round the corner in full uniform. The two guys looked away. They'd think I was a criminal, some lunatic. Fuck it. Let them think it.

"D. D," Eamon said catching up to me. He put his hand on my shoulder.

"Don't," I said.

"Don't be pissed at me. I swear I almost told you. Fucking worst two weeks. I wouldn't have waited any longer. I called him every day," he said.

I knew something was up. I didn't know the something would be this. How could I imagine the unimaginable?

We made it to the end of the alleyway. I found a curb and sat on it. Eamon sat down next to me.

"I hate he did this. I hate he did this to us. He did this to Mom. He hurt Penelope too." Eamon was keeping track on his fingers. "And I've been thinking about this a lot—forget all that other stuff for right now and listen to me. I'm *not* sorry you're my real brother. I'm not. I'm not sorry about that," he said, his voice breaking.

I wasn't sorry about that either. I'd dreamt about it, wished it. That fact was now the crack letting the only light in.

But everything, lies. All of it. And how could I go on lying to Loretta now that I knew the truth? How could Penelope do that to her? Her best friend? Eamon and I were six days apart. *Six days.* Maybe that's why Penelope was so sad all the time. The guilt of it. Maybe she was in love with Calvin. Calvin. *My dad.*

"I met Steve Boone," I said, looking down at my feet. My head was throbbing already from crying and I wasn't even finished yet.

"When? Why didn't you tell me?" Eamon asked.

I glared at him.

"Fuck you," I said.

"I'm sorry. I'm sorry," Eamon said.

"We were going to get a DNA test done," I said, holding my hand straight out at nothing.

"You can get one for Dad but we know it's true. It's like we should've known," Eamon said.

We should've known. The words echoed in my head as I flicked through memories of Calvin never making me feel like an outsider. Of him not once making me feel second-class compared to Eamon. But what, if Penelope hadn't died he wouldn't have gotten to know me? He would've denied me? He would've had me walking around thinking Steve Fucking Boone was my father? I should've never heard of Steve Boone. He was nothing to me. Nothing. *I'm nobody's.*

"This is fucked up. Why'd he want to tell me here? Here? Really?" I said. I used my shirt to cover my face, tented myself.

"I don't know. I think the thought of being alone with you terrifies him. He can't look away. He has to see that shit dead-on. And look, if you want to be alone, get out of here and I'll take care of him. If you want company, come home with me. My shift is over. I cut out early so we could have the rest of the day," he said.

"I'm getting out of here," I said, standing up. I told him to tell Dad I was going. "Who else knows?" I asked him when I was near my truck.

Eamon looked at me.

"Evi knows?" I asked.

"Evi knows," he said, nodding.

"Uncle James, Viv?" I asked.

"I'd guess James knows. I don't know anyone else."

"How could Mom not know?" I asked.

"How could *we* not know?" he asked me back.

No answers—my world completely changed and I had no answers. I knew my biological father was a liar. I knew my biological mother did something deplorable. I knew my best friend—my biological half-brother—kept it a secret from me.

"It was killing me," Eamon said. "I puked, I couldn't sleep."

I turned my back to him, opened my truck door.

"I'm not sorry you're my brother," he said, defiantly.

I started the engine.

☙

I drove. I kept driving. Seventy-five miles out of the city. Penelope taught summer piano lessons at a church in the country back in the day. There was a motel called The Darl Inn. It was still there. A big neon smiling electric blue half-moon, a small orange star twinkling next to it. That was my favorite part when I was a kid— the winking star.

Mom had called as I drove and I answered it, talked to her like normal although it was one of the hardest things I'd ever done. She asked me if I thought they should have their big Fourth of July party at their house or rent a place at the park. Mom sounded good. She sounded happy. That's the thing that would forever keep me from telling her the truth. I wanted Mom to be happy. I was ashamed of what Penelope had done. Would Noah know about this one day? Of course he would. Eamon would tell him. But when? How long would it be his burden to keep from his own grandmother? How would he be able to do that?

I listened to Mom, talked to Mom. I heard the water running in her kitchen. Could see her vividly in my mind. The house, that kitchen, her furry moccasin house shoes. The cloying but familiar peach soap she kept by the sink, the ceramic open-mouthed frog with the soap scrub brush in its mouth.

"Your dad doesn't feel well. He went to bed already. Did y'all have a nice lunch this afternoon?" she asked.

Flickered scenes. The pizza place, Eamon in uniform, me sobbing. Dad sitting there with a dumbass look on his face. *No Mom, we didn't have a nice lunch.* I teared up again, this time out of anger. Frustration. Self-loathing. Pity. *I'm nobody's.*

I was pulling up to The Darl Inn which felt like I'd driven through a portal taking me right back to 1993 when Penelope and I would stay there for the weekend so I could swim. She'd sit by the pool in her sunglasses, reading her glossy magazines, drinking her Diet Cokes, eating her Little Debbies wrapped in crinkly plastic. I missed her all the time. I wanted her to see the man I'd become. I wanted her to see how well I was handling this. I was doing all right in spite of everything. All the secrets, all the lies. There I was, handling my shit. Wasn't I?

"We had a good time," I lied to Mom.

She told me she loved me and I said it back. Told her I'd talk to her later.

I was supposed to hang out with Cassidy that night but I didn't text her. I'd try my best to explain later. I texted Detroit and asked him to watch the shop for me for two days. I needed two days. He said, *of course*, and didn't ask questions. I loved Detroit. I turned my phone off.

I got a room, left and went and got a bottle of whiskey, some beer, a pack of cigarettes. I went to Walmart and got a new pack of boxer shorts, a pair of yellow flip-flops. A pack of white T-shirts. I already had jeans. I bought a paperback with a shimmery gold bold title on the cover. I didn't bother reading the back of it before I slapped it on the conveyor belt.

There was a small balcony attached to my room. A striped white and green lawn chair was on it, an ashtray, a short plastic table. I sat out there and smoked, drank. I got loaded as the full flower moon rose. The next day I woke up and did the same thing. Anytime I got overwhelmed by my thoughts, I took a sip of whiskey. Anytime I thought about how I was a dumbass for not knowing my dad had lied to me my entire life, anytime I thought about how no matter how much we wanted to, none of us could change the past, anytime I thought about how my dad could've at least tried to come up with a secret signal to let me know I was his, something only we would know, but he didn't. Anytime I thought about how eventually I'd have to look into my mom's eyes and pretend like everything was okay. Anytime I thought about the fact this was another pact I'd made—a pact to keep it a secret forever. I thought about punching a hole in the wall but didn't want to pay for it. I sat in the bathtub in my clothes and turned the shower on because I'd seen people do that in movies. I got out and changed into a clean shirt and underwear, let my jeans dry on the balcony railing in the sunshine. I ordered-in Chinese food: a waxy bag of crab rangoon, special fried rice, a sloppy box of greasy, slippery noodles, some egg rolls and plastic packets of thick amber and black sauces.

I turned my phone on. Ignored texts from Cassidy and Frances. Saw one from Eamon. He'd asked where I was. Told me he'd gone by my place.

I wrote him back. *The Darl Inn.*

Do you want to be alone?

I'll talk to you later. Promise. Just handling my shit.

Love you, D.

You too.

I turned my phone back off. Fine. He was allowed to know I was still alive. I appreciated him looking out for me. I wasn't mad at Eamon. I'd rolled it back and forth in my mind...thinking that I should've been angry with him, but I couldn't find it. Searched and searched. It wasn't there. He'd kept this from me, but who was I to say I would have done any different. And I knew how much it had been killing him.

I didn't leave my room except for stepping outside on the balcony overlooking the parking lot. The pool wasn't open yet. There was a taut forest-green tarp on top of it. I rationed my cigarettes, had some whiskey left and all of the beers. I drank and smoked. I read. Took a nap in that lawn chair, my head hanging back and jerking forward to awaken me. The motel rooms were half empty. I heard a couple two doors down having sex. It was quick and didn't arouse me at all which was depressing. I wanted to sleep. I went inside to eat another round of all the food I'd ordered when I heard a knock at the door and opened it to find Evangeline, full-belly pregnant in her rolled-up overalls, a blue scarf tied in her hair.

"Fucking cliché, you coming here, Evangeline," I said, immediately regretful I'd cussed. "I'm sorry. I'm buzzed and pissed off," I said as she made her way inside. I closed the door behind us.

It was a small room, a sad room. I missed my own house, my own bed. I wanted out of there. Maybe seeing Evi's face had snapped me out of it. I went over to the table, started cleaning up.

Evi sat on the edge of the bed. The comforter, surely filthy with strangers' bodily fluids. I wanted to put a towel down for her but I didn't have a clean one. She didn't seem to mind.

"It's nice of you to come here. Again, forgive me for cursing when you came to the door. It's not your fault," I said.

She held up her hands.

"I'm not pissed at Eamon. This isn't his fault either. I'm...I don't know what I am," I said, tossing a plastic fork in the garbage without thinking about whether or not I'd need it later. "This was too far for you to drive. I'm sorry."

"Stop apologizing, Dalton. You're upset and you should be and there's nothing I can say to fix that. But I wanted to come out here so you'd know for sure how much we love you and how important you are to us and how even through the lies and all the messed up things associated with this...you're Eamon's *real* brother. You're his blood, Uncle Dalton," she said, putting both hands on her belly. She looked at me and her bottom lip quivered like a cartoon. Quick tears smoothed down her cheeks.

"I know," I said. She held my hand.

"I'm still processing this too," she said. She took a deep breath in.

"No shit." We both cry-laughed tiny explosions of tears and sniffling.

I laid my head next to her on the bed and asked if she was hungry. Offered her my Chinese food buffet. She laughed through her tears again when she said no.

"You didn't have to come out here," I said.

"I wanted to. And trust me, Eamon doesn't know how to handle this either. I know he usually seems like he has it all together and he *does*, but he's wrecked by this too."

"You told him you were coming all the way out here?"

She nodded. "I told him I was driving out here myself because I wanted to see you. Wanted to make sure you were okay."

"Am I?" I asked her.

"Are any of us?"

I stood up in that too-small stale hotel room that reminded me of Penelope and the family I didn't have. All that had been denied me, but the happy memories too. I rubbed my hands over my face.

"Things make sense now, though," Evi said.

I stepped to the bathroom to get her some toilet paper, some for me too. I handed it to her and she blew her nose. We stopped crying and sat there next to one another on that awful bed. A moment later she took my hand and put it on her belly so I could feel the flutters again.

I took a cold shower to sober all the way up and insisted on driving Evi back home. She left her car in the parking lot of The Darl Inn. We made a quick stop for coffee. Fully-charged for me, decaf for her. When I dropped her off, I sat in my truck and waited until Eamon opened the door. I lifted my hand and told him I'd talk to him later. I got Detroit to give me a ride back out of town to pick up Evi's car. He followed me to drop it off at their place. It was late. I put her keys in the tulip pot on the porch. Detroit dropped me off at home. I thanked him twice before going inside and opening my bedroom windows to let in the night wind. I closed my eyes and let my heart talk to Penelope, to Jesus, to anyone out there who was listening.

V.

Evangeline

I TAKE A HOT, HOT SHOWER AND WASH MY HAIR. I STAND in front of my closet and hold up the yellow dress. God bless Merit for giving me a yellow dress. I hold it up in the dresser mirror. It looks like a hippie bridesmaid's dress. But not a bridesmaid's dress I've ever worn before. I've only been a bridesmaid once when I was in Merit's wedding and we wore black. When Eamon and I got married, Merit was my best girl. Dalton was Eamon's best man. Merit wore a blue dress and Dalton wore a blue tie. The same blue.

God bless Merit for gifting me this overly ruffly yellow dress because I'm putting it on and I'm going on a house date with Dalton. God bless Merit for being such a dear friend to me. There were days after the funeral when she just knew when to come over and stay and when to leave. She made me tea and cookies. Never attempted to force me to talk about anything. She tucked my hair behind my ears when it was long and she didn't say one negative word after Dalton cut it. She just took me to get it fixed and gave me a pair of earrings. I had no idea that when we met in high school we'd hold each other's babies and we'd be in each other's weddings and she'd pour boiling water over chamomile with lavender teabags for me those days I wouldn't eat, those days right after Eamon was killed. That she'd sweep my kitchen floor for me and refill my ice trays because I'd forgotten.

I go over to my jewelry box and start rifling through my earrings. Eamon gave me a pair of dangly black ones. I look in the mirror and hold one of them up to my ear. I watch it swing back and forth. I close my eyes and picture Eamon stepping behind me and slipping his arms around my waist like he used to do when I stood in front of the mirror, picking out my jewelry. I picture him lifting up my hair to kiss my neck.

He is gone and I know I will spend the rest of my life fruitlessly searching for him. I touch my neck and count my heartbeats. I put the earrings in and open my underwear drawer.

My wedding dress was ivory lace and long but not too long. I wore an orange and white polka-dotted bangle bracelet on my right wrist. I wore my grandma's antique diamond earrings. I painted my toes the same peacock-blue color as the ties Eamon and Dalton were wearing. The same blue as Merit's best girl dress. We had our wedding outside. It rained a lot that morning and I called Eamon and told him it was raining the night at the church when I locked my keys in my car.

"I remember. I like how we talk to each other," he said.

"What do you mean?" I asked. I was in the kitchen at my parents' house. My mom was freaking out about my dad having the right shoes on for the wedding, even though it was still hours and hours away. I walked outside and stood underneath the wind chimes. It was July in Kentucky. The air was as humid as breath, but there was a little wind with the rain. Rainbow weather.

"I love that we're always nice to each other. Marry me," he said.

He sounded so happy. I heard Dalton in the background and Calvin too. I heard Dalton say, *gimme that gimme that give it to me* before he got on the line.

"Evi?"

"Dalton," I said, smiling.

"I'm taking Eamon away now. We're getting chili dogs and beers. Afterwards, we're getting all dressed up in the wedding fanciness."

"Okay. I'll see y'all in a little bit," I said, lifting my shoulders up and shaking my head at the sky. I couldn't stop smiling.

"Say goodbye to Evi," Dalton said.

I heard Eamon's voice again, so close to the mouth of the phone, the sound was all muffled and brushy.

"Goodbye, Evangeline. I love you," he said. I told him I loved him too.

At the reception, we danced our first dance together to "One More Night" by Phil Collins and afterwards, we stole a moment alone. Snuck into the empty girl's bathroom to make out. When we were walking out of there, I held onto his hand and watched the back of his black suit vest. The satin, glossy and choppy as water. I remember thinking something bad was going to happen eventually because everything was so perfect. I was so happy and so in love and this is Earth. Those things don't last because they're not meant to.

I put on my matching bra and undies and not because I think Dalton will be seeing my underwear tonight, but because the dress is so nice, I want to wear nice underwear too. I slip the dress over my head and smooth it down. I take a look in the full-length mirror on the back of the door. I pull on a pair of black tights with it and put my slippers back on. *There.* Now it feels more like me. The dress looks better on me than I thought it would. I go to the bathroom and do my eye makeup. Liquid liner and a flick on the top lid. A little blush, some swipes of pale lip gloss. My hair is slowly growing out and I stick a couple bobby pins in it for good measure. I look pretty. I stare at my reflection for a moment longer and realize I look happy and hope it's not an accident. Happiness, an elusive fish I cannot catch whole—only small darting flashes. Feels nasty to consider or wish for happiness. But I also know that without at least a *little* light, things die.

When I walk into the kitchen, Dalton has his back to me. He's in the grey wool suit and it fits him perfectly. Strapping. I look down at my slippers and take them off. Dalton looks so nice, I don't want to blow it. I haven't even seen the front of him yet. I say hey and he turns around.

"Good gravy, look at you," he says. He runs his hand through his hair and I can smell he's put on cologne, but not a lot. I didn't know Dalton had any cologne. Thinking about him sprucing up in the bathroom for me sends warm sparkles from my stomach to my feet.

"You look beautiful," he says. I'm instantly shy.

"Thank you, Dalton. You look mighty handsome yourself. You smell really good," I say, reaching out to hug him.

"It's the food. You're just hungry."

"No. It's you," I say as he squeezes me.

"It's you," he says back to me. He says he liked the slippers.

"Shut up," I say, trying to get free from his arms. But he won't let me go. Not yet.

"What'd you make?" I ask after he releases me. I pull back the kitchen window curtain. The snow has eased up, but is still gorgeously falling slow, like confetti sprinkles on a snow cake.

"I made steak tacos, baked cheesy veggies and rice," Dalton says, looking at me. He opens the oven door to take a look at the rice and I bend down to peek too. "Careful with your dress. You shouldn't be in here yet. Shoo, shoo."

"Where am I supposed to go, my Huckleberry Friend?"

"Go sit in there. Watch yourself something. It's almost done. Now, get," he says, putting on my favorite version of his thickest southern accent.

"I don't want to watch TV."

"Okay. Well, how about you go get the tea lights and light those and put them on the table," Dalton says, lifting the casserole dish off the oven rack and holding it up to check the bottom.

"Did you put the lighter in your suit pocket?"

He nods. I go back over to him and put my hand into the pants pocket. Dalton shakes his head at me. No lighter. He smirks.

"What?" I ask.

"Not that pocket. My vest," he says. I reach my hand in between his coat and vest and dip it into the satin coolness of the little vest pocket and find the plastic lighter. He's still holding the dish up. I've still got my hand in his pocket.

"Got it."

"Got it," he says, still smirking.

"I'm lighting the candles."

"Thank you," he says. I can feel him watching me walk away but I don't turn around.

We were tucked up in this house together the same way on New Year's Eve except Noah was here with us, sleeping. I've always hated New Year's Eve and this year was even worse because it was the first without Eamon. I didn't want to do anything. I didn't want to see anyone. I wanted to wallow in the warmth of my house, but Dalton convinced me to meet him at his bike shop to help do inventory. I went late in the afternoon and strapped Noah to the front of me and helped Dalton count gears and pedals and things I didn't know the names of. His buddy, Detroit, stopped by to invite us to a party his friends were throwing later that night.

"A rager. Don't miss it," Detroit said, putting both his hands on top of the doorway. He leaned into the back room and grinned at us.

"See, Detroit. That's what I love about you. You're the only dude who uses words like *rager*," Dalton said.

"That's a yes?" Detroit looked at me, then down at Noah, who was shaking and shaking the jingly red plastic teething ring he loves so much. "I know this little dude wants to rage in the new year, don't you, dude?" Detroit placed his huge hand on the top of Noah's head. Gentle and sweet.

"He's all booked up. You should've told us earlier. He's got big plans to sleep through the night and give his mama a break," I said and smiled.

"All right. Well hit me up if you change your mind," Detroit said before turning to walk out. He tossed his keys in the air and caught them behind his back.

"Will do. Happy New Year," Dalton said. We echoed each other. When Detroit was gone, Dalton locked the door behind him. "Happy New Year, Noahlicious," he said. Noah reached out for him and smiled a giant gummy smile. I slipped Noah out of the sling. Dalton took him from me.

Noah's little brown body looked so delicate in Dalton's arms. His head looked so small cradled in Dalton's hand. In a moment of sugar-sweet tenderness, Dalton bounced his knees enough to keep Noah happy and started singing "What Are You Doing New Year's Eve?" to him.

"I may hit up that rager, though. But I'll be home before midnight. If you're up, we'll ring it in together. Deal?" he said.

"It's all good. You go rage," I said, making a dismissive swipe with one hand. I used the other to grab a small cardboard box off the shelf so I could finish counting things. Dalton kept singing. Bless his heart.

Noah went to bed easily and after I put him down, I went into the kitchen to make a pot of coffee but never drank it. I remembered I had a bottle of champagne, so I drank that instead. By the time Dalton came home I was lit up like the multi-colored string of lights I'd wrapped around the front porch railing.

"Lookit who's raging now," Dalton said after he'd tossed his keys onto the counter. He twisted off the top of his beer and took a drink. I sat on the back of the couch, pulled my red pompom snow hat down over my eyes. I felt Dalton put his hand on the small of my back.

"I hate New Year's Eve," I moped.

"I know."

"How was the party?"

Dalton plopped onto the couch. I let myself slink next to him and tucked my feet underneath me. I pulled my hat back and we both sat watching the festivities on the flat screen TV in front of us. Confetti falling in a crowded discotheque on the other side of the world somewhere—a black boxy snow globe filled with neon lights and sad people pretending to be happy.

Dalton looked over at me, offered me his beer and I took it.

"This is better," he said.

I took a drink of his beer and before giving it back to him I clinked my right-hand wedding ring against it making a bright, tinkly sound. I did it again.

"Was it fun, was it crazy, what did you do?" I asked.

"I sat at the kitchen table and talked to Detroit. Talked to a couple other dudes I knew from college. I leaned against the doorframe and met some people I didn't know. All the while, fancily drinking cheap beer from a red Dixie cup. Are you jealous yet?"

"Kind of."

He offered his beer to me again but I shook my head no and looked back at the TV. I picked up the remote and clicked it off. Dalton asked if I wanted to play Scrabble.

"Let's make cookies first," I said. I heard Noah make a fussy noise and I went upstairs to check on him but by the time I'd gotten there he'd put himself back to sleep already.

After I made the chocolate chip cookie dough, I slid the baking sheet into the oven. Dalton and I started our Scrabble game at the kitchen table and when I looked at the oven clock I saw that it was five after midnight already.

"Happy New Year," I said. Dalton looked at the clock.

"Hey. Happy New Year," he said back. He got up from his chair and came over to me. Kissed the top of my head.

I flick the lighter off and on and light so many tealights, I lose track. I put some on the mantle over the fireplace, the coffee table, the kitchen table and on top of the piano. I also put some on top of the bookcase and the counter Dalton isn't using for cooking prep. My stomach growls when I am done.

"Perfect timing because everything's finished," Dalton says, wiping his hands on the dishrag. "Do we want to do wine or no? It's not like we haven't been drinking enough. I can go either way. You want to get trashed and tear the house down, let's do it. You want to teetotal and pray, we can do that too. You want to get trashed and pray, I'm your dude." It makes me laugh. I put the lighter on the counter and say one glass of wine sounds good.

"One glass of wine is what we'll do," he says, going to the fridge.

"That suit is like, so nice. I want to reach out and pet it," I say.

"Do it."

"I will," I say.

He closes the fridge and sets the bottle of wine down. I reach out and pet his arm like it's a fickle cat.

"I mean, I touched it already when I went into your pocket for the lighter. But I wanted to pet it again," I say, suddenly embarrassed. I feel like my emotions are all over the place and keeping them in check tonight is more like a pinball game than usual. *Tilt! Tilt!* I step back.

"You do whatever you feel like doing and you don't have to explain yourself to me. How about that?" Dalton says, turning away from me. He gets two Mason jars out of the cabinet and fills them with the rest of the Shiraz I'd forgotten about.

After dinner, Dalton clears his throat as he's putting his dirty plate in the sink. He turns around and leans against the counter, crosses his arms.

"I want to say something and it not be weird or awkward or too much or overwhelming."

I finish what's left of my wine and cross my arms too.

"I don't want it to be weird or awkward or too much or overwhelming either. Whatever it is. So we agree," I say.

"I know how much Eamon loved you. So this is hard for me."

"What is?"

"Having feelings for you."

"Oh."

"Not so-hard-I-can't-do-it-hard. But...I never would've kissed you if you hadn't kissed me first," Dalton says.

Who are we all dressed up in the kitchen like this? Was this first house date thing an awful idea because people who are on first dates usually don't have to talk about their dead husbands and feel every feeling all at once, do they? I feel like I could handle this conversation more easily if I weren't wearing such a brightly colored dress. I wish I was wearing grey like Dalton. It seems like a conversation better suited for grey.

"Right," is all I say.

"But that doesn't mean I didn't think about it a lot. For the past couple of months whenever people would kiss in a movie or whatever, I'd think about what it'd be like to kiss you. No shit," Dalton says.

It feels like a bigger confession than it actually is, but I can tell by the look on his face he's kind of embarrassed about it. It's sweet. I want to say, *really?* I've been questioning him so much lately and it hurts his feelings so I don't.

"I'd feel guilty for thinking about it because I'm not trying to take advantage of you or anything, obviously. Our relationship is so much bigger than that. More important. If we'd never kissed, I'd still want to, but I would've gone on living here like this. It wasn't a make it or break it type deal. Do you know what I'm trying to say?"

"I think so."

"Because as long as you'll let me, I'll be here for you and Noah and I'd love to be his dad as much as you're okay with it because

I grew up thinking my dad had abandoned me. And although the situation was messed up, Calvin *was* there for me. Look, all I'm saying is Noah *deserves* a dad…"

"So did you," I say. Dalton's mouth goes all crooked like it does right before he starts to cry. He looks away from me for a second and nods, bites his bottom lip. He turns back to me.

"So we need to promise each other we agree on that and nothing can happen between us to screw up what we've already decided. We agree that we love each other. We love Eamon and we love Noah. Because if we can't promise each other that, then I can't move. I can't. I'd be paralyzed."

"Okay. I agree."

"Should we type it up and get a notary to sign it?" Dalton says. He opens his arms and I smash my body against his chest so he can wrap them around me.

I nod against the fabric of his suit and close my eyes.

Eamon

I WAS STILL WRITING LETTERS TO EVI AND NOAH IN THE notebook. I'd take it with me in the patrol car, write and write. And if Noah ever considered becoming a cop one day like his old man, like his grandfather, he could read my thoughts about it. How it was important to me, but not so important I couldn't let it go for him. For them. I figured I'd give the notebook to Evi right after she had Noah. Mom had reminded me that I should have a gift for Evi after she had the baby. Told me Dad had given her a necklace after she had me and I wondered if he'd given Penelope something after she had Dalton too.

I knew Dalton and Dad had been talking. Dalton told me. Dad told me too. The three of us hadn't been alone together since the afternoon at the pizza place when Dad told Dalton the truth. We'd had dinner at my parents' but my mom was there. The three of us did a good, proper job of pretending everything was fine. Things like Dalton calling Dad *Dad* had been set in place since we were kids. This was our truth, had always been our truth, would always be our truth. Someday I'd tell Noah I'd grown up not knowing Uncle Dalton was my half-brother, but we'd lived our lives as brothers anyway. We chose to do that, chose not to let a thing like blood trip us up. I thought of how unnecessary it was for us to become blood brothers when we were eight years old, pricking our fingertips in my treehouse with a needle I'd stolen from my mom's sewing kit. We were *born* blood brothers, the blood binding us. And *blest be the tie that binds*. We sung it in church, we creaked open our heart doors and let it pour in.

Evi's baby shower was one of those co-ed baby showers so Dalton was there and a couple other of Evi's friends' husbands. Her mom Rose and my mom threw it at Evi's parents' place. All the guys were out back by the grill. That was something we felt like we could do. Man the meat. Brian and I had a rare day off together. We usually worked shifts that blended into one another and rarely did a work day pass when I didn't see him. His wife Lucy was inside unpacking the cupcakes she'd made. She owned a successful chain of trendy cupcake shops called Be Sweet To Yourself and had won second place on one of those cupcake challenge shows the year before. A while back, Evi had shown me a picture of the cupcakes Lucy was designing for her—on top of each one, there were tiny chocolate nests with baby bluebirds inside. They were perfectly what Evi wanted and I wanted her to have everything she wanted.

Both of our mothers loved huge dinners, parties, events. They'd planned this whole deal together and Evi's mom was also helping my mom put together the menu for the big Fourth of July party my parents were throwing. My parents had been married for thirty-four years. I thought of my mom's favorite picture of her and Penelope, both of them pregnant, about to pop. I thought of my dad and Penelope keeping that secret. The whole thing was like something out of the Old Testament—it reminded me of Moses. How his sister Miriam went and got their mother to come and care for him when he was a baby, right underneath the Pharaoh's nose. I had no choice but to keep it from Mom, to die keeping it from Mom. Mom could never know. Dalton and I had sworn ourselves to it.

Loads of our extended family were there at the shower and Evi's too. Evi's family was smaller than mine. A lot of my family was spread all across the southern states but Mom had told me a month before that she and Evi's mom had invited sixty-five people total. I admired how Evi let everyone else do most of the work. She was hugely pregnant and looked uncomfortable at certain times of the day. Sometimes her belly was stuck out and swollen, rock hard in places, depending on where Baby Noah was positioned. One night I came home after my shift and she was sleeping. I got in bed next to her. She didn't budge. When I put my hand on her belly, Noah was thrashing around inside, like a mischievous animal trying to break free. She slept through it.

After a couple rounds of games I remembered Mom had told me she'd invited Frances to the shower but Frances wasn't there.

"Is Frances in town?" I asked Dalton. We were sitting in lawn chairs out in the backyard grass. The first couple games included me. People had to guess how much both Evi and I weighed when we were born and there was another quiz about us as a couple. There was a cupcake break and another game. Afterwards, Evi was going to open gifts.

"Nope. And I think Cassidy is my accidental work girlfriend anyway," Dalton said.

"She officially works there now?"

"Well, she's there enough. She still has the rest of her mechanic classes and certification. She'll be in California with her mom and brother visiting her grandmother for the rest of the summer.

She'll finish those classes when she gets back here in the fall. She'll be certified by the beginning of the year if everything goes according to plan."

I'd never heard of bike mechanic certification until Dalton opened the shop. I'd never heard of any of that bike stuff until Dalton. I learned something new every time I talked to him about it. I liked listening to him explain things. It was soothing, familiar. Evi leaned against me and I still felt the shadow of Dad keeping such a huge secret from our family. I wondered if anyone besides Uncle James knew. Aunt Vivian had sent us clothes for the baby and soft-covered books. Had my Dad told anyone else? Had Penelope? The secret had been kept well for over thirty years. I resisted or at least did my best to resist the urge to feel sorry for my mom. She wasn't a woman who required or desired pity. If she knew about this and knew I was worried about her she'd gently or not-so-gently smack my face and tell me not to be.

After cupcakes and more food, I was in the kitchen with Brian. He told me our superior was going to talk to me about possibly moving both of us up a rank to lieutenant. Together, the week before, Brian and I had talked a man out of committing suicide. He was hanging off the side of the bridge and I was first on the scene. Between that and the drug cases we'd been working on lately, add in a couple of the other officers retiring or moving away, both Brian and I had been getting lots of praise and positive buzz in the department. Our city had a small town feel when it came to those things and one of the local news stations did a special segment on me, even followed me on some ride-alongs and when I went to a couple of the local universities to speak to their justice administration classes. There were two lieutenant slots opening soon in our department. I'd considered the possibly of my supervisor approaching me about it. It all felt very Michael Corleone. Every time I thought I was close to getting out, something tried to pull me back in. But I was leaving. No one on the force knew about my plans to leave when the baby was born besides Brian.

I hadn't mentioned any of it to Evi. Not the possible promotion, not the plans to leave. I wrote those plans in my notebook, safe in my work locker. I admitted to myself that the promotion was alluring. More money, higher rank. Police officers were taught from day one to prepare for being promoted, to keep a positive attitude, to show leadership skills. I felt confident with mine and had grown up with a father who'd been through the ranks. My dad worked patrol for years when he was younger, and eventually moved up to deputy chief before retiring. He'd made it work for him and up until Evi got pregnant, I was planning on making it work for me too.

Evi didn't ask me to give this up. But maybe she just didn't tell me she worried about getting that hollow, lonesome knock on the door, uniformed officers on our porch, neither one of them me. Or that she thought about which picture of mine they'd use on the news to accompany the story about how I'd died. I let my mind go there although it wasn't often a cop got killed in Louisville. It'd been over fifteen years since the last time. Back when my dad was on the force. My mom had made meals for the grieving widow. All the wives pitched in to babysit the fallen officer's children. My dad went over to help do some of the yard work. Maybe Evangeline remembered hearing about it on the news and had written my obituary in her mind already, whether the newspaper would include my middle initial, the list of all the people I would leave behind. Maybe she'd thought about our house, empty. Maybe she'd thought about herself, draped in black, sitting in the front row at my funeral. The grainy image of Jacqueline Kennedy and the tiniest JFK Jr., saluting.

In spite of everything, she didn't ask me to give it up.

But I was giving it up anyway.

"I'm getting out," I said to Brian. Again. We were standing next to the sink. His wife had just walked out of the kitchen with a tray full of microwaved candy bars so the girls could put them in diapers and play a game where they tried to guess which ones they were.

"I believe you. Wanted to ask again to make sure," Brian said.

He'd been nothing but supportive. I'd made him my mentor from day one, told him he didn't have a choice in the matter which made him laugh. Brian had a great laugh—a muddy rumble. "Lucy would love it if I left. If it's the right choice for you, it's the right choice for you. Family first," he said.

We both knew that in order to do our jobs, sometimes we had to forget *family first*. Sometimes we left *family first* in the locker room, protected behind the metal doors slammed shut.

I would miss things about being a cop. I'd worked hard to get where I was and maybe part of me would always wonder what could've been if I didn't give it up. But I'd made up my mind. I'd tell Evi when we brought Noah home. I'd tell my superior after my paternity leave. I just needed to ride out the next month. One month.

"Have you decided what else you want to do?" Brian asked me. We were alone in the kitchen. Everyone else had gone out back. I turned to see Mom outside, hugging Dalton around his waist. He kissed the top of her head since he towered over her. I turned back to Brian, suddenly overcome with emotion.

"Um. Yeah. Maybe I'll go work at the bike shop with Dalton, y'know?" I said, sniffing and getting down a glass to fill with water.

"Don't forget my brother-in-law works for that construction company. They make good money." He'd mentioned it once before. "You could even work security for fuck's sake. Rent-a-Cops get paid decently if you don't mind teenage punks calling you Rent-a-Cop."

I drank my water.

"Thanks, man," I said. I was done talking about it for now. We went back outside, watched the girls finish the candy bar game. When that was over, Evi opened just about every kind of baby gift imaginable. The members of our families who hadn't traveled to be there had sent things to her parents' house in the mail. Frances had sent onesies up from Austin which Dalton didn't know about. People loved buying things for babies. Our little Noah was so loved, so loved, so loved.

⚭

Evi was worn out that night after the baby shower. We got right in bed although it wasn't near our bedtime. She had her chamomile with lavender tea and I made a cup of yerba maté. She stretched all the way out, then tucked up like a cat. There was a heaping mound of baby gifts in our living room—slick, shiny bags the color of Easter eggs, crinkly rainbow-colored tissue paper and those papery ribbons that curled up and sprung out.

Evi yawned, rubbed her eyes.

"Tomorrow you'll help me put the crib together?" she asked.

"If you pay me for labor," I said, tapping my mouth.

She leaned over to kiss me.

"You have to pay for parts too," I said, tapping my mouth.

"You're such a greedy hard-ass," she said, kissing me again.

"Nothing's free. You know this," I said, leaning over to feel her mouth on mine again. And again.

"You think Dalton's okay?" she asked when we were finished.

I took a deep breath in, let it out.

"I think he will be. He's handling his shit right now the best way he can," I said.

I heard a police siren in the distance, thought of the notebook in my locker and how surprised Evi would be when I gave it to her.

As I was falling asleep I couldn't stop thinking about Evi, Dad, Mom, Dalton, Noah, work, how scary the world was and how it was on me to protect my family. Every decision I was making was in order to protect my family. Protecting Mom from Dad's betrayal, protecting Dad from Dalton, protecting Dalton from himself and the darkness, protecting Noah and Evi from anything that could ever hurt them. I'd read in a baby name book when I was a kid that Eamon meant *guardian*. That's what I was. That was what I got paid to do. That's what I would continue to be. Guardian. Guardian of these streets, this city. Guardian of my home, my little family.

Dalton and I went for an early run the next morning. Too early. I rolled up to the park ten minutes late and apologized.

"Do you think we look alike?" I asked him as we set off. We ran the same four-mile trail through the park often. It was June. The world was buzzing, lush, exploding. Evi was popping soon, her pregnant belly reflected in the green of the trail, the tree branches flush with leaves. It was a birdsong morning and I felt good. Dalton looked like he'd crossed a threshold in his mind about our dad, like he'd let it fully sink in. And now? Now he was floating, like he felt good too.

"I don't think so...not really. Do you?" he asked me.

We were both only beginning to breathe heavily. I found my rhythm and paced myself to remain steady with him. The trail was narrow, our feet drumming.

"I've been thinking about it, looking for it, but no. Maybe we will when we get older?" I said.

"Calvin was with Penelope like that same week he was with Mom. Maybe even the same day. We have no clue what happened. He says it was only once but do you believe him? I don't," Dalton said when we got to the first hill. To my right, a family of rabbits rushed further into the forest. A hawk screamed above us. I felt impossibly alive, pounded my feet against the dirt, my thighs felt so good from the burn.

"I don't think it matters," I said.

Dalton stopped at the top of the hill and stepped off the trail. Put his hands on his waist.

"I think it matters if they were carrying on some sort of torrid love affair for years...maybe he was in love with her. Maybe she was so depressed all the time because she was in love with him but they couldn't be together," he said, breathing hard. He laced his fingers on top of his head.

I stopped and stood next to him.

"I hear you," I said. "You're right. If that's what happened, then it matters."

"The thing is I don't think I want to know. Like, I know enough. I called Steve Boone, told him he was right. I'd found my real father and it wasn't him. I didn't tell him it was Calvin. I apologized and he asked me for what and I said I didn't know. All I know is that Calvin is my dad, he lied about it and now I know the truth. That's enough," he said.

"For *now* it's enough?" I asked. I pushed. I didn't shove.

"Until I get to the point where I've processed it fully, yes," he said.

Dad had asked Dalton if he wanted a paternity test and Dalton said, *why the hell not.* They got one done. Dad was Dad and they had the paper proof that Dalton immediately burned.

Dalton turned and got back on the trail. I followed him. We were quiet the rest of the time. When we were finished and I was standing next to my truck, I gave him a sweaty hug. When I pulled away I took my hands, touched both of his ears.

"We do kind of have the same ears," I said, examining them. Smallish. Attached lobes.

"You think these are Royce ears?" he said.

"Yep. I bet Noah'll have these ears," I said, smiling. I told him I was heading home to put the crib together.

"One month, right?" he asked.

I checked the date. Yes.

"Literally one month from today is her due date."

One month until I could hold Noah and tell him I was his papa. *One month.*

Dalton

I GOT THE SCREEN PRINTER TO PRINT MORE B'S BIKE SHOP logos on tiny T-shirts for Baby Noah in every color they had—school bus yellow, sunset orange, cotton ball white, witchy black, night sky navy, Granny Smith green, azalea pink, morning glory blue, plum purple, heartbeat red, earthy brown, dusky grey—twelve little B's for one little baby. I'd found myself thinking about him a lot, how Eamon being a father would change things. I was looking forward to it, to all of it. My bloodstream flooded with adrenaline-excitement when I thought about getting the phone call that Baby Noah was on his way. I examined those feelings against how I felt when Frances was pregnant with my baby. I put on my brain goggles, held some beakers up to the light.

Specimen one: Having a baby with Frances would've meant being tied to Frances for the rest of my life. I didn't know if I wanted to do that. I didn't try to talk her into getting an abortion. I didn't try to talk her out of it. I truly would've been okay if she'd decided to keep it. She didn't.

Specimen two: Evangeline having Eamon's baby. I felt more excited about Noah than sad about me not having a baby with Frances. I was stoked about my nephew and only a tiny bit jealous I didn't have a family of my own. It wasn't something I'd wanted before, but felt the twitch of realization that once Noah was here, maybe I'd want a child. Maybe I'd wish I was married too. But it was just a twitch. There, and gone again. Quick.

And also.

Specimen three: Penelope and Calvin. What was she thinking? What was he thinking? It would be impossible to be happy in a situation like that. Clearly not the ideal way to bring a child into the world, and yet here I was. Here I am.

I told Frances about Calvin being my dad. One night I drunk-dialed her, told her everything. The next morning she called me first thing, asked if I'd been telling her the truth. She was surprisingly sweet to me about it. Kept saying *oh Dalton I'm so sorry* and it impressed me how she had the ability to surprise me in both good and bad ways, over and over again.

I stood Cassidy up the night I found out about Dad. Once I got home from The Darl Inn I called her and apologized. I didn't tell her what happened but I told her it was important and to say I was feeling fucked up was putting it lightly. She was quick to forgive and I felt guilty about that.

Finally, in June I invited Cassidy to my place. Told her I'd cook for her and she said it could be fun for us to cook together. She was leaving the next week to spend the rest of the summer in Palo Alto. The women in my life were moving away and with Noah coming, that would keep Eamon and Evangeline busy. I resisted the urge to feel abandoned. There were times when I felt like I was beginning to heal from Calvin's revelation but I was still too tender to tell. Like the time I cut my chin skateboarding and had to get stitches. Or when Eamon and I cut our fingers on Halloween when we were kids. That part of my face, that part of my finger felt like it didn't belong to me for a week or so. The part of me that had felt abandoned for all those years was there, tender to the touch. I didn't want to examine those feelings yet but sometimes I creaked open the door, peeked in. And when it was too much, I gave the door a good slam.

Cassidy came over in a dress. She never wore dresses.

"Look at it," she said, holding the hem up and closer so I could see the fabric covered in vintage bicycles. The rose bush tattoo on her upper thigh underneath it. I let my fingertips rest on her skin and she got on tiptoes to kiss my cheek. "I love your long hair, your beard. Have I ever told you?" she said, putting her hand on my face.

"I don't think so. Thank you. Your dress is snazzy. You're snazzy," I said. Sometimes I'd look at her and wonder where she came from. *What are you doing here? No, stay. Stay.*

"Thank you, fine gentleman," she said before she started unloading things from her cloth grocery bag. I reached in and helped.

Fresh chicken thighs and legs, a medium-sized bag of brown rice, a small bag of yellow onions, cilantro and coconut milk, a jalapeño pepper, and four square glass bottles of Indian spices—curries and powders the glory-color of liquid sunshine, red clay earth. She'd bought some black-bottled wine and a tub of lemon sorbet and made herself at home, put them in the fridge and freezer.

"So my mom was married to this guy from Trinidad when I was a kid and he used to make this chicken so spicy it made my eyes water, made my tongue burn from my throat but I *loved* it. I loved it," Cassidy said, acting out her watering eyes, the tongue on fire. She rolled her eyes back in her head and made a yakking sound that made me smile.

"And that's what you're making us tonight," I said.

"Absolutely."

She asked me for a big pot and I got it out for her.

"Technically we're supposed to marinate the chicken for hours but we'll skip that part and rub the spices in. I won't tell if you won't tell," she said.

I locked my mouth, threw away the key. I found a bowl for her so she could make the curry slurry.

"My mom has been married three times, none of those times to my father," Cassidy said. I liked when she told me about her family because she was taking me someplace I couldn't get to on my own. I loved hearing about other people's families. She hadn't asked me about Steve Boone and the paternity test. She didn't press for more info when I stood her up. I asked her if it were okay if I didn't want to talk about it and she said yes. The not-pressing-it part of her made me trust her more. I wanted to trust her.

I was instructed to put the garlic and tomato in my food processor, all three things she'd made sure I had before she came over. I added the onion and black pepper too, the cilantro. Cassidy skinned and rinsed the chicken, put it in a bowl. When I was finished processing my side of things, she used a spoon to scoop it out and covered the chicken.

"So get in here and let's rub it in, since we're skipping the marinating part," she said, motioning her head for me to dig my hands in the bowl. Our hands, together in all that chicken mix. Cassidy linked her pinky with mine and squished. "This sounds so gross," she said. The watery mix and the chicken bones rang against the sides of the glass bowl like bells.

"Sounds delicious," I said.

When that part was finished she heated oil in the pot, added her curry slurry. We put the chicken in the pot, covered it. Lifted the lid after a couple minutes, added water. While that was cooking, I got the rice started.

I had Duke Ellington playing. The first track on a jazz piano album I liked to put on when I couldn't think of anything else.

Ellington, Albert Ammons, Thelonious Monk, Oscar Peterson Trio. It was my go-to whether I was cleaning or getting in the shower or having people over and by people I meant Frances or Evangeline and Eamon. I didn't have other people over very often. I'd avoided having Cassidy over because I didn't know what it would mean to have her in my house. I didn't know what it would mean when the sun set and the moon rose and Cassidy was *still* in my house. Would she stay? Would I want her to? She was extraordinarily easy to be around and had become a Venus flytrap of getting me to open up to her—opening wide and asking me something about myself, snapping shut with me inside once I told her things. There I was in her mouth, telling her things I'd intended on keeping to myself.

There I was in her mouth, having pulled her close to me and kissed her.

Cassidy moved around a lot when she was a kid. Cassidy's grandmother was Nicaraguan so she grew up down there too. Cassidy was one-quarter Nicaraguan, one-quarter black, one-quarter white, one-quarter Costa Rican. Cassidy was a mix of everything gorgeous in this world. Cassidy spoke English and Spanish and some Portuguese. Cassidy had almost gotten married but left the groom at the altar—a runaway bride who ran half a mile away where her best girlfriend, ex-maid of honor was waiting in the car. Cassidy only started biking after her ex moved to Costa Rica and left his bike in her garage. Cassidy's ex only moved to Costa Rica because he'd fallen in love with it after he'd gone down there with her once to visit her family. Cassidy rolled her eyes and grunted when she talked about her exes. Cassidy usually smelled like vanilla but that night Cassidy smelled like coconuts.

"You smell different. You smell really good, but it's different," I said, leaning in.

"You're sure it's not the curry slurry?" she asked, tending to the chicken.

"It's coconuts. This is going to sound nuts but it's the same way my sister-in-law smells. I'm used to it. I dig it. It smells good," I said.

"Gotcha. But for the record, you should've said coconuts. You should've said, 'This is going to sound *coconuts*,'" she said.

"Please forgive me," I said, putting my hand to my chest before I stirred the rice.

"I know your sister-in-law is Evangeline. I got it all up here," she said, pointing to her head.

"Your brother is Gibson," I said.

She nodded.

"Now, we're getting somewhere," she said.

Were we? Were we getting somewhere? The rice was bubbling so I turned it down. Although I opened up to her from time to time, Cassidy could've seen me as closed off. I never told her what happened those nights I escaped to the chintzy comforts of rural Kentucky's The Darl Inn. I wasn't turned off by how much she wanted me which was a thing I'd heard of, but never felt for any woman. Being desired made me desire. My stomach growled and I realized perhaps Cassidy was talking about the food when she'd said, *now we're getting somewhere.* My face warmed with embarrassment. I put the lid on the rice.

When the food was ready, I got down my good bowls, the ones Frances had gotten me. They were thick and deep and purple. We filled them with brown rice first which Cassidy had mixed with a spoonful of creamy coconut milk. We put the chicken on top. We sat at my kitchen table. I poured our wine. And maybe people were being hyperbolic when they talked about food to die for, but I would've been just fine if our Trinidadian chicken meal was my last. That's how good it was. At one point I did an exaggerated overtly sexual moan and asked her if she wanted to come over every night and cook for me. She said absolutely she would.

⚵

After dinner and sorbet, we sat out back on the deck sharing a cigarette, our thighs touching.

"I have a surprise for you," I said.

"Do I need to close my eyes?"

"Why the hell not. Yes. Close your eyes please," I said. I took her hand, led her to the living room, guided her to the end of the couch closest to the piano. Told her to keep them closed. I opened the window for Miss Margaret. She'd thanked me the day before for playing so beautifully and smiled when she'd said it. Patted my arm.

I sat at the piano and played part of a song I knew Cassidy would recognize immediately. I was right. She gasped and I turned to her. She opened her eyes.

"Dalton!"

I kept playing "Cassidy" by Grateful Dead. Her namesong.

"Did you learn this for me or you already knew how to play it?" she asked. For a moment it looked like she might cry. She didn't seem like the kind of girl to cry over something like this and when the moment passed I wondered if I'd imagined it.

"I did not know it. I learned it. I can learn songs fast. I learned it for you," I said.

"This is better than the sex we aren't having," she said by the light of the amber salt lamp I had next to the piano. Her coconut smell evoked yellow and blue surf shacks. Ocean mornings having fish and beer and small oranges for breakfast.

I played a more difficult piece for her I'd only played a few times before. Chopin. Kept my eyes on the sheet music in front of me and everything. I was unabashedly showing off, trying to impress her. It worked. She leaned over and kissed me. And kept kissing me. We were kissing until we weren't.

"Want to know my truth?" I asked her.

"Yes."

"I like kissing you," I said.

"Right. But you don't want to sleep with me," she said.

"Absolutely not true."

"So what's the deal?" she asked.

"I want to do things the right way."

"I don't want to scare you off," she said.

"You're not. You won't." I shook my head no.

"I'm leaving next week and I'll be gone until September. What will be here when I come back?" she asked, tapping the spot on my chest holding my bloody, thumping heart.

"I will," I said.

"Be sweet to yourself," she said. And I knew she meant about all of the things I wasn't telling her. *Be sweet to yourself.*

I started playing "Cassidy" again and she did end up spending the night in my bed but we didn't have sex although things happened that made us both moan. Both warm and wavy. Both panting and sweating in the June night heat with the windows open and the frogs and crickets behind my house so loud I thought Jesus had appeared in the clouds. I could've sworn I heard the trumpet sound.

I'd been avoiding Dad because I didn't feel comfortable around him anymore. I didn't want to recognize anything about myself in him and feel stupid for not recognizing it sooner.

But one day when I knew he was home alone, I went over there. He was in his chair. I sat down on the couch, watched him cry.

"Did you love Penelope?" I asked.

He sniffed and blew his nose.

"Yes. I loved her because Loretta loved her so much," he said.

The TV was on, the sound turned down—an infomercial for some old Westerns on DVD.

"So how could you do something like that when you knew how much Mom loved her? That's—" I stopped, kept myself from cursing in front of him, in his house. "That's messed up. That's the *worst* possible thing you could've done." I said slowly. If Penelope were there I would've told her the same thing.

"I know that," he said.

My face, as calm as a coin.

"It was obviously the biggest mistake of my life, but you're a blessing," he said, leaning towards me.

"Was Penelope in love with you?"

"I don't know."

I searched my heart for the glimmer of truth, the sharp needle-point of a lie. I felt neither. My radar was off and I couldn't root myself about it. Penelope was close-mouthed about her passion-ate feelings for anything else besides music and me. She'd never pretended to be in love with Steve Boone and I knew nothing about her past relationships outside of little bits Mom would spill into conversation sometimes.

"I swear it only happened once," he said.

I imagined it happening on a wet, dark, desperate night. I imagined it happening on a sunny, warm morning, Penelope's eyes barely open, her brain swimming deep in a bath of prescrip-tion sleep. I imagined Dad coming back home, taking off his uni-form or whatever he was wearing, climbing into bed with Mom, his body permanently watermarked with Penelope. Stained.

"I just do not see how you could've done something like that...how you could keep it from Mom and E and me for so long. I—" I ran out of words. He looked pitiful there in his chair, crying. This time, silently begging me to keep his secret. I sat there with my head in my hands for a while before I left. I was no closer to knowing what I wanted to know, had no clearer vision of the past that had been hidden so well from me. I wanted to ask him how he juggled those emotions, how he separated his feelings for Eamon, his legitimate child, from his feelings for me, the bastard. But I realized that in his heart, he probably *hadn't* separated his feelings. It wasn't like he introduced Eamon as one way and me as another. I could still hear him vividly saying, *these are my boys* when we were younger, anytime we met someone new at the police station, anytime we ran into anyone he knew when we were out in the world.

I was so small the first time he took both Eamon and me to

work with him. We got suckers and sat on the floor under the captain's desk while Dad laughed and talked to him. One of the new female officers came into the room and asked, *and who are these little dumplings underneath here?* And Dad said, *these are my boys.* I remembered it because I pretended like what he was saying was one-hundred percent true. I had a police officer for a dad and he claimed me. Called me his boy, even when I thought I wasn't his.

Cassidy was gone and I'd miss her. Couple days after I talked to Dad alone, Eamon told me Evi's doctor said there was a possibility Noah could come earlier. He told me he knew for sure he was leaving police officer life behind once Noah was born. We were at our parents' and he told me this quietly because he didn't want them to know yet. He hadn't told Evi. Just Brian and me.

Evi and Mom were in the kitchen making popcorn and we were going to watch old home movies together. I wasn't entirely in the mood for it but hadn't wanted to say no. I felt an ache and couldn't place it until I realized it was Cassidy being gone but so what? Was it because Frances was gone too? I didn't even have a girl to hang out with. Eamon had a wife and a baby boy on the way. I had a bike shop, an old truck. I had a rented house. I had a dead mom and a father who didn't want to publicly claim me. I was going to the dark spot in my brain, my heart. That dark spot was lifted temporarily when I knew Eamon was serious about quitting the force.

"I know you're serious, man. I'm excited for you," I said quietly after we were sure Mom was out of earshot. She'd walked past us a moment earlier and touched the back of my neck, remarking on how long my hair had gotten.

Eamon looked a lot like our Dad when he was thinking. He stood across from me in the hallway, making that familiar face.

"I am serious," he said. "But The Pact stands." He slapped my shoulder before walking off.

It'd become a corny inside joke for us but something about it made me feel slightly panicky, like being miles away from home and suddenly wondering if I'd left the oven on. We all sat down in the living room and watched the home movies like we did at least once a year.

Eamon's favorite: He and I are playing touch football in the backyard but then he decides he wants it to be tackle. Dad is holding the camera close to my face. I have the football safely tucked under my arm. Eamon is offscreen and suddenly he tackles me. I go down hard, flip him over, start pounding away at him with my tiny fists. Dad says, *these are my boys* into the camera mic and pans to Mom in a floppy sunhat, sitting in the lawn chair next to him, drinking sweet tea with lemon, the ice clinking against the glass.

Evi's favorite: Eamon is a crawling baby, laughing. He is on the kitchen floor with Dad and Mom comes in the door. Eamon cries as soon as he sees her. Mom says, *he cries when he sees me in case he needs something, he wants to let me know.* She scoops him up in her arms and touches his chin with her index finger, kisses his mouth. Dad turns the camera off.

Mom's favorite: She and Penelope are standing in their overalls, waving at the camera. They are both mere days away from giving birth to Eamon and me. They hold hands and someone off-camera takes a photograph. The photograph hung in my parents' foyer. I looked at it and saw two mothers, both mine.

Dad's favorite: When they took Eamon and me down to Disney World not long after Penelope died. Eamon and I have Mickey ears with our names stitched on them and we are twelve years old and mortified but we let Dad take the video anyway because even back then, we could recognize that one day...one day in the future we would get a kick out of it. We knew the timestamp of nostalgia had a way of tilting things like that in our favor.

My favorite: A small moment when Eamon and I are ten. Christmastime. Penelope got us matching *Jurassic Park* sweatshirts. Eamon and I are sitting in front of the tree, holding the sweatshirts in front of us. Penelope would only be with us for one more Christmas. Mom has the video camera and it turns off and back on again. Penelope is at the piano playing Christmas carols and looks happy. I join her on the piano bench and we play one together. She does the pedals. *Soft, sostenuto, sustaining*—she would instruct me quietly when I was very young and still learning—the pedal names from left to right. I am wearing my sweatshirt. We both look so happy. Dad is wearing a Santa Claus hat. Penelope knows Calvin is my biological father but nothing in her face reveals that, even when I stared at the screen, even when I knew what I was looking for. Penelope throws her head back and laughs brightly. Christmas-tree-light-in-a-dark-room bright.

We watched those videos, Mom alternating between digging her hand in the popcorn bowl, wiping it off and flipping through the home movie DVDs in the binder next to her. Evi made her way to the floor, sitting with her back up against the couch.

"It is *very* uncomfortable growing an entire person," she said, adjusting herself. "Noah tucks a foot up in my ribcage, in this same spot and he won't budge."

"Eamon did the same thing," Mom said, pointing. For a moment I almost forgot she wasn't my biological mother and waited for her to mention what I was like in utero. No. The womb that bore me had been burned away, cremated and buried. The seed, in the chair across the room.

"The only thing that would work to move him was crawling around on my hands and knees like this," Mom said, assuming the position.

Evi got on her hands and knees too. She crawled in front of us, turned at the couch.

"Are you kidding me, I think he's moving!" Evi said by the time she'd made it to the kitchen.

At times I couldn't stand to look at Dad. I hated being in his presence. I looked over at him sitting there in his chair and I thought about how I hadn't known him at all and probably never would. I'd never know him like Eamon did and that was what made me jealous. I felt dizzy and wanted to leave but Mom started giggling as she was crawling around on the floor. Eamon started laughing too. Soon the room was filled with bubbly laughter and I shook my head at them. If someone had been recording video of that moment, it oddly would've gone on my list of favorites. The night had started with me in a foul mood, thinking about everylittlething about my life I didn't enjoy. Everything I felt cheated out of. But it'd ended like this. The dog-eared possibility of a feeling I could save for later. Endings were as important as beginnings.

VI.

Evangeline

NOAH WAS BORN AT FOUR FIFTY-FIVE IN THE MORNING. Once we were all settled in my hospital room and my dad and Calvin had left together so they could come back with a decent breakfast for all of us, Dalton softly tapped on the door. Loretta told him it was safe to come in.

He walked in sleepy-eyed, carrying a cup of coffee and suddenly, I wanted one. I hadn't had a cup of real coffee in months; I was scared it would hurt the baby. And even though I was planning on nursing Noah whenever he wanted, I figured a sip of real coffee wouldn't hurt us. I held out both of my hands to Dalton and he handed me his cup of coffee without missing a beat. He leaned over and kissed my forehead as I took a careful sip. Loretta stood up and handed Noah to Dalton—a blue and white swaddled bundle of summer baby joy in the middle of a room missing some air. I asked my mom if she would open the window for me. I wanted to feel a breeze because a breeze would feel like Eamon was in the room. Like how when I was in third grade, I'd go to my Orthodox Jewish best friend's house for Seder and we'd leave the door open so Elijah could slip in.

Loretta and my mom were taking turns oohing and aahing over which parts of Noah looked most like me and most like Eamon and most like other people in both of our families. Loretta was complaining the bed was too close to the window and Noah would catch a cold although it was at least eighty-five degrees outside and the sun hadn't fully come up yet.

What I remember so vividly is Dalton never made me feel like I was second to Noah. Loretta and my mom were overly concerned with Noah having what he needed and my mom was very gracious in letting Loretta hold Noah first and for longer. Noah was all that was left of Eamon. But Dalton went out of his way to dote on me, ask me if I needed anything. He seemed equally impressed with the wonder of a newborn baby *and* his mother, who'd done the hardest bits of work. He stood next to me and I sat up in bed. He nodded towards the tiny bundle of Noah he was holding in his arms. I was impressed Dalton wasn't skittish or weird about holding a baby.

"So you're the little dude who's been kicking me," Dalton said to him, so softly.

I thought about how Noah would see Dalton looking back at him and wonder who *he* was. How I would look down at Noah and wonder who he was. How I could make a person with someone who wasn't here anymore.

My dad and Calvin came back and we ate breakfast. Afterwards, Mom said they'd all step out to give me rest. I sent for the nurse to come and take Noah to the nursery. Merit and some other ballet girls texted and said for me to call them as soon as I woke up so they could come see me. Dalton was the last person out of the room; he sat down on the edge of the bed before he left.

"I'm going downstairs to buy Noah a football," Dalton said, wiping his eyes.

The fluffy football stays in the rocking chair in Noah's room, most of the time. Sometimes Dalton picks it up and lies on his back and throws it up in the air and catches it while we're talking. I like to watch how he throws it and how he holds it after he catches it. Sometimes he looks over at me then back up at the ball. He never drops it.

Dalton is reaching up into the cabinet for something when I hear the glass breaking. I turn over my shoulder to see Eamon's black U of L mug smashed on the kitchen floor. It's not shattered and scattered, but it's broken into big chunks—the handle, some of the side and the rest of it.

"Fuck fuck fuck," Dalton says in a voice I've never heard him use before. It sounds thin and fragile.

"It's okay. We can fix it," I say, crouching.

"I don't think so."

I hold it up for him and show him it's only in a few pieces. It can be glued.

"But it won't be perfect," he says.

"It doesn't matter."

"Evangeline, it matters. It *does* matter."

"We can fix it," I say, standing straight again.

"That's not what I'm talking about."

"What *are* you talking about?"

"I need some air," he says, loosening his tie. He walks towards the front door and opens it. The snow-cold air takes my breath. I've never seen him this panicky before. Not when Eamon died, not when Noah was fussing and fussing. Never. I don't know what to do. I watch him grab his coat and throw it on. He pulls his snow hat on his head and goes into his pockets for his gloves. I do the same thing. Get my big coat from the rack. My hat, gloves and boots. I hold the hem of my dress up so it won't get snow on it, but maybe it doesn't matter. I feel like I'm in one of the period pieces I love so much, wildly chasing a man out into the snow in my best dress.

"I need some air," he says again.

I'm so nervous. I feel sick. I tell him.

"You should go back inside. I need some air. We've been trapped in the house," he says.

"Trapped? You feel trapped here. I told you that yesterday but you denied it. I knew it," I say. I feel sicker.

"No. It's not what I meant. I meant the snow, the lack of being able to get out in the world. Do not read into this. I didn't mean *trapped*. Evi, you know what I mean!" he says, raising his voice.

"Wait. Are you mad at me? I have no clue what happened back there. You're upset the mug broke?" I ask. A snowplow is scraping its way up the street. The snow is still falling and everything is quiet except for the truck's metallic scraping and our boots crunching.

"Did you hear that?" Dalton asks. He turns around to look at me for the first time since the mug fell in the kitchen. His cheeks are flushed.

Before I can answer, I hear it.

Caesura.

A low growling—stretching above us, a deep crack in the sky.

Eamon

MY PARENTS' FOURTH OF JULY PARTY WAS DOPE. DAD
spent an ungodly amount of money on fireworks. He said it was
not only because of the Fourth but also because my birthday was
five days away, Dalton's six days after, Evi's two weeks out. We were
all July babies and Noah would be too. Dad put his wallet and
guilt and frustration and pain into those fireworks, both mine
and Evi's families oohing and aahing as his glittered penance
shot straight up into the sky and popped—raining sparkles all lit
up and out and back down again. Exploding. Transforming.

I'd worked overnight and slept before Evi and I went to the
party. Frances was back in town for the holiday and Dalton
brought her along. I'd walked past her talking to Evi, heard Frances say she felt like she'd commit suicide if she had to be pregnant
for nine *whole* months and didn't Evi just want to die? My sweet
Evi shook her head and kindly replied, *no, Frances, I don't want to*

die. And I thought, *I don't want to die either.* It was the kind of day that made me want to live forever. The entire neighborhood was abuzz and my cousin's kids had brought their friends. I walked into the kitchen and saw kids I'd never seen before. I patted one red-haired boy on the top of his head and didn't realize it was Brian's kid until he'd run out the back door, the screen slamming hard. Brian was working but Lucy must've come in when I wasn't looking.

One of my little cousins asked me if I'd ever shot a bad guy. I told him no. He asked if I'd ever pulled my gun on a bad guy. I told him yes. Several times. Another asked if I'd come to his summer camp for career week and I happily agreed, told him yes, unless Baby Noah was coming into the world that day.

"Baby Noah is coming so soon!" he said, before running through the grass towards another small group of kids.

I sat down and had a beer, watched the sun begin to fade away. We'd set fireworks off already but the big bonanza would begin once the sun had fully gone down. I was overstimulated. I rooted myself in my chair, my belly full of baked beans, potato salad, cheeseburgers and apple pie. I watched Evi talking to her mother. Her dad and mine were putting more dogs on the grill. My mom and Dalton were loading up the cooler with more ice.

When I thought about who I'd be when I was no longer a police officer, I pictured a long darkened corridor, a tunnel with a swinging lightbulb at the end, the brick exposed. A door. And I couldn't find out what was behind the door until I turned the knob. I felt a stinging impatience to open that door, to hold my son, to catch the swinging lightbulb—careful not to burn my hand—steady it. Still it.

I had another beer once the big fireworks show was starting. Evi was next to me drinking a tall glass of lemon water. All of that colored light flashed across the widening sky, sprinkling down at the river. Wispy wires of electricity, green and blue and white and red and orange, spinning webs across the sky. The humid Kentucky summer air, thick with grey smoke. In a backyard of a house across the river, colored specks of children held flickery paper golden-lit lanterns in the air and let them go. I felt my breath catch in my throat, watching them. I didn't know why.

My shift was over on the morning of July 11, but I heard the street name I'd just passed on the police scanner. Domestic disturbance. The same residence had called 911 a week earlier. I told the operator I was close. I heard Brian's voice on the radio saying he'd swing by too. Both of us would be there, take care of it.

The night before, I'd kissed Evi's belly after I'd kissed her mouth. Noah was due to come into the world in less than three weeks.

"I love you. Be safe," she'd said. Like always.

Before I locked the door behind me I went back inside and kissed her again. Told her I loved her.

It was quiet at the residence. I got there before Brian, parked my patrol car in front of the house. I went to the door and knocked. A man identified himself as the stepfather of an unruly teenager in the house. I asked the man if he had any weapons inside. I heard a clattering and put my hand on my gun. I'd done this plenty of times before. I knew what I was doing. We had stepped down off the porch, I had my hand on my gun. I was watching the house. I knew what I was doing. I turned to see Brian's patrol car coming towards us, gravel-pops dusting the peachy-gold early morning light.

It wasn't the gravel popping so close to me. I heard the sound, a familiar sound. Gunshots. Loud. Close.

Caesura.

A word I'd heard from Evi. Or maybe Dalton. It was a musical term or a ballet term. It was a lemony word when it caught the light. It meant break or pause. My adrenaline did not pause. I heard that word in my breath and brain, felt my heart beating wildly. I heard another gunshot too. Another. The grass was wet when I fell back and I was leaving. I was going. I heard Brian's voice near me, close. He told me I'd be okay. He told me to hang on. *Hang on, Eamon. Eamon, stay with me.* He told me help was on the way and *officer down* was detached from meaning. The words I'd written in my notebook, locked away at work. Those secrets. *Evi, I'm getting out.* Maybe Brian could give them to Evi. I'd been shot but I would be okay. This wasn't the end. I was reaching for the knob, steadying the light. Maybe Noah and I would be in the hospital at the same time. Maybe we would be roomies. I would see my son. I would see my wife. This was not the end. Grey radio static, birds singing. I prayed. *Jesus. Jesus.*

Caesura.

It was a pause.

Only a pause.

How could it be the end?

Sergeant Eamon Royce, thirty-two, was killed in the line of duty on Monday, July 11 while attempting to investigate a domestic disturbance. Sergeant Royce had been on the force for ten years. Originally from Louisville, Eamon was born on July 9 to Calvin and Loretta Royce. He played football at Indian Hills High School and graduated from Western Kentucky University with a degree in criminal justice. He enjoyed fishing, especially with his family on their trips to the Upper Peninsula. He also loved cheesy eighties music and power ballads. Eamon was a kind man, an excellent leader and role model for the community. He was a devoted husband, son, brother and friend. He loved Jesus and a good snowstorm. He was a member of Oak Grove Baptist Church, where he had once worked security. He met his wife Evangeline Royce (née Cooper), also a member, there, and liked to say that for him, it was love at first sight. Eamon was funny and full of life, almost impossibly so. He was light in a dark room and will be so greatly missed. He is survived by Evangeline and their unborn child, who Evangeline and Eamon have already named Noah. Eamon is also survived by his parents and his brother and best friend, Dalton Berkeley-Royce, as well as a big family of numerous aunts, uncles and cousins. The Royce family would like to thank the local and national communities for their kindness and continued outpouring of support. Services will be held at Oak Grove Baptist Church on Saturday, July 16 at 10:00 AM with visitation from 5-8 PM on Friday, July 15. Interment will be in La Grange Cemetery.

Dalton

CAESURA.

My brother Eamon was dead and the world kept going.

But not mine.

Not my world.

Fuck the rest of the world.

Mine stopped.

Not paused.

Stopped.

I found Evangeline peeing across the kitchen floor before her legs gave out. I stepped around the puddle and picked her up. She was delirious and I was only able to hold it together because she couldn't. I put her on the floor of the bathroom and told her I was covering my eyes and I did. I covered my eyes and wiggled her wet leggings off, her underwear too. I opened my eyes only to go to the bedroom and grab a fresh pair of underwear for her.

I closed my eyes again when I got back to the bathroom. I didn't see her swollen naked pregnant belly, but my fingertips brushed against the skin of it as I wiped her up the best I could with a wet towel, shimmied her underwear up where it belonged. I picked her up and took her upstairs to the bedroom, put her in bed. She was wailing. It took everything inside me not to cover my ears and run out the front door, screaming. I called my parents, I called her parents. I called Merit. I called Detroit and told him. I called Cassidy, told her. I called Frances.

I don't remember making any of those calls.

I got another towel from the bathroom closet and a bottle of neon-blue spray from underneath the kitchen sink and cleaned up Evi's pee puddle. I put the dirty towel in the hamper. I had spent so many nights in Eamon and Evangeline's house. I knew where everything was, where everything went. My world had stopped and life had changed forever but the hamper was still in the corner of their bedroom. The clean towels were still on the bottom shelf of the bathroom closet.

I got Evi a glass of water with lemon and sat next to her in bed, both of us weeping. Evi keened—a ghostly sound I'd never heard before. Never wanted to hear again. She screamed and swiped at the glass of water, sent it smashing against the wall where the glass split and the water splashed to the floor. She cried *where is he where is he where did he go* in between heavy sobs and didn't stop repeating it until her mother Rose came into the bedroom, her bloodshot crying eyes rimmed with neon pink. Rose put her hand on Evi's back and shushed her and rubbed. Evi's sobs clenched my heart in a vise. Perhaps I could've been in denial if it weren't for Evi's keening.

"Will you open the window for me?" Evi said later that night. It was raining.

The sheets were getting wet. The wind was blowing hard. There was no thunder.

"I don't know where Eamon is," she said. "I can't find him."

I slept on her floor, at the foot of her bed. I knew she was asleep again when the crying stopped. She woke up in the middle of the night, crying and gasping. Rose was asleep in the blue bedroom and she stepped over me, convinced Evi to take a thick oval white pill with a full glass of lemon water. Rose went back to the blue bedroom. Evi slept again.

Merit came and brought food. Salads with fruit, sandwiches, two trays of lasagna for freezing. She made chamomile with lavender tea for Evangeline and took it to her even when Evi refused to drink it. Evi would only drink lemon water. Evi wouldn't leave her bedroom. After we made Eamon's funeral arrangements, Merit lured her to the kitchen with hot water and lemon and warm almond cookies. While Evi was in the kitchen, I changed the sheets on her bed.

Three different pedals on a piano, three different beating hearts in this house. *Soft, sostenuto, sustaining.* I played piano in the morning and evenings. A way to start and end our days together. On the days I went into work late, I played "Moonlight Sonata" while Noah was having his rice cereal and cinnamon apples. I played "Moon River" while Evi nursed Noah to sleep at night. Sun-white "Clair de Lune" mornings. Moon-blue "In A Sentimental Mood" nights.

I started leaving petals around the house for Evangeline. *Zuzu's petals.* She would be in the shower and come out to pink petals on the bathroom counter. I usually bought the flowers at the grocery store, de-petaled them, threw the thorny long stems in the bed of my truck.

"What is this?" she asked softly, making a cup with one hand and scooping the pink petals into it with the other.

"Zuzu's petals. To…remember we need to hang in there," I said. My coping mechanism was holding her up, reminding her to not let go of the will to live. Holding Evi up became *my* new will to live. My reason. What no one tells you about grief is that you don't want to figure out a way to *live* with it—you want the part of you that hurts to *die* instead. Living with it isn't an option—a part of you *has* to die. Part of me died with Penelope, part of me died out at The Darl Inn after I found out about Calvin. I knew a part of me would have to die with Eamon. I killed those parts of myself. That's what my anger was for. I blew through the second stage of grief and put it to good use.

On that early morning when Noah was born and I held him for the first time, I told him Eamon was his father and he loved him very much. I told him I was his Uncle Dalton and I'd do anything for him to protect him for the rest of my life. I held him and cried. I went down to the gift shop and bought him a soft, fuzzy football. Evi brought him home in the school bus yellow B's T-shirt I'd had made for him.

By Christmastime we were both deep into the depression stage of grief. The short, dark, cold days had taken our breath away. My beard was back and I was growing out my hair again. Evi was too. I'd taken to using her coconut shampoo when I slept over and showered. I told Cassidy that when she came into the shop and sniffed me, identifying it. Cassidy was one class away from being a certified bike mechanic and I'd already told her she was hired. Eamon's death unplugged something inside of me and I was unable to keep things from her. I filtered myself with Evi in a way I didn't have to with Cassidy because Evi was closer. Cassidy was further away.

I could vent to her about the unfairness of Eamon being taken from us so early. *He was so fucking young,* I'd say and not be shy about crying in front of her. I tried my best to let Evi take the grieving wheel when I was around her. He was her husband, the father of her child. It felt unfair for me to hoard the grief from her. But with Cassidy, I could. I'd wonder aloud to her if Eamon knew something like this was coming for him and he just kept it from us. Cassidy said she didn't believe in things like that and I liked that about her. She didn't scare easily. I could be messier with her, spill all over the place, clean myself up before I saw Evi again.

Most nights after I closed the shop, I headed straight to Evi's and was back at the shop sunrise-early, practically sleepwalking after being up with Noah for so much of the night. If I heard him and Evi didn't, I would get up and creep quietly to his room after getting a fresh bottle of breast milk from the fridge. I'd close the door to Noah's bedroom and feed him, rock him back to sleep. I remembered Eamon telling me the color and would never forget it. *Electric pickle juice.* Most nights Noah and I would remain sleeping in that rocking chair until the crick in my neck would wake me up. I'd look at his tiny Royce ears in the dark. They were the same as mine. The same as Eamon's. I'd carefully put Noah in his crib and get back in bed in the blue bedroom. I always stayed in the blue bedroom when I slept over.

When Evi asked me to move in, it felt like I could let out the breath I'd been holding. The lease on my house was up. I told my neighbor Miss Margaret I was moving and even though it was freezing, I opened my living room window that entire week before moving and played piano so she could hear it. I moved all my stuff into Evangeline's and worried everyone we knew would think I was trying to take Eamon's place. I voiced these concerns to Mom and Dad one night when I'd gone over for dinner. Mom had made chicken and dumplings. Evi and Noah were supposed to be coming over too after she stopped by to visit her parents.

Mom's chicken and dumplings were Eamon's favorite. She bowed her head to pray and when she was finished she wiped her eyes with the cloth napkin at her elbow.

"It won't be long until I'll go home to be with Eamon and

Penelope and baby Thomas," she said. I opened my mouth to challenge her on it but she held a finger up at me. "Whether it's tonight or twenty years from now don't matter. You are taking care of your family and that's what's important. Eamon would've done the same thing for you," she said, her voice grief-weary.

"Nobody knew this would happen. All we can do now is deal with it best we can," Dad said.

I remembered exactly what they said and filed the words away because I'd knew I'd refer back to them whenever I felt as weary as Mom's voice. She'd lost so much. If her heart kept beating and she kept going after losing so much I could do it too. I could do this.

Acceptance. When did it happen? Was it the day I put the box of Eamon's stuff in the garage and covered it up with a blanket so Evi wouldn't have to see it when she went down there to get in the freezer? Was it the day I finally took his running shoes out of the foyer and put them out in the garage too? Was it the day that customer came into the bike shop after having moved away and back again and asked how my brother was doing and I told him my brother had been killed in the line of duty? Was it that day? Was it the first day Noah grinned his gummy grin at me with his daddy's syrupy-brown eyes flashing as I held him up high and swooped him back down again? Was it that day? Was it the day I strapped Noah to me and took him out in the garage so I could work on a bike I'd found in someone's curbside trash? Was it that day? Was it the day Frances told me if I was going to live with Evangeline, if I was going to *play house* with Evangeline and try to take Eamon's place then she and I were done forever and I told her, *then it looks like we're done forever*. Was it that day? I'm asking because I don't know what day it was.

There have been several key changes in my life. Moments I knew would affect the rest of it, forever. Loretta telling me Penelope was gone—permanent key change, would never return to the original. Finding out Calvin was my real father. Eamon dying. Eamon, the unfinished melody that would haunt me as long as I lived. No music, no voice, nothing would ever sound the same again. My heart, my soul, everything. *Modulation.*

VII.

Evangeline

THUNDERSNOW.

Quiet.

More thundersnow.

I look up at the billowy pink-greyness over our heads. The street lamp flickers. *Eamon.*

"Are you okay?" I ask him.

"I'm not mad at you." Dalton shakes his head.

"What's wrong?" I ask. Should I be more upset than I am? Why aren't I? The mug isn't a big deal. Truly. We'll glue it and put it back and it doesn't matter. Eamon wouldn't care. He never cared about stuff like that.

My legs are freezing. So is my face.

"Because the mug broke—" I say, trying to get him talking. Explaining himself.

"That was part of it. I'm so…I'm so obsessed with doing this the right way. Obsessed with not making any mistakes. Not even one," he says.

He starts talking about how that's impossible because God is in control, not us. How it's both liberating and restricting. How in his mind he had this whole perfect date night at home planned out with dinner and his suit and then the mug broke. The mug breaking is proof. I stop him. I hold out my hand and grab his arm again and snatch him around because at this point we're still walking in the middle of the road, the snow falling all around us, complicated grumbles of thunder echoing off the dark emptiness of the neighborhood. Our untied boots clomping next to each other, keeping time.

"Proof of what?" I say.

"Proof things can happen and there's nothing we can do about it."

"Do you think either of us needs more proof of that?" I've twisted my face up into such an uncomfortable position, it's giving me a headache. "After your mom dying when you were so young and not knowing your dad was your dad and after both of us losing Eamon like that…and me being a mom like this and Noah never meeting his dad…do you really think we need a reminder terrible, awful things happen every day?" I feel like a bird because my voice is so screechy and this ridiculous dress and this coat. I'm flapping my arms.

"I'm just nervous, that's all," Dalton says.

"It's too cold out here. Let's go back. Can we please go back?"

"I do not want to let him down. Not Eamon, not Noah. And I don't want to let *you* down, either. I'm obsessed with doing all of this right," he says.

Dalton and I stand there in the silence between us as the snow-plow scrapes and scrapes and scrapes and scrapes.

"Evi, I'm going to walk to Cassidy's place. I promise I'm coming back," he says.

"This is about Cassidy?" I ask. The darkish broken bright of my heart is twisted. Why would I ever have thought he was mine and only mine? No matter what he's told me. There is someone else and there will probably always be someone else because no matter how hard I wish it or pray for it, Dalton is not mine and he never was.

"This is not about Cassidy. But I need to talk to her," he says.

I turn and begin walking away. There is nothing left for me to do.

"Evi. I have to tell her to her face that it's over. She's been a good friend to me. She's been there for me. I owe her this," he says behind me.

"Are you saying I'm not there for you?"

"Absolutely not! Why are you saying these things?"

"Because you freaked out on me and you've never freaked out on me!" I say, turning around.

The snowplow is scraping next to us now. Loud. We have to walk in the opposite direction of our house in order to stay on the street and avoid knee-high snow drifts.

"I'm sorry. I'm sorry about what happened in there and I'm sorry I have to do this but I promise I'm coming back, I promise I love you, I promise you can trust me," he says, his white breath rolling out in heated puffs.

"Just use your key. I'm locking the door," I say, swivelling to walk back towards the house.

"Evi," he says.

"I'm cold," I say.

I don't turn around. I don't cry until I get in the house and lock the door.

Dalton

"JUST USE YOUR KEY. I'M LOCKING THE DOOR," EVI SAYS, swivelling to walk back towards the house.

"Evi," I say.

"I'm cold," she says.

Cassidy was in California when Eamon was killed. It took a while to fall back together when she returned to Kentucky. I found comfort there, where I always had. I hadn't lied to Evi. Cassidy and I still never slept together, but we were clearly more than friends. I turn around and head to her place. I text her I'm on the way.

Eamon's favorite mug is broken and material things don't matter, but besides Noah, they're all we have left. I'm very protective of his stuff. Living in his house, holding his baby, seeing his mug still in the cabinet matter. Loving his wife matters. I love Eamon's wife and Eamon is gone. I love Eamon's wife more than I love Cassidy, but I *do* love Cassidy. Enough. I love Cassidy enough to tell her to her face that I love Evangeline.

It's at least a mile and a half to Cassidy's and I'm walking slow in the ice and snow so I don't break both ankles. This may not have been my best idea, walking miles in a blizzard and ice storm but I had to get out before Eamon's ghost suffocated me. I had to get out before Eamon's ghost suffocated me, because I would've let it.

Cassidy opens the door in her pajamas and smiles at me.

"You walked here?" she asks, looking at her empty driveway.

I stomp the snow off my boots before going inside.

"Are you wearing a suit? This is fancy," she says, looking at my pants, guessing at what else is hidden under my winter coat.

I take off my hat. I don't say anything.

"What's wrong?" she asks.

She's made hot chocolate and cookies. She has been waiting for me. Not only tonight, but for a while. She's been waiting for me. The darkish broken bright of my heart is twisted when I sit down and tell her I love Evangeline and Evangeline and I are making a go but not just a go. Evangeline and I are glued together with something stronger than both of us. I don't drink Cassidy's hot chocolate, I don't eat her cookies. I tell her I want her to keep her job as bike mechanic at B's. I tell her I've been drinking all day. I tell her the winter has been so hard and she hugs me. She says she loves me but she understands and I don't know whether or not to believe her but she says she'll keep her job. She says she knows how hard Eamon's death is for me. She says I don't need to apologize for grieving.

I am wonderstruck at having never confused grief with love.

There can be no grief *without* love but the love I feel for Evi is protected and untouched by grief. I love her through and through. This love is so pure and pristine and gleaming, it hurts my eyes.

Cassidy gives me a bag of criss-cross peanut butter cookies to take with me. I eat one of them as I crunch-walk through the slow snow. I stomp my boots off when I get back home. I unlock the door and Evi is on the couch in her pajamas. The yellow dress, a puddle on the floor at her feet.

Evangeline

DALTON UNLOCKS THE DOOR AND I AM ON THE COUCH IN my pajamas. The yellow dress, a puddle on the floor at my feet.

When Dalton moved into this house, I never truly felt like it was out of pity even when I tried to talk myself into it. I know I didn't pressure him into it. It was an organic movement—a cat stretching, the sun peeking from behind a cloud, a fluffy chick cracking through an egg. There were moments when neither of us knew what we were doing, but we did it anyway. We made dinners together and put Noah in his high chair, taking turns feeding him. We didn't correct people when they complimented Noah for looking just like his daddy, turning to Dalton with smiles. We'd created a home together out of necessity, a harbor. We'd created a home for Noah and he was *our* baby. He and Dalton had the same ears. There were times when I could see Dalton in his face, the scrunch of his nose. Noah was mine and Eamon's baby and he was mine and Dalton's baby too. He was the Royce's baby and my parents' baby too. I wanted to scream and laugh and weep when I thought about how proud Eamon would be of us if he *could* see what we were doing and I believed he could see what we were doing. I believed he could see us from Heaven. He was the flickering light. Although there'd been times when I didn't know what I believed, now I was certain. I believed he was loving us from all the way up there and he could feel us loving him back.

Dalton takes his coat off and gets on his knees in front of me.

"Leeny, will you marry me? Someday? I know you'll need some time, but whenever you're ready, I'll marry you. I know it won't fix us but I want to marry you."

Dalton

I TAKE MY COAT OFF AND GET ON MY KNEES IN FRONT OF her. "Leeny, will you marry me? Someday? I know you'll need some time, but whenever you're ready, I'll marry you. I know it won't fix us but I want to marry you," I say.

She leans forward to kiss me and I kiss her back. The kiss is yes before she says yes.

"You want a whole mess of kids running around here?" She laughs and blinks her watery eyes, shakes her head at me. "There's so much we haven't even talked about."

"We've been through it. It's already happened to us. I'm good with this. You and me and Noah. Maybe eventually we'd get a dog," I say. We've already made our case to God for being a fairly sturdy team together.

"You'd change your mind, Dalton, you would. You'd want your own kid."

"Yes. Absolutely. With you, I would." I nod.

"And what if I didn't want another baby?"

"Fine. Then we'd get two dogs," I say.

Evi laughs a little and keeps looking at me, won't let it go.

"One day I'd love to have a baby with you. Yes. That is true. But that fact doesn't make *this* any less *enough* for me," I say, taking her face in my hands.

"Is this how you always talk to girls on your first date?"

I shake my head no.

The latch is lifted.

Evangeline

THE LATCH IS LIFTED.

Dalton picks me up and takes me to the bed and we are together there. There, we are together. It is new and it is different. We both feel the weight of that newness, that difference pressing on us, rolling over us, surrounding us. Dalton is so careful with me I have to ask him to touch me in the ways he hasn't before. His breathy chorus of *are you sure* and *is this okay* warm against my ear. His weight, that weight heavy on me. My *yes* and *yes* and *please* in the dark—our solemn, lusty call and response. A new hymn. I bite my bottom lip so hard it bleeds and I cry a lot when I come. Dalton goes to the bathroom and cries afterwards too.

The snow has stopped.

Dalton tells me he knows sometimes when we're together like that I'll think about Eamon. He says it doesn't bother him—a bold, confident declaration that pulls me under, drowns me in sleep.

The next morning Dalton is looking in the bathroom closet for the extra scrapers so he can get the ice off his truck and he finds the secret box—the stuff from Eamon's locker. Dalton tells me he only peeked to see what was in there and as soon as he saw it was Eamon's, he brought it to me. He asks me if I want to look in it before he puts it in the garage.

I am in bed with my knitting needles cast on with the beginning stitches of a new blue wool sweater I am knitting for Dalton, a trashy celebrity magazine and a mug of lemony rooibos. I feel okay, brave enough to open the box.

I find a small black leather notebook, a water bottle, a pair of socks, a tube of cherry ChapStick. I smell the socks first. I am disappointed they only smell like our house and not like Eamon anymore. I put them on my feet. I smooth the cherry ChapStick across my lips, rub them together.

I hear Dalton go out the front door, I hear him scraping ice off his truck. I open the notebook and find letters Eamon has written to Noah and me.

Dear Evangeline,

I am writing you this because I'm not telling you yet but I want to let you know I will give up being a police officer for you, for Noah. I love you for not asking me to but I will give it up for you. When Noah is born I am resigning. I can find a job doing something else. Maybe I could teach criminal justice? I could be happy digging ditches if it meant I got to come home to you and our baby. I love you both so much.

I read it over and over again. I read the others with my hands shaking, my chin trembling, my tears blurring everything. I toss the yarn and knitting needles onto the floor, spill my tea all over the bed and sob into my hands.

Eamon was leaving. If God had let him live a few more days until Noah was born, Eamon would've resigned. He wouldn't have been killed. If Noah had been born a few days earlier, maybe this wouldn't have happened.

Dalton

EAMON WAS LEAVING. IF GOD HAD LET HIM LIVE A FEW more days until Noah was born, Eamon would've resigned. He wouldn't have been killed. If Noah had been born a few days earlier, maybe this wouldn't have happened.

When I go back inside, Evi is sitting on the bed, the quilt stained with tea, Eamon's box in front of her. She is crying. She points at the little black notebook and I pick it up and flip through it to find letters to Evi and Noah. He talks about leaving the force, getting another job. I know this sets back her healing and my eyes fill with tears.

> Dear Noah,
>   Man, oh man I am crazy about you and have only laid eyes on

you via this thing called an ultrasound which makes you look like a freaky hollow monster in black and white. I can't wait to take you fishing with your Uncle Dalton, your grandpa, your Great Uncle James. It's so beautiful up there, Noah. You will love it. We'll have boys' time. And later your mom and I will have to have a little girl so she won't feel left out and they can have girls' time. It's important early on to learn how to make a woman happy, son. I'll tell you more about that later.

 Love,
 Your Papa
 Your Daddy
 (You can decide what you want to call me later.)

There is a whole book of them and I get on the bed with Evi and we laugh and cry, reading them aloud. It feels like Eamon is right there with us. It always feels like it, but feels like it even more with his words in the room. Those words he'd kept a secret from us, they are reaching out to us now. They will never leave us. The lamp on the nightstand flickers. Evi takes the little notebook in her hands and clutches it to her chest. I kiss the top of her head and leave her bedroom to go out in the snow-covered world. To let her have some more time alone. I drive around to check out the roads. I stop at the one coffee shop open and get a small cup. I drive past B's to see how it looks in so much snow. I go to Evi's parents' to pick up Baby Noah and bring him home.

Evangeline

EAMON'S VOICE IS IN OUR BEDROOM AGAIN AND I AM
shattered and grief-heavy. I change the tea-stained sheets and
feel the lifting. Now Noah is on my bed, grabbing at his feet and
making his shiny baby sounds. I read Noah the letters his daddy
had written him. I read Noah about all of the things his daddy
wanted to show him and teach him about the world and I promise Noah I'll keep reading them to him until he can read them
himself. I am leaning on the lifting; I can feel it. Slow.

Slow. I can feel it. But more than feeling it, I can *see* it.
   I can see it now. I can *see* it. The latch is lifted, the snow has
stopped. It is God revealed, it is fact wrapped in the haze of
mystery. It is a vision—a shimmery light escaping mirage. It is a

mirror behind a scarf, the scarf slinked away. It is a velvet blind-fold pulled over my eyes, then off. I will start teaching ballet again. The Littlest Sprouts are in their proper rows in front of me, the mirror. Dalton is at the piano, ready to play. I look over at him. Noah is at my parents'. Safe.

The lights will flicker and I'll think of Eamon.

Oh, Eamon.

I'll say, "Okay. Let's begin."

I can see it.

One October, Dalton and I will get married in our jeans at B's with the golden turquoise sunset light in my hair. Only my parents and the Royces and Merit holding Baby Noah and Detroit and Cassidy will be there. The Royces will keep Noah for the next couple days afterwards and Dalton and I will make love like it's saving our souls, our mouths sweet-rich with leftover coconut wedding cake. We will make Mirabelle on an October night so she will have a July birthday like the rest of us. I can see it. And when Noah is older he will put his hands straight up in the air and he will be squealing and coming down the slide so fast. Dalton will bend to scoop him up and spin him around. I will lift my hand to my eyes to block the sun so I can watch them. I will be weeding the vegetable garden with a black-feather-haired baby slung around me—a girl with Dalton's nose and my eyes, the Royce ears. I can see it. Me, dancing again. *Swan Lake.* My parents and Merit and Dalton and the Royces in the front row, minus one—an empty seat. But *feeling* Eamon close to me when I am center stage, stretched and lifted up, up, up, to the sky. I can see it. Like how if you put your thumb over the end of a spraying garden hose it'll make a rainbow. A surprise. It's almost an accident. You have to look for it or you'll miss it. You have to hold it perfectly still in the right light.

I can hear it coming. Healing. The train tracks leading to my heart are warmed by it. I can put my hand there and feel it hot. It is rattling towards me. Rumbling. The buzzing sound of a flickering light at the end of the tunnel. A grief train rumbling away from us. A healing train coming our way. My heart, Dalton's heart, Eamon's heart, the hearts of our babies. Everything. In rhythm. All of it—glowing and glowing—light spilling and pouring and rushing through the cracks of the bits glued back together. This shattered life. This broken bright.

Da capo

MIRABELLE DOVE BERKELEY-ROYCE

Born
July 7

Acknowledgements

A GIANT, OVER-THE-MOON THANKS TO MY LITERARY AGENT Kerry D'Agostino who is not only a true treasure and delight to work with, but also an incredible editor and a kind, lovely person. Thank you so much for believing in me and my books, Kerry. And thank you to everyone at Curtis Brown, Ltd. for making beautiful things happen. Another giant, over-the-moon thanks to Betsy Teter, Meg Reid, Kate McMullen, Latria Graham, Kalee Lineberger and everyone at Hub City Press. What a dream to work with these women! It takes a lot of people to make a book! Thank you for believing in me, thank you for believing in this book. Thank you to my early readers and three of my dearest friends—Sarah Jarboe, Teri Vlassopoulos and Steve Karas. Thank you to Lindsay Hunter, Megan Stielstra, Porochista Khakpour, Bonnie Nadzam, Alexander Chee, Kima Jones and everyone at

Jack Jones Literary Arts for inspiration and blessings and time. Thank you to Otis Redding, Kip Moore, Sturgill Simpson, Bon Iver, Fleetwood Mac and yacht rock. Thank you, dear reader. Thank you to the characters in this book, in my heart, who refuse to let me go. Thank you to my mom and dad and brother— Jennifer and Winfried and WC—for loving me fully and for being there, always. Thank you to R and A—our baby girl and baby boy—for sharing me with my words. And to Loran William—my husband, my lover, my heart—thank you always for your kindness and patience, for making me tea and dinners, for encouraging me, for believing in me, for being my most trusted reader, for your easy acceptance of my wildness and for loving me like Jesus does. I absolutely couldn't do this without you. I love you.

Paperback Extras

A PEN Open Book Award Nominee, LEESA CROSS-SMITH
has been a finalist for the Flannery O'Connor Award for
Short Fiction and Iowa Short Fiction Award. She is the
author of the short story collection *Every Kiss a War* and lives
in Louisville, KY.

FACEBOOK: Leesa Cross-Smith
TWITTER: @LeesaCrossSmith
INSTAGRAM: @leesacrosssmith

A NOTE FROM THE AUTHOR

I STARTED WRITING A VERSION OF WHISKEY & RIBBONS NOT long before September 11, 2001. I wanted to write a short story about two best friends and a woman who loved them both equally. I also considered writing it as a play and a screenplay, too. After September 11, I couldn't write anymore because the world was too dark, too confusing, too sad. I put the story away, wrote very little and finished college. In 2003, I began writing obituaries for our local newspaper and in 2004, my husband and I welcomed our first baby, our daughter, into the world. I wasn't reading very much and I was writing even less. In 2005, a local police officer was killed and although that thankfully doesn't happen very often around here, the pain and shock of it turned our city upside down with sadness. I was especially attuned to local deaths because of writing obituaries but I was no longer working at the newspaper—I was a full-time mom. The police officer's funeral was broadcast live on television. I held my daughter and cried watching the spring rain as Jesus wept. This young man's funeral, his grieving widow, his family and friends. It was heartbreaking—a senseless, sudden act of violence.

By 2010 I'd had another baby, our son, and was a full-time mom to two children. By the time they were both in school during the days, I decided to put together a collection of short stories and I kept thinking about *Whiskey & Ribbons* and the story I'd abandoned back in 2001. I knew I wanted there to be a smallish cast of characters and I decided to make one of the main characters, Eamon, a police officer and to have him ripped away from his wife and their unborn child, his best friend and adopted brother. And since I love snowed-in stories, I decided to restart the story with the idea that the reader would meet Eamon's adopted brother, Dalton, and Eamon's wife, Evangeline, six months after Eamon's death, during a blizzard that has trapped them inside for the weekend. I decided that Dalton and Evangeline would be snowed in together without Eamon and Evangeline's six-month-old baby Noah—that Noah would be safe and warm at Evangeline's parents' place. I was particularly interested in the idea that Evangeline and Dalton would begin admitting their tricky feelings for one another while attempting to piece their shattered lives back together and move forward, however impossible that seemed. I finished the story and submitted it to Carve Magazine's Raymond Carver Short Story contest and didn't tell a soul about it besides my husband because I was embarrassed and shy about entering, assured that it wouldn't win. But it did. It won Editor's Choice. I included it in my debut short story collection *Every Kiss A War*.

I put *Whiskey & Ribbons* away and wrote two more books. But I never stopped thinking about Eamon and Evangeline and Dalton. In the short story, I'd written from only Evangeline's point of view but I knew I wanted to write a longer version, including Eamon and Dalton's points of view as well. I attempted writing Eamon's obituary first, had to stop and cry into my hands because killing him felt too real because he had become so real to me and I'd fallen in love with him. Again, I put the book away, unable to finish it, unsure of how to approach it. But one day I was watching *Mozart In The Jungle*, not really even thinking about writing and it occurred to me that I could try writing a novel-length version of *Whiskey & Ribbons* as a piece of music. So I researched fugues…pieces of music with more than one voice. I read a lot about fugues and how composers intertwined voices and how sometimes one voice can drop away and leave the others. I decided to write *Whiskey & Ribbons* as a fugue with three distinct voices, three distinct points of view throughout the course of the novel. And after Eamon's death, only two voices remain.

I wanted the voices to echo one another. There are some phrases that are repeated by all three of the characters. I wanted the reader to know exactly who was speaking even without the header telling them who it was. I wanted the reader to feel equally close and emotionally connected to all three of them. I wanted all three of them to have secrets and rich inner lives. I wanted the reader to get to the last page and feel like they knew these characters, had shared space with them and understood their hearts and actions and motivations. I wanted the book to resemble music because Evangeline is a ballerina and Dalton is a pianist and music is very important to them, a huge part of who they are and who they've always been been and it's something they share, together.

More than anything I wanted to do justice to good, flawed, kind-hearted people whose lives are broken by trauma and sudden tragedy. A story that can be held up to the light, that shimmers with hope, even in the darkest of circumstances, even under the heaviest fog of grief. I wanted to tell their story with compassion and tenderness and kisses, too. *Whiskey & Ribbons* took a bit shy of two decades to come together properly, but I know in my heart it was worth the wait.

LEESA CROSS-SMITH TALKS
WITH LATRIA GRAHAM

LATRIA GRAHAM: There's a 20-year arc between when this story was started in school, and its publication with Hub City Press. Can you talk a bit more about *Whiskey and Ribbon*'s origins and how it developed?

LEESA CROSS-SMITH: I started it when I was in college. Originally it was a simple story about a woman who was torn between two brothers/adopted brothers/best friends.

A local police officer in my town was killed right after my daughter was born. I started thinking about his widow and how her life looked now, and felt now, and I was so touched by it not just because those things always affect me but because I just had a baby and I was so dependent on my husband. I just couldn't stop thinking about that and tying that to the story I started in college. You're always encouraged in writing to dig into those really dark places. I was compelled to continue working on it, so it just kept coming back to me. I made it a short story, and then I couldn't stop thinking about it, so I just kept writing it and made it a novel.

LG: I was listening to the Spotify playlist that accompanies the book. There's classical, there's country, there's the Grateful Dead in this lineup. Even the way the novel opens is musical. What does music do for you as a creative?

LCS: I always make a playlist to everything I'm working on, so it's always been something that I do, whether I'm assigning a song to a specific character, or creating a mood. So I'll always have something in mind to create a mood, or I will say to myself, "I want to write a story, like how this song makes me feel."

LG: What role did you intend for music to have in the novel?

LCS: Originally I had no idea how to structure this novel. It drove me crazy. I would go on long walks, I would walk three miles. I would just think about it, and I couldn't, I absolutely could not figure out how to structure it.

While reading, I came across the idea of a fugue, which is defined as a piece of music that intertwines several different voices, some of them repetitious, and then a voice drops out. That's exactly what I needed to do when I was putting this book together. I have their voices come together as if they're all singing a song, and then we have Eamon's voice drop out.

LG: Everybody thinks of Kentucky, musically, as a country music kind of place. I don't know whether or not you agree with this, I see the state as a middle ground for music—where rock, bluegrass, country, hip-hop, and blues intersect.

LCS: We have so many dope hip hop artists here in Louisville. There's rock, and there is a lot of bluegrass, and then there's a lot of punk bands in the 90s, and a lot of alternative music and stuff like that. My Morning Jacket is from here, and they're super alternative. Kentuckians know how much diversity there is, but then people in other places, yeah they will ask if we ride horses.

Louisville is a big city. A lot of people don't really know that, but in *Whiskey & Ribbons*, what I'm trying to show is that there's

Black people who live in Louisville and it's wild, but yeah, they get married too. They go out to dinner, they go to work, they own businesses. There's black people here, you know, dancing and listening to music. And they get in fights, and they have sex, and they get hungry. Eamon is a Black dude and he listens to Grateful Dead.

LG: What do you wish people understood about Kentucky?

LCS: There are people here existing in that middle space. It's just a matter of listening, which I think a lot of people don't do, especially in this climate. So there's a lot to say there but I think it requires a lot observation, which people aren't that good at. It's easier to make snap judgements, or rely on what you see on television if you've never been to a place—the way people think California is all about surfing.

LG: I understand that this may be more of a craft question, but when reading the book I realized that a lot of the power in this novel was gained by the restraint—not saying too much, letting glances and touches linger instead of spelling them out. How did you know which moments to prune and which you should allow to bloom?

LCS: I cut everything about the kid who killed Eamon, because that wasn't important to me. It really is just an isolated, random act of violence. There's so many people in families that have to deal with that. They don't have the answers. There's no court case. The kid is also deceased now. There's just nothing else to say. It's just a tragedy. So that's something I stripped down a lot and took outside completely.

In terms of allowing sections to bloom, when I talked to my editor, I really thought really hard and wanted to make sure what we had in there were a lot of the really comfortable, intimate moments between Evi and Dalton when they're snowed in together. I wanted it to be so confessional, and they know each other so well, but then there's intimacy there that has not been breached out of respect. Creating that intimacy was important to me. And one other part, in terms of blooming was allowing the reader feel Evi's jealousy and anxiety she has about Dalton potentially being in love with another woman.

LG: I know you draw inspiration from your surroundings but what helps you keep going when you're in a real rut?

LCS: I'm stubborn. I am, for lack of a better word, a finisher. I feel blessed because I'm really easily inspired, if that's a term. I'm really easily inspired. I can see a man's cuffs on TV, or the way someone steps out of their house, or something like that, and I'll get a story I could write from that. So it's really not the inspiration, it's just keeping in the flow of it that's hard. The publishing business is designed to break you down, designed to make you want to give up. I have this desire to dig in and be like, "No, I said I was going to finish this, I'm going to finish it." I'm okay with letting things go if I know they're not working or something but *Whiskey & Ribbons* would not let me go.

LG: I know the internet literary community helped you with some of those moments—you've been very candid on Twitter about what goes into your writing and what it took to make this debut novel happen. What did the internet literary space do for you at the start of your writing career?

LCS: The internet is how I learned. I was not a part of an MFA program. I did not have my MFA because I couldn't afford it. And so I really just would see that people in MFA programs are reading like a craft book, and then reading a book of short stories, and I'd go and see where they got published, and I would go to those literary magazines and see if I liked their stuff there. And if I did, I would send them my stuff. And that's kind of where I started. So I started reading a lot of what people were writing and then when

I loved it, I would write them immediately and be like, "I loved this." My husband and I started our own literary magazine. And so that really helped a lot. I made a lot of connections, and ended up connecting with the man who published my short story collection, through the literary magazine. And so I made a lot of connections that way because then I got to spotlight people, which I feel far more comfortable doing than the spotlight being on me. I wanted to add something positive. I really do think that kind of community is what you make it.

What were your expectations before starting this book?

Do you think Evangeline and Dalton would've kissed if not for being snowed in? Do you think the circumstances leaned themselves to this action, or do you think Evangeline had been thinking about this before?

Dalton carries a lot of the emotional burden in the book, perhaps even more than Evangeline. What do you think about how he handles his emotions?

Do you think Dalton and Frances were truly in love at any point?

Do you think it was wrong of Eamon to keep Calvin's secret from Dalton? What reasons can you think of for why Eamon did so?

Do you see Eamon as more dominant in his and Dalton's relationship? Do you seem them as equals?

How do you think Eamon would feel about Evangeline and Dalton deciding to be together?

How do you think Evangeline and Dalton should handle telling Noah that Dalton is his biological uncle? What would you do in that situation?

Do you think Evangeline and Dalton will stay happily married? Why or why not?

If you could ask the author one question about *Whiskey & Ribbons*, what would it be?

HUB CITY PRESS

HUB CITY PRESS is a non-profit independent press in Spartan-burg, SC that publishes well-crafted, high-quality works by new and established authors, with an emphasis on the Southern experience. We are committed to high-caliber novels, short stories, poetry, plays, memoir, and works emphasizing regional culture and history. We are particularly interested in books with a strong sense of place.

Hub City Press is an imprint of the non-profit Hub City Writers Project, founded in 1995 to foster a sense of community through the literary arts. Our metaphor of organization purposely looks backward to the nineteenth century when Spartanburg was known as the "hub city," a place where railroads converged and departed.

RECENT HUB CITY PRESS TITLES

The Magnetic Girl • Jessica Handler

What Luck, This Life • Kathryn Scwhille

The Wooden King • Thomas McConnell

Ember • Brock Adams

Strangers to Temptation • Scott Gould

Over the Plain Houses • Julia Franks

Minnow • James E. McTeer II

Pasture Art • Marlin Barton

New Baskerville ITC Pro 11 / 14.7